EMAN

Winner of the 2013 Amazon.ca First Novel Award
Finalist for the CBA Libris Award
A CBC Best Book of 2013
A *National Post* Best Book of the Year
A *Chatelaine* Book Club Pick
An Indigo Books "Heather's Pick"

"Grady uses his skills to keep his prose quiet, spacious and neat, showing us how his characters navigate racial politics without telling us what to think about it. . . . *Emancipation Day* is an engaging look at when and where true co-existence and polite tolerance dissolve into prejudice and power struggle. That's a fully contemporary issue, and one that's entirely Canadian." *The Globe and Mail*

"A startling book, one that will likely be celebrated come awards season." *National Post*

"A masterwork of storytelling examining race relations, denial and misconceptions, and what they do to three generations of a Canadian family. Grady does not tie things up in a neat bundle for the reader here. Like life itself, *Emancipation Day* is gritty, messy, surprising and poignant. It is an unvarnished look at life in Canada in the middle of the last century and the profound influence our thoughts and actions have on the lives of others." *Telegraph Journal*

"A stellar debut. This literary novel is set in the heart of the big-band era. . . . The music swings. So does the story. Though Grady portrays the complexities of race and racial politics, there's nothing overtly didactic here. It's a novel of ideas that succeeds precisely because it's also a good story." *Winnipeg Free Press*

"Grady's novel reads with the velvety tempo of the jazz music of its day. Like a deft conductor, he seamlessly brings in his main characters' voices in alternating chapters throughout the novel. . . . For Jack, the eternal dilemma is whether we can successfully carve out a future if we reject our past. The answer occupies a distinctly grey area, one Wayne Grady fearlessly explores to expose heated race relations and the masks we all assume." *Chatelaine*

"These lines are not only pitch-perfect in the way they convey William Henry's voice, they are a lovely example of one of the gifts literature offers us: the possibility of learning from the mistakes of the characters we meet and grow to care for." *The Gazette* (Montreal)

"A haunting tale of shame, denial, racism and the intricacy of family relationships." *The News* (UK)

"A haunting, memorable, believable portrait of a man so desperate to deny his heritage that he imperils his very soul." Lawrence Hill, author of *The Book of Negroes*

"A brave book to challenge every reader's thinking on race, family, fear, and love. Profound and compelling." Annabel Lyon, author of *The Sweet Girl*

"This finely wrought novel navigates the complexities of love, race, and loyalties of choice. With a deft hand, Grady convinces us that whatever appearances may suggest, nothing is ever black and white." Vincent Lam, author of *The Headmaster's Wager* and *Bloodletting and Miraculous Cures*

"Grady's masterful novel is a compelling story about secrets and shame, denial and self-discovery, racism, and love that goes deeper than skin deep. Grady shows how the ties of family bind and also set us free. This novel is unforgettable." Lisa Moore, author of *Caught*

WAYNE GRADY

· A NOVEL ·

EMANCIPATION DAY

ANCHOR CANADA

Library and Archives Canada Cataloguing in Publication data
is available upon request

ISBN 978-0-385-67768-4

Cover and text design by Terri Nimmo
Cover image by francois dion / Getty Images
Printed and bound in the USA

Published in Canada by Anchor Canada,
a division of Random House of Canada Limited,
a Penguin Random House Company

www.penguinrandomhouse.ca

10 9 8 7 6 5 4 3 2 1

Penguin
Random House
ANCHOR CANADA

To my parents, Albert and Zoë Grady:

Requiescatis in pace.

And, always, to Merilyn.

PART I

WILLIAM HENRY

William Henry Lewis, of W. H. Lewis & Sons, Ltd., Plasterers, Willie to his wife, Will to his brother and friends, the Old Man to his sons, Pop to his daughter, William Henry to his mama who was living in Ypsilanti or Cassopolis, no one was certain where or even if she was still alive, she'd be in her nineties, and also William Henry to himself, sat regally in his father's ancient barber chair, his hands spread across his knees under the blue pinstriped barber's bib, and watched himself in the large wall mirror while his brother, Harlan, shaved his chin. Harlan had owned this barbershop off the lobby of the British-American Hotel since the death of their father, Andrew Jackson Lewis, who fell dead from this very chair onto this very terrazzo floor on a hot Saturday in July of 1911, thirty-two years ago now, after a longer than usual bout of drinking during which he had taken to sleeping in the barbershop rather than going home to his wife and family. Harlan lived upstairs in one of the hotel's smaller rooms, and kept two chairs going even though there was just the one barber, also worked as night watch-man at Lansberry's Pharmacy across the street after six p.m., also played Stepin Fetchit for the hotel's white manager, also shone shoes out in the lobby if anyone asked him to. There was nothing William Henry loved more than being shaved by his brother Harlan.

William Henry had been coming to the shop every day to have his morning shave and occasionally his hair trimmed since the day after their father's funeral, a habit that had not altered with his marriage to Josie the year after, nor upon the birth of their three children, despite the many times it would have been more convenient, because of work or the drink, to stay home and shave himself or not be shaved at all. William Henry was vain about this, he knew it, others knew it, too, and said so, but all flesh was vanity, and he liked the routine of it, it was like going to church except that church cost money and his brother never charged him a nickel, nor so much as mentioned money even to remark upon the absence of it. His coming here was a comfort to them both. They'd been doing it too long now for him to say he looked forward to it, it would be like saying he looked forward to breathing, or to the Detroit River flowing past. Thirty-two years was a long time. He tried to think of something he could start now that would go on for thirty-two more years, but he couldn't think of a thing. Maybe something his son, Benny, could do with him every day, but what? When you came to think of it, there weren't many things in life you did every day and liked doing.

Harlan talked and William Henry mostly listened or read the Detroit *Free Press* or the Windsor *Daily Star*, even though, as he would say if there were another customer waiting, "the *Free Press* ain't free and stars don't come out in the daytime," now and then grunting when he agreed or disagreed with something he read or his brother said. There was always something new to listen to or read about. These days it was the war. The many coloureds who were migrating north to work in the Detroit armament factories. The many whites who were moving out of downtown Detroit for that very reason. The war was none of his or Harlan's concern, except that it did affect business. Folks had worn their hair long during the Depression, Harlan said, almost over their collars, but now that the war was on they seemed to prefer a more military cut, even the civilians, and not just the coloureds. Everyone wanted to look like they just been called up, or would be any day now, or else just got back and wanted everyone to know it. William Henry countered with how the plastering business had picked up, too, what with every-one wanting little one-room apartments in their houses to rent to the new workers, or for when the soldiers returned. He liked the smell of the toilet water Harlan used, and the talcum powder that he sprinkled on the brush before whisking the cut hairs off the back of a customer's neck. His own hair was thin and wavy, not wiry like some, his brother had no trouble getting even a fine-toothed comb through it, and his skin was light enough that when he did go to church he sat right up at the front and did not look around. He could have been called up for service, but he was too old. Fifty-two. Old as a poker deck.

"What's that boy of yours up to today, Will?" Harlan said, finishing up a cheek. He lightly touched the underside of William Henry's chin with the tip of his forefinger, and William Henry tilted his head back so that his brother could get at his throat.

"Benny?" said William Henry. "Same as usual, I guess. Business is slow."

"I meant Jackson. He helpin' you out?"

William Henry grunted. He saw Harlan stop and look at him in the mirror, the razor poised in the air like a bandleader's baton. Harlan favoured Jackson, always had. So did his mother. Jackson was her heart. It was always Jackson this and Jackson that. A person would think Jackson was Harlan's son, not William Henry's. The truth was, Jackson was a disappointment. Worse than that, a disgrace.

"He helps some," William Henry said. "His heart ain't in it, though."

"That so."

"Some people ain't cut out for hard work."

"Barberin's hard work," Harlan said, as though William Henry had been referring to him. "On your feet all day, breathin' in little bits of hair. Remember how Daddy got so he couldn't close the scissors no more, his fingers were so swole up?"

"Yours gettin' like that?"

"Startin' to."

There was a pause accompanied by the scrape of straight razor on stubble. William Henry thought about his own grip on a trowel. When Harlan stopped to run the blade under the hot water tap, William Henry said, "That's the arthritis settin' in."

Harlan wiped the extra shaving cream off William Henry's neck and wrapped a warm, scented, damp towel around his face, covering his nose and forehead. William Henry closed his eyes and breathed in the fragrant steam, his favourite moment of the whole shave. It took him back to when his wife, Josie, had been in service in his father's house, after they got her from the Hôtel-Dieu orphanage. They'd had some money then, and Mama needed looking after. He would watch Josie make beds and be aware of her even when she was in another room, when she opened the windows to let in fresh air and the warm scent of lilacs filled the house. He thought then she would make a fine wife, and she had agreed, but his father had put his foot down even though they were as dark as she was. No son of mine marryin' no servant girl. But then the old man died and all opposition to the marriage died with him, because Mama just packed up and left the house to him and Harlan while she went back to somewhere in Michigan, maybe Kalamazoo or Lansing, Harlan said with a salesman who came to her door one day selling clothespins, but that didn't make it so, Harlan saying it. Harlan would say anything to keep the air from going flat around him.

He found himself remembering the walk up Ouellette Avenue in September to the registry office with Josie on his arm, to get their marriage licence. He was nervous as a cat, but she was calm and collected. The nuns at the orphanage hadn't told them much about her other than her name, Josephine Rickman, and that she might have been dark from being Jewish. Something about her father being a bandleader, but that didn't make sense to anybody, so they ignored it. Josie herself maintained that her father was a minister in the African Methodist Episcopal Church, and had moved back to Indiana, but she might have said that to scandalize the nuns.

"What'll we say your mama's name was, Josie?" William Henry asked her when they were halfway to the registry office. He thought they'd best get that part straight, at least.

"Mildred, you know that."

"Mildred what?"

"Mildred Hughes."

"That gonna be your name, then? Josie Hughes?"

"I took after my daddy's name. Josephine Constance O'Sullivan Rickman."

"Where'n hell you get all them names from?"

"Constance the name the nuns give me at the orphanage. I don't know where O'Sullivan come from, that was part of my daddy's name. You just put it down like I told you. Josephine Constance O'Sullivan Rickman."

"An' how old are you, Miss Josie-fine Constance O'Sullivan Hughes Rickman Soon-To-Be Lewis?"

"How old do I gotta be?"

"I dunno, eighteen, I guess."

"Then say I'm twenty."

"You ain't no twenty. I'm twenty. We can't both be twenty."

"Why not, anyway?"

"Look suspicious."

"No it don't. Lots of people is twenty. Eighteen look suspicious."

He had to admit she was better at hiding things than he was.

But at the registry office the white clerk behind the counter took a shrewd look at Josie and said that if she was twenty he'd eat his hat, but he filled out the form for them anyway.

"You people don't hold back none, do you?" the clerk said. "Might as well make it legal."

Then the idiot filled the form out wrong. Where the form asked for Name of Wife the clerk wrote "Josephine Constance Rickman." There wasn't space for all them other names. In the box marked Place of Birth, for William Henry the man wrote "Windsor," but Josie didn't know where she was born so he just shook his head and wrote her name again, this time leaving out the Constance. And in the box marked Spinster or Widow, he put "Coloured."

"Coloured a state of marriage now, is it?" Josie said, she always did have a tongue on her, but the clerk didn't even look up. And on William Henry's form, under Nationality, the clerk again wrote "Coloured." It was like he was registering mongrel pups at the city pound. Josie glared at the man and held her peace, like the nuns taught her. But he had to practically drag her out of there.

"You got a drink in one of them things?" William Henry said to Harlan when the towel had cooled and been unwrapped from his face and the bottles of variously coloured lotions and ointments appeared in front of him, twinned in the mirror. He looked at the clock on the wall above the bathroom door. Going on eleven. A good time to start. It wasn't first thing in the morning. He'd resisted long enough to convince himself that he had the urge under control. He had eaten bacon and eggs and toast and coffee at breakfast time or a little after, and kept it down. He had talked to Josie about the house in Walkerville he and Benny and Jackson were working on, tearing down a plaster wall. Thirsty work. Lots of people drank at noon, and it was almost noon now. "I know you keep some somewhere. Where is it?"

"I got some bay rum," Harlan said, unpinning the bib from William Henry's neck and stepping on the pedal that lowered the chair with a pneumatic sigh of relief.

A collar of tissue paper remained around William Henry's neck, and he tore it off and leaned towards the mirror. Where had Harlan put his damned eyeglasses? They had speckles of paint on them, he'd forgotten to clean them after work yesterday. Was it yesterday? The day before?

"Just a tot, then," he said. "Just a bracer."

Harlan laughed. It was their old joke. "If you're going to drink aftershave, Will, I got a better brand in my cupboard."

Harlan opened the cupboard above the sink and took out a

bottle of Kentucky bourbon and two shot glasses. Their father was from Kentucky, it was a connection to him. Everything they did meant something.

"Here," he said, pouring, "slap some of this on your face."

"You're a good man, Harlan."

"To sitting in this chair," Harlan said, raising his glass. "To Daddy."

"To Daddy," William Henry said, standing up.

Nothing ever tasted so good as the first drink of the day.

JACK

Their orders came at six in the morning. Full kit, battle dress, look sharp. Jack stuffed everything into his kitbag, made his cot and dragged his duffle and trombone down to the parade square along with the forty other members of the Navy Band, not knowing what was up. It was dark and wet, as usual, snowing and raining at the same time, a bitter wind coming in off the Atlantic. Greatcoats and oilskins over their Mae Wests. The hundred and seventy-six crewmen they were to accompany to their ship fell in behind the band, waiting to be paraded down Prince of Wales to the St. John's dock-yard. Black drizzle made the faint light leaking from behind the blackout curtains in the admin buildings surrounding the parade square look like marker buoys in fog, more a warning than a comfort.

His head was still pounding from the night before. He needed a smoke. He'd been playing a dance at the K of C, the Knights of Columbus Hall in St. John's, a few of the guys from the Navy Band, him on drums and trombone, Frank Sterling on trumpet and cornet, Rory Johnston on piano, Ken Bradley on bass, others who came and went. They called themselves the King's Men only they said it fast, *Kingsmen*. They were supposed to finish at twenty-three hundred, but they stayed on, playing for the drunks and the diehards. They did it for fun, mostly, but there were girls there, some of them V-girls. V-girls also did it for fun. There were some nice girls, like Vivian, who'd brought him sandwiches during the break one night and, the next week, let him walk her home. Sweet kid, didn't have a clue. He'd asked her out last week and she'd gone, too, no questions asked, but she was a real tease. Her eyes tell me yes, yes, yes, but her knees tell me no, no, no. Still, she might get him places he couldn't go by himself. He'd call her when he got back to barracks. He didn't know what music did for the other guys, maybe it helped with the boredom or cut through the fear, but for him it meant fitting in, belonging, five guys sneaking up on the enemy under cover of sound. And it wasn't all pack up your troubles, either, it was Goodman and Miller and the Dorseys, it was "Moonlight Serenade" and "Boogie Woogie Bugle Boy." Frank was a whiz on the cornet, they were all good. All good together.

Across the square a driver and his mate were tossing kitbags and horn cases into a covered truck, water running off their helmets.

"What's the deal?" Jack asked Frank.

"Fucked if I know."

"I need a smoke."

"I need a drink," someone else chimed in. Gutterson.

"I need an Aspirin." Frank.

"I need a girl." Johnston.

"I got a girl," said Jack, "in Kalamazoo." Laughter.

He'd always been quick with the jokes. He fronted the King's Men because he could tell a joke and knew the lyrics to all the songs. Got people on their feet. Give him the first bar and he'd sing the whole song, he loved it, the looks on the faces of the dancers when the music got to them. When a person is singing he looks you straight in the eye, ever notice that? He wasn't himself anymore when he was a frontman, he was someone else, like an actor, someone with no past outside the song. He sang with his heart, like he was proposing to his best girl, like he was talking his way into barracks after lights-out. Honest, Corp, I've grown accustomed to your face. That always got a laugh. Like last night, when they finally rolled out of the K of C, "*Rolling home (dead drunk)*," they didn't know they were going to be called up at six a.m. Get a few pints in us and we're all linked arms and swaggering down the sidewalk, holding each other up, "*Happy is the day when a sailor gets his pay, as we go rolling rolling home (dead drunk!)*." That was another reason he chose the Navy, for the songs. Sea songs older than hymns, old as the sea itself. Name one goddamned Army song, go ahead. There were Air Force songs, *Off we go, into the wild blue yonder*, but what was wilder or bluer than the sea? Not the sky, not here in Newfoundland, it wasn't, it might be wild but it sure wasn't blue. Battleship grey when it wasn't pitch black.

Well, he wasn't rolling home now, he was freezing his balls off on a parade square in HMCS *Avalon* in St. John's bloody Newfoundland with the rest of the Navy Band, and these poor devils waiting behind them to be marched down to their ship. Crew change for one of the destroyer escorts, he guessed. They did this every day, two sometimes three times a day, not usually this early, not usually in the dark, but always this many. In the four months he'd been here, the band must have sent ten thousand men off on convoy duty. A lot of them never came back. He no longer looked at their faces. The band played something rousing to lift the men's spirits as they marched them down Prince of Wales, past the warehouses and the few flag-waving citizens who still showed up, over to the Navy docks, saw them onto their ships to their likely deaths, then turned around and marched themselves back to headquarters where the next condemned crew was waiting for the same treatment.

When the Chief finally marched them out, it was close to oh seven hundred, still too dark to see the music on their lyres. They played from memory, Sousa's "Salvation Army," which he'd been playing since Sea Cadets. Rain beaded on his horn and froze, collected on his cap and ran down his neck. Thank God he could play the trombone with gloves on, and that he'd coated it with cold cream to keep the rain off the brass. A handful of locals maybe walking to work stopped to wave or shout a word of encouragement. School kids ran along the sidewalk beside them, throwing pebbles at the bass drum.

When they reached the Navy docks, something broke in the routine. Instead of splitting them into two parallel lines so the band could play as the men continued up and onto the ship, the Chief marched the band straight up the gangway and onto the foredeck, where they looked about them like a bunch of cats that had just been dumped out of a sack. HMCS *Assiniboine*. Destroyer escort, like he'd thought, but what the fuck were they doing on it? The band was formed into six lines and stood at ease, feet twelve inches apart, instruments ready at their sides.

"We're going to sea," someone behind him said quietly. Sounded like Seddidge.

"No we're not," Frank said. "Some bigwig just wants a show."

"We are."

"We can't be," Jack said.

"Why the fuck not?"

"Because that's why I joined the band, so I wouldn't have to go to sea."

There were sniggers among the ranks, but Jack was serious. The Chief turned and glared. A low rumbling sound, like kettle drums tuned to E, and tremors coming up from the metal deck through the soles of their boots. The ship's engines had started; the deck crew was getting ready to cast off. Jesus, they hadn't prepared him for active duty. A few fire drills in the Armouries in Toronto, a lecture on chain of command. If a gunnery rating tells you to get out of the fucking way, get out of the fucking way. If a ranking officer tells you to get out of the fucking way, jump overboard. Officers wore caps with scrambled egg on their visors: salute it. The Chief was a non-commissioned officer, promoted from the ranks, one of the boys. Don't salute him and don't call him sir. Ordinary seamen were nothing, useful for holding hoses and clearing clogged scuppers. Four ways you could be killed in the Navy: aircraft from above, U-boat from below, destroyer from in front, cowardice from within. What about stupidity? Stupidity was cowardice. Ignorance, ditto. And how many ways to make it out alive? One: luck. And if you were a bandsman standing on the deck of a ship in wartime in the snow in the dark holding a frozen trombone, you were one unlucky son of a bitch.

Except it wasn't completely dark anymore. Jack could see across the *Assiniboine*'s foredeck to the harbour, where a dozen other ships lay at anchor. Two huge grey hulks crawling with ants: troopships. Some of the names on the warships he could make out through the rain. HMCS *Shawinigan*, corvette. HMCS *Esquimalt*, HMCS *Clayoquot*, minesweepers. Half a dozen merchant vessels: M/V *Bay D'Espoir*. M/V *Connaught*. Fucking escort duty, then. Maybe they'd be escorting the merchantmen to Halifax, two days each way, or possibly to New York, a week.

They'd lost three ships to U-boats on that run last month. You didn't notice the empty bunks in the barracks anymore, except you did. Above the ships' radar antennas the black headland of Cape Spear, a thin line of white froth barely swelling at its base, shielded them from the open sea. Beyond that was nothing, water, black and cold and unimaginably deep, with lots of corpses in uniform at the bottom of it.

When the ship cleared the harbour gates the Chief dismissed them and the boson piped them below to the mess deck. Their kitbags were already there, neatly stowed beside their instrument cases and a pile of curious-looking cloth batons that turned out to be rolled-up hammocks. Twelve men to a mess, one mess for each of the trades: signalmen, firemen, gunnery mates, stokers. Jack, Frank and some of the other bandsmen fell in with the gunnery mates. They slung their micks over steam pipes, vent housings, odd hooks, wherever they could find a billet. Below them, metal tables and lockers were bolted to the decks and the bulkheads. Nothing was made of wood. When a torpedo struck, one of the gunnery mates told them, wood splintered and flew through the air, killing more ratings than compression or drowning. Metal just buckled and melted. "Fucking slave ship," Frank muttered. Jack laughed, but his hands were shaking and they'd barely left port. He looked for a porthole but there wasn't one, they must be below the waterline, a half inch of steel between them and oblivion. Knowing he was underwater made him feel as though he were drowning. Over the intercom they were ordered to bring their instruments to the forward hold, D Deck, to be stowed under rope netting until needed. Soft, red light in the passageways, couldn't see your hand in front of your face. "Blacker than Toby's arse down here," Jack said. You had to claw your way back up the gangway to C Deck for chow. By then, the ship was well underway. The tremor he'd felt earlier became a full-fledged shudder as they listed slightly into the open sea, the engines rising to maybe F-sharp. Standing in line for chow he could see the flat, grey, foam-flecked ocean and smell fresh air through an open scuttle. He took in huge draughts of it, as though he'd been holding his breath against a smell. A dozen merchant ships through one scuttle, another dozen through the next. A huge convoy.

Frank came back from a reconnaissance mission among the regular sailors ahead of them in line.

"We're not going to Halifax," he said. "We're on the Derry Run, escort duty across the North Atlantic. Fifty ships. We hand the merchantmen over to the British at the MOMP, the Mid-Ocean Meeting Point, somewhere off Iceland. Then it's R and R," he said, grinning.

"Oh good, rest and relaxation."

"No, refuel and return. Three fucking weeks at sea. Maybe longer."

Jack's stomach tightened and his ears buzzed. "Why us? We're not combat, we're bandsmen."

"They send us to sea every six months to dry us out."

"What, no rum on board?"

"I didn't pack any, did you?"

"Fucking hell."

The crew worked four-hour watches: the first from oh eight hundred to twelve hundred hours; the middle watch, twelve to sixteen hundred; and the morning watch, sixteen to twenty hundred, then the first again. A day was four hours on, eight hours off, then four on and eight off. Everything done by bells. Goddamned bells rang every half-hour: one bell, two bells, up to eight bells, change of watch. Jack pulled the twelve-to-sixteen-hundred and midnight-to-oh-four-hundred: hell's bells. He spent his first noon watch on the boat deck, manning Fire Station H, portside boat deck, with petty officer second-class Spoonerman or Spoonerson, and two other ordinary seamen, Trilling and Sinclair, neither of them bandsmen. Salt water freezing to the rails. He could already feel the beginnings of seasickness, the slight dizziness, the weakness in the knees. He'd sometimes felt light-headed on the Detroit ferry, but that trip lasted only half an hour, and he'd put it down mostly to booze. This was something else. This went deeper.

The four of them spent the watch either sitting on the hose locker or standing in the lee of a lifeboat, smoking and telling lies about the girls they'd left behind. They called the women "parties." Jack thought about Vivian. He'd phone her when he got back, but she'd probably have someone else by then. Sweet little party like that, it was a wonder some officer hadn't got his hooks into her already. What did she see in a guy like him? He held on to the ship's rail with one hand, keeping the other in the pocket of his greatcoat, staring out at the ocean, unable to go forward, afraid to go back.

His stomach began to feel worse when they lost sight of land. He spent the eight hours between watches lying in his hammock, trying not to throw up. He thought he'd be all right as long as he didn't eat, but at twelve hundred hours he went above decks, emerging from the blood-red light into the sudden, silent star-light, and was sick. It was like being drunk, only all the time.

One relatively calm night, Spoonerson told them about taking his survivor's leave in Ireland after the *Ottawa*, a sister destroyer escort, went down. He'd been billeted in a castle beside a pub and had fucked a barmaid named Cathleen every night for two weeks, or so he said. When his leave was up she tried to cut her wrists with a broken wineglass. Jack leaned his elbows on the taffrail and watched the way the moon lit up the spit left behind by the props. This was all bullshit, he thought. Who would be fool enough to kill herself over Spoonerson?

"The *Ottawa* was a beautiful destroyer, though," Spoonerson said after a while. "Went down right about where we are now, thirty-two merchantmen in the ring, except it was a Sunday and not so fucking cold. Thirteenth of September, 1942. Out on a hunt, wolfpack caught her. Sixty-five survivors from a crew of a hundred and seventy-eight." Spoonerson leaned over the rail and spat into the propwash, a tribute to all drowned seamen. "First torpedo came through the fo'c'sle on the port side, into the signalmen's mess where thirty men were sleeping. Rudder smashed all to shit, and when the sub's commander saw she couldn't manoeuvre, he angled off and torpedoed her again, this time hitting her amidships on the starboard side, right in the boilers. She went down like a stone, captain with her. Me and a few others was picked up by the *Arvida*, took us all the way to Londonderry."

Jack looked at Spoonerson's ribbons. He might have been telling the truth. But then why was he still a second-class PO doing fire duty? No one was who they said they were.

On his fourth day out he was worse but thought if he tried to eat something he would get his sea legs, so just before noon he climbed up to the mess for chow. The sea had become rougher if anything, not stormy exactly but moody, as though on a slow burn, biding its time, and the clouds on the horizon were always low and dark. Someone said they were over the Grand Banks, where the water was shallow and easily rucked. As soon as he entered the mess, the smell of frying sausages sent him running for the side. After that, all he could think of was the ship's heaving, the deck slowly rising under him, and just when he thought the ship was about to flip over it would begin to go back down. A pause, as though the ship were lowering itself for him to jump into the sea, and then the whole thing would start again the other way. Jesus, the sweat running down his rib cage, the roaring in his ears. *Rolling home* . . . He felt hollow and filled with sound, like a cave in a windstorm. Or maybe like a horn. Thank Christ he didn't have to blow one now. He stood at the rail for the entire watch, feet sliding on the slick metal, wishing the ship would just keep canting for once and dump him over the side. He didn't report to sickbay, although he knew plenty who did. Sickness was cowardice. Next worse thing to deserting your post. Frank told him to eat, keep something in his guts, so he went up to the mess for mid-rats before his night watch and what did he see? Two pumpkin pies set out on the table. At first he thought they were walnuts on top, then they moved. Cockroaches. He puked all down his uniform front, inside his tunic. Seamen stepped around him. "Christ, Lewis, get the fuck down to sickbay."

He had to crawl on his hands and knees, couldn't stand up his stomach hurt so much, he just wanted to lie down in it and die, but he made it to the hatch, through the blackout cheaters and out onto the fantail, where he lay on his stomach clawing at the deck mat with his fingernails to keep from sliding over the stern. Couldn't move another inch. Fuck it, let them put him on charge, let a sniper see him. But it was Sinclair and Trilling who found him.

"Well, look at this sorry excuse for a seaman," Sinclair said. He stood wavering on the deck, as though trying to keep his balance. "He don't look human at all. He couldn't be drunk, now, could he?"

"No," said Trilling. "We're drunk, and he looks worse'n us."

Jack tried to speak but he had no breath. All his stomach could do was tighten and heave. I'm all right, boys, he thought, leave me alone, I'll be fine.

"I think he is, though." Sinclair leaned unsteadily over Jack and nudged him with his boot. "Drunk, I mean."

"Maybe we should give him some water," Trilling said. "Whaddaya say, Jack, ol' boy? You wanna cold shower? Sober you up a bit?" Sinclair was unfurling the three-inch hose from its housing on the afterdeck. "That's the ticket!" shouted Trilling, and together they turned the water on him, a jet so strong it took both of them to hold it, laughing so hard they nearly washed him overboard. Jack wrapped his arms around a stanchion as his legs swung over the side, and he stared down at the propwash glowing phosphorescent in the glowering sea, still puking, through his nose, now, from terror. His cap filled with water and the chin-strap started to choke him, then it broke. He looked up into the white faces of his tormenters and screamed. What had he done to deserve this? Why did they hate him? What did they know?

When they shut the hose off and left him, his greatcoat froze to the deck. He didn't know if he was still hugging the stanchion or if his coat was the only thing keeping him on the ship. His last thought before passing out was that his mother would look into her tea leaves in the morning and see a floating cap with his name stencilled on it. She would tell his father he had drowned.

Their ghostly faces were still leering at him when he came to, and it took him a long second to realize he was in sickbay, lying on a metal cot. Pipes hissed above his head. Orderlies scurried about, the ship rolling more than ever, but he felt better, no, he felt numb, they must have given him something. He lay for a long time afraid to move, hearing the kettle drums' pulse through the sides of his cot. His hands were wrapped in bandages.

A man wearing a white smock came up to him. He was older, probably an officer but the smock covered his pips. He looked more like a businessman to Jack, like he was going to sell him insurance or something: hair neatly brushed, nails cut short and filed smooth.

"Ordinary Seaman Jack Lewis," the man said, reading his clipboard.

"Sir."

"I'm Surgeon Captain Barnes, chief medical officer on board. You're a lucky man."

"Am I, sir?" Barnes. Dr. Barnes. It couldn't be. Jack felt his palms sweat under their bandages.

"Your mates thought you were drunk."

"I wasn't."

"I've determined that. Worse case of seasickness I've ever seen. Where're you from, anyway? Saskatchewan?"

"No, sir. Windsor."

"Nova Scotia?"

"No, sir. Ontario. Across from Detroit."

The man looked amused. "I know where Windsor is," he said. "I'm from there myself."

Jesus. It *was* Dr. Barnes. "Wish I was there now, sir."

"Hmm. Well, you'll have to stay where you are for a bit. Until your hands improve and we can take those bandages off. Couple of days. They were pretty badly frozen. We should be into the storm good and proper by then. Think you can manage?"

"No, sir."

"Good man," he said, and left.

Jack stared after him. Doc Barnes, Peter's fucking father. The one man in the whole goddamned Navy who had reason to kill him. Had Peter written to him? He felt his stomach and chest start to go and he thought about calling for a bedpan. Whatever the doc had given him was either taking hold or wearing off. Half an hour went by and no one came to his cot. Maybe Barnes had poisoned him and was waiting for him to die. Eventually, an orderly padded up and placed a bottle of pills on the metal bedstand.

"The MO says you're to take these for seasickness."

"I already have seasickness," he said.

"Take one every four hours. Every time you hear eight bells, take a pill. Got that?"

He nodded and the orderly left. He looked at the bottle. "Pill #2-183," but no name on the label. The pills were pale yellow, like powdered piss. How the fuck was he supposed to take them with his hands wrapped in bandages? But of course he wouldn't take them anyway, in case Barnes had recognized him. A chief medical officer could get away with anything, even murder.

He'd never met the doc in Windsor because he'd gone off to war before Jack had joined the All-Whites, but he remembered the photograph in Peter's house, on a small table under a lamp with a fringed shade. It was always early evening when he'd visited Peter and Peter's mother, Della. He and Peter would stand by a window in the upstairs parlour, blackout curtain askew, looking down onto the street through the leaves of a giant chestnut. Black smoke over Detroit, Jack's own face reflected in the glass, hollows where his eyes should have been and his pale ears sticking out. He looked like a frightened raccoon. Were his cheekbones too high? Della was behind them, knitting. He watched her reflection in the window as she crossed her legs, swinging her foot in time to the needles, the little pucker of concentration making her lips look poised for a kiss. He turned his head for a better look at his own profile in the window. A little too high? He'd kiss her if she ever gave him the chance.

"They threw a woman off the Belle Isle Bridge."

What woman? Who were "they"?

When he woke up, Frank Sterling was standing beside his cot. "Hello, Jack," he said. "I hear they had to chip you off the deck with ice scrapers."

Jack held up his bandaged hands. "I could have died, the bastards."

"They're being disciplined," Frank said happily.

"For what? Attempted murder?"

"Naw, unauthorized use of firefighting equipment. An hour's rifle drill every morning at oh six hundred. I've been reassigned to your station, me and Merrifield."

This was good news. He liked Frank, although he didn't trust him all that much. He was older, twenty-three or four, came from a posh town somewhere near Toronto, father a lawyer or something, Frank was always vague about what. Jack could smell money, and Frank had the smell in spades. He was built like a prizefighter, buzz cut, heavily browed and bull necked, but he didn't have a boxer's stance. Stood with his feet apart. Doing his bit for the country but not taking it too seriously. Lots waiting for him when the war was over, in it for some kind of lark, the lawyer's boy who could have been an officer or maybe even ducked the war altogether, but joined the ranks instead and befriended people like Jack. You couldn't trust someone if you didn't know their motives. But maybe he and Frank weren't so different after all: they both wanted to see how the other half lived.

"Any action yet?" Jack asked.

"No. Quiet as a mouse. Bad weather keeps the U-boats under, apparently. But we'll soon be crossing the Pit, said to be swarming with the enemy. If we get one on the ASDIC we could be out for a long time."

Jack groaned. He'd heard of ships that had stayed out for months, their crews not even getting shore leave for over a year. He looked at the bottle of pills. "You getting seasick at all, Frank?"

"Yeah," he said, touching his stomach. "Been feeding the fish all morning."

"You should take these pills," Jack said. "I don't need them anymore."

"Really?" Frank picked up the bottle and read the label.

"Thanks, bud," he said, spilling a few into his hand and putting them in the pocket of his dungarees. "Mighty white of you."

Jack looked up at the ceiling. "Don't mention it."

After three days the orderly cut Jack's bandages off with a pair of scissors. The skin beneath them was as pale as skimmed milk and he marvelled at it, the black hairs on the backs of his hands lying flat, like grass after a flood. On the fourth day he was back on watch, this time with Frank and Merrifield, but he still felt like death on a plate. Merrifield was an easygoing Nova Scotian who'd been a bosun's mate on any number of whaling and sealing ships, according to him, before joining the Navy. Jack picked up a new cap from ship's stores, but it had HMCS *Assiniboine* on it instead of HMCS *Avalon*, the Navy base in St. John's that was his posting, and he didn't like it. It felt like a transfer, like he'd never get back on solid ground. And they didn't have his size: the strap dangled comically under his chin. The weather had calmed but the fog was so thick he could barely see the width of the ship, the sea a vague menace, something alive but unseen, forgotten for long stretches until suddenly remembered and dreaded, like a debt.

He was still regularly sick, but he didn't take the pills; he wouldn't have kept them down long enough, anyway. He wondered how Frank was doing with them. He ate his salt cod (which they called sewer trout), or chipped beef on toast (shit on a shingle), then ran to the side to send it all over the rail.

Chipped beef came out looking like a chocolate milkshake. Creamed corn cut a lovely golden arc through the fog. Every smell set him off. Soap, aftershave, cigarette smoke, burning coal. But he wouldn't go back to Dr. Barnes.

He was mustering for noon watch when the fog lifted, as though someone had raised a blackout curtain. Jesus, the sea was big. High overhead, a lone gull's muted cry cut through the wind whistling through the rigging. Then the alert sounded: Action stations! U-boat off the port bow. They had both been cruising through the fog, the *Assiniboine* trailing behind the convoy and the U-boat waiting just below the surface for stragglers. Radar apparently hadn't picked it up in the ground clutter. PO Spoonerson stood at the rail under the companionway, calmly smoking and calling back to Jack and Frank to remain at their post. "She's that close we can't get our big guns down low enough," he said. "Cripes, Lewis, if her hatch was open you could puke your lunch right down into her. She's trying to get far enough away from us to dive. Can't dive this close or we'd be on her in a minute with the depth charges."

"We're *chasing* her?" Jack yelled. He was standing beside the PO.

"Bloody right we're chasing her," Merrifield called back.

"What if it's a trap? What if the U-boat captain's the same one who blew the *Ottawa* to hell?"

"We're going to ram her," the PO shouted.

Oh Jesus, thought Jack, Jesus, Mary and Joseph. He and Frank ran to the rail to have a look. Spoonerson told them to get back to the hose locker, but he didn't push it so they stayed. Jack had never seen a U-boat before, hadn't seen anything of the enemy at all. He realized that the war, up to this point, had been a rumour, news of something happening somewhere else. German planes didn't fly over St. John's. Torpedo netting kept the U-boats out of the harbour. The sub was longer than the *Assiniboine* but only half as wide, and with green water streaming along her glistening flanks she looked sleek as a giant fish, a whale or a leviathan, something mysterious and black and dangerous. Something biblical. He saw that the sub was not fleeing but manoeuvring for position—he *knew* it!—attempting to put some distance between the vessels so she could turn and launch a torpedo, and that the *Assiniboine*'s captain was trying to stay with her in case she submerged. They'd be sitting ducks.

Staccato gunfire erupted from the *Assiniboine*'s foredeck: the gunners were firing on the submarine to keep the Germans from getting a crew to their own deck-mounted artillery. Jack couldn't see many of the *Assiniboine*'s crew, a few at the rail like him and Frank, the rest at their action stations or behind baffles. What must it have been like in the U-boat? Jack realized with a start that there were men inside the submarine, that this wasn't them against a machine or a monster from the depths, it was them against other men. Their own deck guns were ineffective, and the sub soon had its half-inch swung around and trained on the *Assiniboine*'s bridge.

"Get back to your stations!" Spoonerson shouted, and Jack and Frank scrambled behind the fire station baffle. As soon as he lost sight of the ocean, he started feeling sick again. His head tried to lift itself from his shoulders. He heard a sharp *budda-budda*, a snare drum beaten on its rim, and an almost simultaneous clangour from above and behind them, followed by a searing roar. The Germans had hit a stack of gasoline cans stored under a tarp on the upper deck, fuel for the lifeboats and runabout, stupid place to put them. Jack could feel the heat from the flames on his face. Liquid fire began running along the boat deck, then towards them down the gangway and into the scuppers as the ship's bow rose into the chase. He remembered what flames could do to flesh. He froze. Then Merrifield shoved him aside and began paying out the three-inch. "Take it!" he shouted, and Jack gripped the hose's nozzle and ran with it towards the advancing flames, Frank following. "Don't bother trying to put it out!" Merrifield called after them. "Just wash it over the side before it hits the companionway and goes below. Show a leg, now!"

The hose stiffened in his hands as Merrifield opened the hydrant, and he and Frank grappled along the deck towards the flames. Crews on the upper decks were washing down fire, some of it landing on the lifeboats and some of it on them. Jack and Frank hosed off the boat canopies first, then washed the main fire into the scuppers, where it spilled into the sea and hissed like molten metal. He was sweating despite the spray blowing back into his face. He wanted to rip off some part of his uniform but didn't dare take his hands off the hose. Frank turned to him and was about to speak when the ship gave a violent shudder and listed strongly to port, throwing both of them against the fo'c'sle. They were going down. Jack cried out, dropped the hose in panic, and it snaked away from him, spitting water in all directions.

"Why the fuck did you do that?" Frank yelled, spittles of fire spilling around his head from the upper deck, and at that moment Jack hated him, hated the look of fear in his eyes mirroring his own. It was as though Jack had shared some private part of himself he had not meant to reveal. But they were all sinking, what did it matter? He didn't belong here, he was a Windsor boy; his father had been right, this wasn't their war. Merrifield saw the writhing hose, ran over and stepped on its brass head, stilling it. The ship righted.

To avoid looking at Frank, Jack grabbed the hose from under Merrifield's boot, then leaned over the side to search for the U-boat. She'd gone down and was slowly bobbing back to the surface, a long, silver gash showing on her portside.

"We rammed her!" Frank said.

The *Assiniboine* cut throttle and came about in a tight arc while, on the foredeck, the artillery crew lowered the forward Y-gun into position. Flame burst from the gun's muzzle and Jack watched the black dots appear along the U-boat's hull. They seemed unnecessary, for the U-boat was obviously finished. Still, you never knew. Air was bubbling out of her through the shell holes. Her nose lifted from the green water as though she were sniffing the air for the scent of land, and in seconds she began sliding backwards and was gone. It was over, his first kill. He realized he'd been gripping the rail so hard his gloves had frozen to it and his hands were numb. He heard the pipe to lower boats, and then the sound of davits and winches. It wasn't over.

"Get those boats in the water!" the bosun yelled. "Look sharp to it!"

When he looked down at the sea again, he saw the oil slick, like the blood of the sunken U-boat, shimmering in the pale winter sunlight, spreading in a calm circle above the vanished sub. Then, within the slick's circumference, objects floated to the surface. At first Jack thought they were just clothing and blankets. Then he realized he was looking at men. Some of them waved their arms and started swimming through the oil towards the ship, but many were unmoving, churned to the surface by underwater turbulence. Their blackened bodies emerged momentarily from the darkness, twisted and rolled and then vanished back into the depths. Islands of flame from the *Assiniboine* floated in the water between the ship and the living men. He watched as the little fire patches attached and grew into larger islands, then into bright continents, until the whole slick was a vortex of black, acrid smoke. The ship's cutters were in the water now, their crews rowing hard towards the inferno. The few survivors, the mere handful who had managed to swim clear of the oil, were hauled up into the boats.

Some of the men lying on the bottom of the open cutters wore German uniforms, but others were soot-stained men in civilian clothing—pinstriped suits, camel overcoats and street shoes. It was as though the exploding sub had torn a hole in the ocean, sucked up bodies from Windsor and Detroit and was now spewing them to the surface. He had seen this before, seen fire floating on water, seen bodies blackened by flame. He tried to turn away, but instead found his eyes searching the boats for the one dark face he had come this far to forget.

Within a week he was back in sickbay. He hadn't kept food or even water down for days. He stared up at the ceiling, imagining he was a bird flying over a snow-covered expanse of solid ice, looking for land. The orderly told him his fever was 102 and rising. On the cot next to his, an accident case sat, brown and gaunt, propped against a pillow, with a bandage over his right eye and forehead.

"Fell down the aft companionway," he said, "carrying a tray of wineglasses up to the officers' mess. I'll get a medal for it." He grinned. His hair stuck out at odd angles from under the bandage. "What you got?"

Just then Doc Barnes came in.

"Have you been taking the pills?" he asked Jack.

"Yes, sir," Jack replied. Taking them and giving them to Frank.

"Every four hours?"

"On the bell, sir."

"Hmm. We'll try upping the dosage. They're new. Dr. Penfield at the Montreal Neurological Institute at McGill developed them. Navy's trying them out for him. Makes you a kind of guinea pig, Lewis. I'll give you some more, and this time, take them as required. Whenever you feel nausea coming on. Got that?"

"I'll be eating them like candy, sir."

"Try to keep track. If we can establish the proper dosage for you chronic cases it'll be a big step forward."

Jack decided to risk it. He hadn't detected any signs of recognition from the doc, but not knowing for sure was eating him up. "You're Peter's father, aren't you, sir," he said, trying to make his face look innocent.

"You know my son?" the doctor said, frowning.

"We were in the Sea Cadet band together. The All-Whites."

"Ah. Small world, isn't it." He stood peering at Jack as though trying to place him, then appeared to give it up. "In any case," he said, "we'll keep you here until you're rehydrated." At the door he turned. "We have to get you back to Windsor in one piece, don't we?"

Now what the fuck did that mean?

Still, it sounded as though he didn't mean to kill him. Maybe Peter hadn't said anything, after all. You couldn't trust anyone to do the obvious. He took two pills and felt all right for an hour, and when the icefield above his cot began heaving and breaking up again he took two more. He lay under the sheet in a cold sweat, unable to close his eyes, remembering the writhing bodies in the water, the strangers in the lifeboats. They must have hit some kind of weather system, the ship was bucking swells fore and aft as well as rolling from side to side. The bulkhead was being wrenched one way while the deck under him torqued in another. The war hero next to him was asleep. Jack took two more pills and, when he could close his eyes without getting sick, he fell asleep, too.

When he woke up, Surgeon Captain Barnes was sitting on a chair at the foot of his cot, writing something on his clipboard. Jack stared at the silver snake on his cap badge. The ship was so steady he thought they must have docked. And the air smelled fresh. Someone had sluiced the scuppers. What a relief. There was a glass of water with a straw in it on his nightstand, and he sat up and took a sip. He looked over at the next cot and saw not the war hero but two gasoline pumps with his father's truck parked beside them. The driver's door was open but there was no driver in sight. Through the open door he saw a woman in the passenger seat, smoking a cigarette and showing a lot of leg.

"Della?" he said.

Dr. Barnes eyed him. "What was that, bandsman?"

"Nothing, sir. How much do I owe you?"

"Owe me?"

"For the gas, sir."

Jack had to distract the doctor. Barnes must not look behind him and see his wife in Jack's truck. Jack heard the Dodge door slam and saw that someone had climbed into the driver's seat. It was his brother, Benny. Benny and Della? "You son of a bitch!" he yelled. "Find your own party!" Benny started the truck, drove it across the street and parked in front of the Ambassador Motel. Jack tried to get up and run but he was strapped into his cot.

"Steady on, bandsman," the doctor said. "How many of those pills have you taken?"

Behind the doctor's back, Frank Sterling and Ken Bradley were setting up their music stands. Rory Johnston came in carrying a bass drum with *W. H. Lewis & Sons, Plasterers* painted on the head and he began assembling the hi-hat and snare. Jack's father was standing at the microphone and Frank waved Jack up to the bandstand. Christ, couldn't he see he was sick? The doctor, still scribbling away, seemed unconcerned that behind the King's Men a huge hole had opened in the ship's side and a German U-boat was nosing its way into sickbay, sniffing for the *Assiniboine*'s boilers.

"Are you hallucinating, bandsman?" asked the doctor, standing up and facing him. "Are you seeing things?" In his hand he held a key chain in the shape of the Ambassador Bridge.

"I don't think so, sir."

"How many people are in this room?"

Jack looked around. Della and Benny had disappeared into Unit Six.

The doctor made a note. "Who were you talking to just now?"

"Myself, sir." It was true.

"You seem to be in some distress."

"Not really, sir." But seeing Della again, the line of her nylon stocking slightly askew, her skirt swinging as she walked towards the motel with Benny, who wouldn't be distressed? If the doc could see what he saw, he'd be in some distress himself. If there was a doc.

What was in those fucking pills? He looked at the band. They had changed into tuxedos and were smearing their faces and hands with black greasepaint. "Down Where the Swanee River Flows." No, not Al Jolson, he hated Al Jolson. And Dixieland, they burned people down in Dixie. A hatch opened in the U-boat and Hitler began climbing down a Jacob's ladder into sickbay. As the Führer stepped onto the deck the rope ladder became a hose, and then a noose around his father's neck, and Frank and the band struck up a Dixieland version of "St. James Infirmary." Jack twisted against the restraints in his cot, calling out in terror, but not loud enough to drown out Della's screams of pleasure coming from the motel.

VIVIAN

Mary Parsons was right, he looked so much like Frank Sinatra it took your breath away. Triangular face, curly black hair plastered to his forehead, a grin like a fox who knows where the chickens are kept, that was Jack Lewis, Newfoundland's newest singing sensation, as they called him on the marconi. Except he wasn't from Newfoundland, was he. Mary Parsons said every time she saw him she had to bite her knuckles to keep herself from screaming, but Mary Parsons was Catholic and Catholics were given to hysterics. Vivian's family was Church of England, solid as a rock. He did look like Frank Sinatra, but when that American sailor took her to see *Step Lively* at Fort Pepperrell, she hadn't liked Sinatra at all. Too brash. Jack Lewis thought he looked brash, but he wasn't quite pulling it off. Something about his eyes, well, they weren't blue for one thing, but it wasn't just that, there was a kind of pleading behind them, a coaxing, like they were saying, "Go along with me on this." Like even before tonight they'd been in something sinful together. She'd once found Mary Parsons smoking a cigarette in school, and Mary had given her a look like that: "Don't tell Matron." And she hadn't.

But if you didn't know better, if you forgot you were in the Knights of Columbus Hostel in St. John's, Newfoundland, and if you squinted up at the stage through the smoke and the darkness and the dancing couples, well, you might think it was Frank Sinatra up there, but you'd have to wonder what Frank Sinatra was doing in St. John's, looking like a lost kid. That was the difference—the real Frank Sinatra never looked lost.

Since she was at the K of C dance as a volunteer, selling lunches to raise money for the war effort, during the break she took a tray of sandwiches and tea to the band in the back room. The King's Men, they called themselves. They were drinking beer, which wasn't allowed but she didn't say anything. They were from the Navy Band down at HMCS *Avalon*. She'd seen them many times, parading back and forth from the base to the dockyards whenever a convoy sailed. They looked right smart in their dark blue uniforms, with white puttees and dickie fronts. But St. John's was full of men from away, and a girl had to be careful. She served him last, when there were just two halves left on the tray. By the time she got to him, she'd worked herself into a fine tizzy. He looked at her and she felt caught. There was only the tray between them.

He pointed at the sandwiches and asked, "What kind are they?"

"Fish. Mary Parsons made them and she's Catholic."

"What's that got to do with anything?"

Mainlanders didn't know much, did they. "The fish is left over from last night," she said. "Friday," she added when he looked at her blankly.

"Leftover fish," he said. "And tea." He took a swig from his beer bottle. "Just like home."

From close up he was handsome as all get out. His eyes seemed to pull her in and she had trouble keeping the tray straight. He was a bit wound up, she could tell that, it might be from being on stage but she hoped it was from being near her. He was tanned, like a fisherman, maybe he came from somewhere warm. She sensed a need in him that she liked because she thought it was a need she could fulfill. Everyone had needs, her parents, her sister, her younger brother, but satisfying their needs was something she had to do, she didn't have a choice in the matter. With this man, though, this stranger, she felt in her body that his were needs she would be happy to look after. His woollen uniform had dark stains down the back and his white dickie was soaked. She almost asked if he wanted her to find him a towel.

"You eat a lot of fish where you come from, do you?" she said, surprised that her voice was working.

"Enough."

"Where's it come from, then?"

"From a can."

"You mean from a tin."

"Yeah, from a tin can," he said. "How come your skin is so white? Don't you ever get any sun?"

"This is Newfoundland, Mr. Lewis. Have you seen any sun lately?" She should have called him Ordinary Seaman Lewis, but that sounded vulgar.

"My name's Jack," he said, holding out his hand. There was an awkward moment as she shifted the tray to her left hand and shook his with her right. His felt cold and bony, as if she were shaking a frog. It didn't repel her, though. It told her he was as nervous as she was.

"I'll call you Jack Tar," she said.

"That's a sailor, ain't it? That's me, then. Jack Tar," and he sang: "*I was born upon the deep blue sea.*"

He hadn't been, she thought. He hadn't been anywhere near the sea before. And she hadn't been anywhere else. "Well," she said, "if you don't want a sandwich . . . " She began turning from him.

"Wait." He reached out and held his hand a few inches from her chest, pretending to be choosing a sandwich. "They both look so nice," he said, looking up at her and smiling into her eyes. He thinks I'm a V-girl. Am I? Her arms ached from holding the tray, but she couldn't move. She could feel the heat from his hand through her blouse. "What's your name?" he asked.

"I'll never tell."

"Come on, I'll bet I can guess."

"Go ahead and try."

"Lily White."

"No," she said. "It's Vivian. Vivian Clift." It was only part of her name, but it was close enough.

Finally he looked down at her tray and took a sandwich. She almost stepped back, as though he had let go of her. "Thanks for the grub, Vivian Clift. Got a song you like? I'll sing it for you next set."

But she couldn't think of a song she liked, couldn't think of any song at all, not even one she didn't like. Her mind was still on his hand, its heat. "I'm not staying," she said. "I've got to get home."

"Too bad," he said, biting into his sandwich. "How much for the sandwich?"

"It's on the house," she said.

"Thanks." He washed the sandwich down with the last of his beer. "See you around, then, Lily White."

Not since she was a girl had she been dismissed so suddenly, as though she had failed a simple test. All the way home, as she crossed Buckmaster's Field and walked along Duckworth and up Admiralty Road, the street lights out and the houses and storefronts dark in the blackout, she remembered tons of songs she liked. They rolled off her tongue like the names of her father's ships. "Always." "Smoke Gets in Your Eyes." "I'm in the Mood for Love." What a dolt she was. "That Old Black Magic." "Don't Sit Under the Apple Tree." It wasn't as though she liked him. He was exactly like Frank Sinatra after all. Vain. Full of himself. Dangerous. She liked the lost little boy on stage, not the bantam rooster in the back room. "I'll Be Seeing You." "People Will Say We're in Love." "You Stepped Out of a Dream." Oh, shut up!

The next Saturday night when the announcer at VONF, the radio station that broadcast the K of C dances, introduced the King's Men and asked listeners to call in with requests, she rang at the start of the broadcast. Her fingers trembled so much she could hardly dial. "Tell Newfoundland's newest singing sensation that it's Lily White on the line," she said to the woman who answered. "Tell him she wants to hear 'Till We Meet Again.'"

He rang the house the next morning, one of the other girls had given him her number. She was at work at Baird's department store and her sister, Iris, answered. "Are all the girls in your family named after flowers?" he'd asked her sister, and Iris hadn't known what he was talking about. She said he sounded coarse and had a funny accent, but she still told him where Vivian worked, and he turned up at Baird's just before noon to ask her out for lunch. Strange, but he seemed smaller standing up, not much taller than she was and she was only five-two. He'd had a tailor alter his uniform by widening the bell-bottoms; they were so wide that in the ladies' wear department outside the accounts office he looked like he was trying on a long woollen skirt. She told him so and he laughed. "I'm afraid of drowning," he said. "With these cuffs I can get my pants off quicker if I fall overboard."

"That's fine talk," she said. "Here we are, only just met, and you talking about taking your trousers off."

My God, what was he going to think? To cover her embarrassment, she told him that Newfoundland men wore hip boots when they went to sea. "When a man falls overboard," she said, "his boots fill with water and carry him to the bottom."

Jack said, "Oh," as if he were in pain, and stopped, clapped both hands to his stomach and bent over. She touched his back. It was like touching the flank of a wild animal.

"Are you all right?"

"Why don't they just learn to swim?" he gasped. His face had gone white. "What would be the point of swimming," she said, "if your boat went down fifty miles from shore?"

He took her to a restaurant on Water Street, a workingman's café, narrow and dark and smelling of stale beer and fried fish. There was the rattle of cutlery on thick china and a drone of people talking, like the low sound of airplanes flying overhead. He led her through a pall of tobacco smoke to a booth at the back, almost at the kitchen door. Some of the other booths were filled with men from her father's warehouse, which was just down the street. "Afternoon, miss," they said, one after another, tugging at their cloth caps. They eyed Jack with suspicion, a fella from away with a local girl. Her father was ninety miles south in Ferryland, but he would know about this by suppertime.

"You have a lot of men friends," Jack said when they were seated.

"Jealous?" she asked.

"Naw, not me."

He'd taken off his cap and set it on the bench beside him, and his tightly waved, brilliantined hair shone in the dim light. He took a comb from his pocket and drew it over his temple, watching her, and then put it in an inside pocket of his tunic. She cleared her throat.

"The men work for my father," she said.

"All of them?"

"Most of them."

He whistled. "And here I thought you were just a typing clerk at Baird's."

"No you didn't," she said. "Whoever gave you my telephone number must have told you who I was."

"Naw," he said. "All I did was look up Lily White in the directory."

"Liar."

But she laughed and he reached across the table for her hand. There it was again, that need, "*Let me have this*," but she no longer thought he was just being fresh. He had a musician's hands, so thin his knuckles looked like walnuts in the fingers of a leather glove.

"What are you doing in St. John's?" he asked.

What was anybody doing in St. John's? "Living with my sister and her husband Freddie, and the twins." She withdrew her hand. She didn't want him touching her. Well, she did, but not here, not like this, not yet. "Is your band playing at the hostel again tonight?"

"You bet. Have you thought of another song you like?"

"Anything will do," she said.

"Sorry, don't know that one."

She laughed. God, she was giddy as a spring lamb. But he laughed, too. "I'll probably be busy at home tonight, anyway."

Playing with him like this was a dangerous game, like jumping from ice pan to ice pan in the Ferryland harbour. Watch your step, girl.

"Are those waves natural?" he asked.

"Are yours?" she countered.

"Naw," he said, sitting back. "That's what Brylcreem's for." He took the comb from his pocket and ran it through his hair again. A nervous tic. She found it reassuring.

She ended up going, of course. She gave the twins their bath and put them to bed, then put on a grey pleated skirt, her open-necked blouse with the pearl buttons and her checked tailored jacket. Very Gene Tierney. Even while she was putting on her lipstick she told Iris she wasn't going. But she couldn't resist the tug at her heart.

The band was already playing when she arrived at the K of C. Jack saw her come in and broke into a smile, waving to her from the stage. He wasn't playing drums this time, he was holding a trombone and standing at the front of the stage. She waved back, wriggling her fingers idiotically. Blushing, she sat at a table by herself and watched the others dance. The floor was so crowded she lost sight of the stage, but she could hear the trombone. Someone had cut out paper stars and pasted them to the ceiling, above the steam pipes. She hadn't noticed them before. Twice she took her turn at the service table and sold soft drinks and sandwiches and cigarettes. Maybe he would join her on his break.

It was as though she were testing herself. Not dancing with anyone, sitting alone, looking for any excuse to stand up and catch Jack's eye and smile at him. How much of this could she take? She was almost painfully sensitive, especially to Jack and what he was doing on the stage, as though every nerve had been rubbed raw and now she was pouring salt on them. It angered her, how silly she was getting, even envying his trombone when he put his lips to it. Get a grip on yourself. But how delicate his fingers on the slide, and what a smooth moan it made when he blew into it. She tilted her head to catch his voice when he sang, to hear him through the noisy crowd around the service table, as though hers were the only ears she wanted his words to reach.

When the band took its first break, he did come down to sit with her instead of going into the back room with his mates to drink beer. His forehead glistened and his hair hung in ringlets down one side of his face. She was conscious of the other girls watching them. Envious or resentful, she couldn't tell. She took a hankie from her purse and put it on the table in front of him, an offering. He looked at it but didn't pick it up. "Thanks," he said. He lit a cigarette and drank Coca-Cola from a bottle. "Fag?" he asked her, holding out a pack of Lucky Strikes.

"No, thank you."

"You don't smoke? You don't dance, either, I noticed. What else don't you do?"

"Lots," she said archly, then relented. "I never learned how to dance." The truth was she didn't like jitterbugging. She thought it was a fad that would pass, and then she'd just have to learn a new one anyway, so why bother? Instead, it kept getting more and more complicated, with the men doing the breakaway and the girls flying up into the air step to show off their nylon stockings. "Never had the right partner, I guess."

"I could teach you. I'm a whiz at it."

"I bet you are."

"Used to dance with my sister back home."

So he did have a family. "What's her name?"

A pause. "Alvina."

"Where's home, then?" She realized he'd not mentioned where he was from. With most people it would have been the first thing they talked about.

"Windsor. Ever heard of it?"

"No. Where's it at, then?"

"Across the river from Detroit."

She wasn't sure where Detroit was, either, but at least she'd heard of it. Something to do with motor cars. Her father bought his cars in England, brought them across strapped to the deck of one of the company's merchant vessels. Not since the war started, of course.

"My sister and me went across to the dance halls in Detroit. They had live bands, all the big names. Glenn Miller, Benny Goodman, Guy Lombardo. Glenn runs the American Army Air Force Band now. You ever hear them play 'In the Mood'?"

"On the marconi, yes. It's nice."

"And Tommy Dorsey. I'll play a little Tommy Dorsey for you next set. You're staying this time, ain't you?"

"I suppose I will."

"Here, have a drink."

He pushed his Coke bottle across the table and she put it to her lips, aware that his had just touched it. The Coke was warm and burned her throat.

"You've put rum in it!" she said, coughing.

"Good old Newfie Screech. Sailor's best friend."

"It's awful," she said, pushing the bottle back to his side of the table.

"Where are you from when you're not living with your sister?"

She told him she belonged to Ferryland, down the South Shore.

"Well, I better get back up there," he said, nodding at the stage. "Stick around till the bitter end and I'll walk you home."

"Maybe," she said.

"Say you will?"

"Why should I?"

"Just because," he said.

He was a flirt, she wouldn't trust him for a minute, but when he stood up and passed behind her she found herself leaning her head back and letting her hair brush his arm.

When the band returned to the stage they played two fast numbers to get the mampus on the floor. She almost wished she could join them, the smiling girls tossing their hair from their glistening foreheads, the men standing between songs with their arms around the girls' waists. That was an aspect of dancing she hadn't considered. Then Jack went to the microphone and announced that the next song was going out to Miss Lily White from Ferryland. He put a mute in the bell of his trombone and played "I'm Getting Sentimental Over You," Tommy Dorsey's signature tune. He played it slowly, not as high as Dorsey but more sensual, the muted notes sliding into one another and flowing out into the room like liquid smoke. On the floor, couples sank into one another, barely moving their feet. She felt the sound soak into her back and arms and chest. She held his Coke bottle in her hands and watched a couple she knew, a girl who worked in a dry cleaner's and a corporal from the Canadian air base. Seeing them together made the idea of herself and Jack seem possible. The music brought the pair closer and closer until the girl's head was resting on her partner's chest, as though she were listening to his heart.

The thought that Jack was playing, and that he was doing this for her, made her dizzy.

Later that night, at Iris's front door, she let him kiss her. Then she didn't see or hear from him again for three weeks.

"Throw him back, Viv, he's by-catch," Iris said when Vivian told her about the kiss the next day. "Forget him."

But she went over it a thousand times in her mind. They had been talking on the porch, saying good night. In the summer the porch was shaded with ivy, but now, in December, the dry leaves rattled in the wind and they stood close together to stay warm. Jack opened his greatcoat and wrapped her in it with him. There was no porch light because of the blackout, but the half moon was bright enough that she could see him clearly, especially his eyes. It was later than she usually came home but she wasn't tired. In fact, she'd never been so wide awake. They both kept bringing up new things to talk about. He wanted to know everything about her. He made her feel interesting.

"Why did you say you *belong* to Ferryland?"

"That's just how we talk. I belong to Ferryland. You belong to Windsor."

"Not me, kid," he said, looking away. "Not that place."

"Where do you belong to, then?" She broke away from the warmth of his greatcoat and leaned back against the door.

He lit a cigarette and grinned. There was always that hesitation before he spoke, as though he wanted to be certain of saying the right thing. Not the thing that was true, but the thing that put him in the best light.

"I belong to the Navy," he said, exhaling smoke.

"You can't belong to a thing, you belong to a place. Where you came from."

She didn't know why she was being so insistent about it. She actually agreed with him, at least in theory. He seemed to bring out the contrariness in her. And anyway, she didn't like to think of him belonging to the Navy. It was like belonging to the war. What would he belong to when the war ended?

"Don't you want to go back to Windsor?"

"Why should I?"

"Your family's there. It's where you belong."

"No, it ain't," he said. "You get born, you grow up and you leave. That's the way it is, see?" He threw his cigarette into a snowbank in the garden, as though he had lost interest in it, and put his hands in his coat pockets. "Why can't I belong to where I'm going?"

She thought about that. The war had torn up so many people, sent them to places they hadn't known about before, and not all of them would go back home. "I don't want to stay in Newfoundland forever," she said. "I want to travel, learn about new things."

"And never come back," he said.

"Oh, I'd come back, of course I would."

He half turned as if to go, and she remained leaning against the door, as if to let him. She felt irritated, as though they'd been arguing and he was refusing to make up. She didn't want him to leave. She knew he'd been expecting her to ask him in, it was cold out here on the porch, but she could never, not with her nieces upstairs and Iris maybe waiting up. Had she been too standoffish, was that it, too cool? Had he given up on her because she wasn't a V-girl? "The V doesn't stand for virgin, honey," Iris always said. But then he seemed to change his mind about leaving, and suddenly leaned into her, resting himself against her, smelling of cigarettes and bay rum. She'd had to thrust her pelvis out to keep from collapsing against the door, and he must have taken that for encouragement. His lips tasted metallic, probably from the trombone. He pressed into her, his chest against hers, his hands under her coat cupping the small of her back, the kiss itself almost incidental. His hands travelled up and down her back. Was she returning his kiss? Was she? She didn't know. It didn't feel like music, not slow and smooth. She put her hands on his shoulders, but one of them moved involuntarily to the back of his neck, felt his muscles tighten, and yes, she did thrust back. She was back inside his greatcoat, and the warmth of his body felt good. She didn't thrust too much, she told Iris, nothing lewd, more as though she were bracing herself. What else could a girl do?

"Stay away from him, that's what," Iris said.

"Why?"

"Viv, darling, he's a *sailor*."

"No, he's not, he's a musician." Iris wouldn't appreciate the difference. But seeing, no, *feeling* what Jack could do with music told her that he was different, special, that a person didn't get that good at something unless it was already part of him. And part of her. Surely only someone who already had beauty inside them could make such beautiful music. "He's only a sailor because of the war," she said. "You should hear him play. The sound goes right through you."

"So does cod liver oil."

"Oh Iris, don't be vulgar. Please."

"Father rang this evening while you were out."

Vivian groaned. "What did he say?"

"He gave me hell for letting you traipse about town on your own."

"I wasn't traipsing. And I wasn't alone. We were in a restaurant, having lunch."

"Five thousand Yanks in the colony, he said, and I've got to keep you away from all of them."

"Well, you needn't worry. Jack isn't a Yank and he won't call again, I'm sure of it."

"Oh, he'll call, all right. If he doesn't, he's worse than a Yank. He's an idiot."

But he didn't call that week or the next, and when she turned on the marconi on Saturday night it wasn't the King's Men doing the Voice of Newfoundland broadcast but another band, the Starlighters, and she thought, Well, then, that's cut it. She stayed away from the K of C, resigned herself to spinsterhood. She

to nothing, tea and toast, changed into her nightgown and slippers and stretched out on the sofa with the cushions around her and the blackout curtains drawn against the harsh sunlight. She loved Iris's living room. It was exactly the right size, big enough for really comfortable furniture but small enough to feel cozy. It was the kind of room she would want if she were married. A living room should be lived in, she told herself, thinking of her mother's waking room, which was opened only for funerals and when the Anglican minister came to tea. That made her think of Jack. She tried to read Thomas Raddall's new book, *Roger Sudden*, but it didn't hold her attention. Bigger fish, she kept thinking. But there weren't, and anyway, Jack was a perfectly good-sized fish. Big enough to take her away from Newfoundland and show her how other people lived. She wasn't like Iris, who had been off the island only once in her life and hadn't liked it. For their honeymoon, she and Freddie had gone to Brazil on a company ship with a load of salt cod. They'd stayed in Rio de Janeiro while the ship called at ports farther south. They had taken a cable car up Sugarloaf Mountain, in the middle of the bay, and ridden a bus up to the base of the Finger of God. The place was, Iris said, merely squalid. She had not felt comfortable at all. She described the *favelas*, where the poor blacks lived in shacks terraced down the mountainside like so much accumulated debris. Dogs and babies, that's all you saw and heard. Little pickaninnies with their hair all matted and something wrong with their eyes. Freddie told her about the half-naked Negro men loading sacks of coffee, the smell of fruit in the market stalls in the early morning before the mist had burned off the hillsides.

Finally, after almost a month had gone by and Vivian had given up all hope of ever seeing him again, Jack rang. It was a Friday night, a week before Christmas. He'd been to sea, he said. "Escort duty, almost to Ireland and back. Even bandsmen have to go to sea sometimes," he said.

"You could have told a person."

"No, I couldn't. I didn't know myself until the last minute, none of us did. Loose lips sink ships."

As soon as he said it she realized she ought to have trusted him. All the while she'd been mooning around St. John's he'd been on a ship at sea, fighting the enemy. He might have been killed. Just that morning she'd been reading the Newfoundland *Bulletin*, which gave all kinds of unsettling news about soldiers and airmen and sailors wounded and lost. She'd looked for names she recognized. "*Signaller Edward Flanagan of the 166th (Newfoundland) Field Regiment and Corporal Duncan J. Mercer who was serving with the Canadian Army have been killed in action. Pilot Officer Kevin J. Evans and Sergeant Walter Sweetapple, both serving with the R.A.F., have been killed in air accidents. Gunner Frederick Robertson died on September 15th at a Military Hospital at Shrewsbury.*" Jack's name might easily have been among them. What would she have done?

Chastened, she agreed to see him again. Longed to see him again. She would go to the K of C on Saturday and watch him play, and they could talk during breaks, she would like that, she said.

"And I could walk you home again."

And she said, "Yes."

"And what about during the week?"

"I work during the week."

"Can't you get a day off?"

No, she couldn't, not unless she called in sick again. And if she did that, she would have to stay home and let Iris look after her. With the war economy, the store had never been so busy, and Mr. Baird was a friend of her father's. But everyone was taking time off work to do their Christmas shopping. "I might be able to get an extra hour for lunch one day," she said. Not much of a war effort, was it? "Tuesday," she said. "Don't come to the store. I'll meet you someplace."

"Where?"

She couldn't think. Her father had spies everywhere. "The train station," she said, "at the lower end of Water Street. It has a lunch counter."

The train station was full of people, mostly men in uniform but many in fedoras and civilian clothes, government men, she guessed, although more interesting than that. Movie actors, perhaps, a scene from *Heaven Can Wait*. They didn't look local, anyway. Those in uniform were either American GIs going back to their base at Stephenville or airmen from Fort Pepperrell, the U.S. Air Force base on the shore of Quidi Vidi Lake that she'd heard had been laid out in the shape of a cowboy hat. She didn't know where the civilians were going. Off the island, presumably, off the map. They sat at the tables or on the benches reading newspapers, or paced back and forth in the waiting area, smoking. There were a few other women, WRENs and local girls kissing their Yankee boyfriends goodbye. She would kiss Jack like that when he got there. He would swoop her up in his arms and say, "The war can wait."

She thought he wasn't there yet, and then she saw him. He had a table, and had placed his greatcoat and cap on the chair beside him, saving a place for her. And on the table was a glass of Coke for him and a pot of tea for her. That was all it took. He was the only one in the station in a Navy uniform. He looked so young, a little boy in a sailor's suit. He saw her and waved and she waved back. Eyes turned in her direction.

He put his greatcoat on the table, then took it off the table and placed it on the floor under his chair, then put his cap on the table, then took it off the table and placed it on top of his greatcoat, where it fell to the floor. She picked it up and put it on her lap when she sat down. They decided on fish and chips. Jack took a flask from inside his tunic and topped up his glass of Coke. He offered to pour some into her teacup, but she said, "Thanks but no thanks." She didn't know anyone who drank in the middle of the day, not even her father.

"This place gives me the creeps," he said, looking around the crowded room.

"Why? It's just a train station."

Something had changed in him. He was uncomfortable. She

wished she'd thought of somewhere more private for their first date, even Baird's would have been better than this.

"Any one of these bums could be a spy," he said, indicating the men in civilian dress. "On the Derry Run we sank this U-boat, see, then we had to stop and pick up the survivors. There weren't many. We had to go out in boats and hook them out of the water. The brass wanted to know what ship they'd been attached to, for intelligence." He paused and took a drink.

"How awful," she said.

That mocking look had gone out of his eyes. Three long weeks at sea had taken the confidence out of him, and although she hadn't liked his cockiness, she liked this nervousness even less.

She wondered if the German government sent out something like the *Bulletin*, if there were German women sitting in their kitchens at this very moment reading of the deaths of husbands or brothers or fiancés. Men who'd died fighting for something the women didn't believe in. Of course there were. She wanted to take his hand, to draw him closer to her, closer than the war, and stop him from speaking these horrors. But she didn't, and he went on.

"Some of the bodies were wearing ordinary clothes, suits, socks, ties—just like these guys. You'd think they were us, except they were German spies, going to be put ashore in Halifax or St. John's to pose as Canadians, mingle with the sailors and GIs in the bars, get them talking, find out what their orders are. They had theatre tickets in their pockets for movies playing that week, and ration booklets, matches from St. John's and Halifax nightclubs. They had passports with Canadian names, home addresses in Ontario and Manitoba, letters from sweethearts, photos of wives and children."

"Where did they get all those things?"

"From our guys who were shot in Europe, that's where," he said.

She gasped.

"Yeah," he said. "Remember what I said about loose lips?" He nodded towards a group of civilians standing by the Departures sign. "They could all be spies. You can't tell anything about a person just by the way he looks." He looked at her for so long she thought she had missed something.

"Not you, Jack," she said. "You're exactly what you look like."

"Yeah," he said. "That's right. You're safe with me."

She put her hand lightly on his arm.

"We could buy two tickets and be a thousand miles away by this time tomorrow," he said. "The sky's the limit. What do you say?"

Was that a proposal? The war had brought the world to Newfoundland, to her door. Hadn't she wanted the world? Yes, but she wanted to leave the island to see it, not have it hauled aboard like some thrashing sea creature. And now he, too, wanted to be on the move, get off the island, see something. Where was a thousand miles away? She read down the column of figures on the Departures sign. There was a train leaving for Port-aux-Basques at one o'clock, in time to catch the late ferry to North Sydney. It didn't seem very adventuresome, but it would be a start.

"You just got back," she said.

"Three weeks at sea." He shuddered. "I'm no good at it. I should have joined the Army, like them." He looked at the American GIs with their girlfriends.

"Is Windsor a port, then?"

"Not like St. John's. It's on a river."

"How do you cross the river?"

"There's a ferry, a bridge, and a tunnel big enough to drive cars through."

"I'd like to see that," she said. Was she being too bold? She didn't care. She wanted to know more about him. "What do you do in Windsor?"

"Work for my father," he said, his voice gloomier than ever. Then he seemed to perk up. He finished his Coke, caught the waitress's eye and ordered another. She thought she had better get back to work, but she wanted to hear about his father. "He owns a construction company in Windsor," Jack said. He made a square with his hands, like a sign: "'W. H. Lewis and Sons Limited.' There's me and my brother, Benny, and Dad's brother, Uncle Harley, when we need him. If we get too many houses to do we hire more people. It's a classy outfit. Not as big as *your* father's, of course, but big enough. We did the Fox Theatre in Detroit. You ever hear of it?"

"Can't say I have."

"Huge job. Took six months."

"Do you like construction work?" she asked.

"Naw, I hate it. That's why I took up music. Joined up as

soon as I could. To get away, see?"

"Get away from Windsor?"

"The work, the family, all that . . . " He stopped to light a cigarette. All that what? The waitress came with his drink. This time he drank half of it before taking his arm from her hand and refilling the glass with rum.

"Why do you want to get away from your family?" she asked.

He looked at her as though she had asked an odd question. "A fella's got to strike out on his own." He reached over and took her hand. "Don't you think so?"

"This is an island, Jack. I've never been off it. People are born here, live here all their lives, and die without ever knowing a thing about the rest of the world. Maybe you don't realize it, but people here look down their noses at people like you."

He pulled his hand away as though she'd burned it.

"I don't mean you, silly," she said, taking his hand back. "I mean anyone from away, soldiers and sailors. They complain about you all the time, as if you're the ones who've invaded us, not the Germans." Jack took a drink with his free hand. "They don't complain about you risking your lives to keep U-boats and spies out of our harbour, but would you mind keeping your dirty paws off our daughters, thank you?"

He looked at her blankly. She hadn't realized how strongly she felt until she'd said it. Now indignation filled her on his behalf, the injustice of it. People like Jack should be thanked. Newfoundlanders should get down on their knees and thank God for these men.

"You're not like them, though, are you?" he said.

"No, Jack, I'm not."

"You don't mind me putting my dirty paws on you?" He held one of her fingers, it was her ring finger, and rubbed his thumb gently along its side, then brushed it lightly over the little V where the finger joined the body of her hand. It made her throat throb. Maybe she was a V-girl after all.

"The war," he said, not letting go of her hand, pressing his finger into the V. "It won't last much longer."

If she had wanted to, if she still had control of her limbs, she would have withdrawn her hand from his at that instant. She would have changed the subject, told him that at Baird's they were having a special on razor blades, he should tell his buddies, or that in May the harbour at Ferryland filled with migrating birds—baccalieus, turnstones, sandpipers—and that her father was fanatical about them. But she didn't say that. Or anything. She didn't want him to think that his hand was dirty, or that she looked down her nose at him, and she knew by saying nothing, by letting this moment pass unremarked upon, she was saying yes to something, and that later to pretend that nothing had transpired between them would be to go back on a promise.

"I guess you'd better come over some evening," she said, her voice trembling, "to meet Iris and Freddie and the twins."

JACK

He thought he'd left family behind when he joined up and got out of Windsor, but he'd been wrong. He'd go to her house if she wanted him to, he was on his way now, wasn't he? But he'd be damned if he was going to start comparing families with her. People from Windsor didn't go around poking their noses into other people's families. You never knew what might turn up.

Admiralty Road was in a good part of town. He walked with his fists stuffed into his greatcoat pockets, peering through the gathering dusk at the house numbers until he came to a gate marked 17. He'd been here before, when he walked her home after the dance, but it had been dark and his mind had been elsewhere. He stopped, his hand on the latch of the wrought-iron gate, and looked up. Christ, the place was a fucking palace. Even the chimneys had turrets. He said he'd meet her sister, not the Queen of England. Through the gate he could see where snow had slid off the roof and piled on top of flower beds under the mullioned windows. Fuck this. It was back to the barracks for him, or down to the Caribou Club, where his mates would be swilling beer and playing darts or writing to their sweethearts, minding their own business. But he'd told Frank he had a date, so he couldn't go back early. Everyone would think he'd been stood up. Was the gate locked from the inside to keep people like him out? He began to turn away. He was cold and his feet were wet. He was in the wrong part of town. Then, through the fence and across a narrow strip of snow-covered lawn, he saw a blackout curtain move and then fall back, and a few seconds later the front door opened.

"Are you going to stand out there all night?" Vivian called.

He pushed on the gate and it swung open easily. Vivian stood on the porch, wearing a green skirt and a fuzzy sweater with fake pearl buttons, at least he assumed they were fake. She had her arms wrapped around herself and her knees slightly bent, and she was shivering. But smiling, and her eyes didn't look cold at all. She took his arm and drew him into the shadow of the porch so he could kiss her. When she took him in, the family was waiting, standing back from the door like they thought he might have the Spanish flu. He stomped the snow off his boots on a small rug in the vestibule and unbuttoned his greatcoat.

"This is my sister, Iris," Vivian said, "and this is her husband, Freddie, and these are the twins, Sadie and Beverley. Everyone, this is Jack."

The house smelled of floor wax and cooking. He smiled at the faces lined up in front of him. Iris looked like trouble, Freddie looked henpecked, and the two little girls looked like he had double vision.

"How do you tell them apart?" he asked. He looked down at everyone's feet. Slippers. Should he take off his boots?

"Iris is the one in the dress," Freddie said, laughing at his own joke.

Jack looked at Vivian. "I meant the twins."

"Here, old boy," Freddie said, "let me take your coat."

"There's a bottle in it," Jack said. He rummaged in his pocket and found it. "Rum. I thought you might like it."

"How thoughtful," said Iris, taking the bottle of Screech. "I'll just take it in the kitchen and make some tea." She turned and walked towards a confusion of rooms at the back of the house, nothing as simple as a hallway. Vivian followed her.

"It's about all you can get these days," Jack said to Freddie. He'd grown to like rum. His father and brother and his Uncle Harley drank beer and sometimes bourbon. He was looking forward to going into the British-American Hotel in Windsor and ordering Lamb's Navy dark and a Coke. His father would say he was putting on the Ritz.

He wished Vivian hadn't followed Iris. He stood looking around the vestibule while Freddie hung up his wet coat. The closet doors were narrow and high, arched at the top like the doors of an Anglican church. High ceilings, you'd need scaffolding to plaster them. Good work, though, some fancy cove mouldings at the corners and a rosette in the centre, all hand-made of course. But no ceiling fixture, someone had taken that down. Nice cathedral effect in the living room when Freddie led him into it, but the room itself was disappointing, even shabby: worn furniture, magazines and books lying about, lampshades askew. Only the blackout curtains were decent. He would have thought people like them would be tidier, more careful about how things looked, especially when they were having company. Freddie straightened a rug with his foot and motioned him to a chesterfield covered with little square pillows. Why pillows? Did someone sleep there? Was he supposed to move them or sit on them? But the twins ran ahead giggling and jumped on the chesterfield, so he took one of the tired-looking stuffed chairs. There were two pillows on it. He moved one aside and sat on the other. Where the hell was Vivian?

"We'll have our tot in a minute," Freddie said. He was tall, elegant, with a kind of Jimmy Stewart look. Long, fair hair combed straight back, razor cut at the neck, never seen a hat. He was wearing dress pants and a wool sweater buttoned up the front over a white shirt and no tie. Jack liked his face, angular but open, no venom in it, rather a kind of innocence, like he'd be a soft touch. "We've been drinking mostly wine lately," Freddie went on, sitting in the chair opposite the chesterfield. There was a coal fire in the grate and Freddie poked at it, sending a spray of sparks out onto the hardwood floor, where he kicked at them vaguely with his slippered foot. "Fortunately we had a load in before the war started, got it put down in the cellar. Argentine," he said, looking up. Jack nodded. "Quite good, actually."

"Yes," Jack agreed. "It gives off a good heat."

Freddie smiled uncertainly. "Nice way of putting it."

The twins were sitting in temporary truce on the chesterfield, watching their father play with the fire. "And how old are you?" Jack asked them.

"Seven and three-quarters," one of them said, and the other one continued, "and Mommy's twenty-eight, and Auntie Viv is nineteen, and Daddy's thirty-two."

"How old are you?" asked the first one.

"I'm eighteen." He bit his tongue; he should have said twenty.

"I sleep with Sadie," said the one who must have been Beverley, "and Mommy sleeps with Daddy, and Auntie Viv sleeps with herself."

"Who do you sleep with?" Sadie asked him.

"That's enough, girls," Freddie said.

"I sleep with thirty-five men in a barracks," said Jack.

The twins howled. "What's a *barracks*?" Beverley asked.

"A big building with lots of beds in it." Two long rows of cots, eighteen to a side, each with its drumhead of white woollen blanket with a single black stripe, and a metal locker, regimental numbers stencilled on the door. The blanket itched. He'd got used to the snoring and farting and drunken roughhousing. In fact, he liked it. It was what men did. The incessantly polished, unforgiving linoleum floor reflected the square of light coming through the window in the bathroom door, and he liked that, too.

"That's a *hospital*!" said Sadie knowingly.

"Mommy and Auntie Viv seem to be taking a long time with the rum," said Freddie. "Why don't you two go and see if they're leaving any for us."

The twins scampered off and Freddie turned to Jack. "Vivian tells us you're from Ontario somewhere. Windsor, is it?"

Jack noticed the way they called her Viv amongst themselves, but Vivian when addressing him, as though her name was their private possession, not to be used by strangers. "Windsor, yes," he said. "Across from Detroit."

"Never been there, I'm afraid. Been to Toronto a few times."

"What line of work are you in?" Jack asked, man to man.

"Oh, import and export. Feeding the troops and all that."

"Import and export?"

"Our people bring in fish, and we pack it up and ship it off to Merrie Olde on the Derry Run. We also bring sugar and rum up from the Islands, bit of coffee and cocoa. Surprised the Germans haven't got *us* blocked off. Torpedo the odd fishing boat and the whole fleet would stay in harbour. That'd starve the Brits out. Your lot's doing a fine job of keeping the U-boats out of Cabot Strait."

His lot? "Not me," Jack said. "I'm just a bandsman."

"Not a bit of it," Freddie protested. "Morale is everything. You must know that."

"I guess so."

"You've done wonders for Vivian's morale, I can tell you. Regular droop before you came along." Freddie went back to poking at the fire. "What do your people do in Windsor, if you don't mind my asking?"

His people? He bloody well did mind. "They build houses."

Freddie started to say something, but then Iris and Vivian came in carrying trays and trailing the twins.

"Wait, girls, just wait, for heaven's sake," Iris said, setting her tray precariously on top of the books and magazines on the low coffee table in front of the chesterfield. On the tray were a teapot, four cups, a stack of saucers and a plate of cookies. Vivian placed her tray on a side table. It held an ice bucket, two tumblers and a bottle of rum—not the one he'd brought.

"Cookies!" said the twins in unison.

"Make them yourself, Auntie Viv?" Jack asked Vivian.

"Vivian can't boil water—can you, love?" Iris said.

"I can make toast."

"Yes, but you have to pull the blackout curtains first in case the wardens think you're signalling the Germans with the flames."

"Iris, that happened once."

"Will you have some tea, Jack?" Iris asked. "Or do you prefer rum?" Everything she said had an edge to it, a secret meaning she would hint at but was not willing to share outright.

"I'll have a bit of the serum, if you don't mind," he said. Was that polite enough for her?

Iris laughed, not entirely pleasantly, and got up to pour the tea. Jack wondered what it was she was so disappointed in. She didn't know anything about him.

"You don't like going to sea, I hear."

"It's not that I don't like it," he said. "I get seasick. The doc thought I was going to die out there. I spent most of the run hanging over the side with the dry heaves."

"We have men working for us who are just the same," said Iris. "Still, they go out every day to fish."

"Mommy, what's the dry heaves?" asked one of the twins.

"I've read somewhere," said Freddie, "that Polynesians actually boast about getting seasick. And they're the best sailors in the world."

"Mommy, what's the dry heaves?"

"Not now, girls."

Jack gave Vivian his best Frank Sinatra smile. She looked lovely, sitting on the chesterfield beside the twins, hands folded in her lap, knees slanted demurely a few degrees away from him. Pretty as a pin-up. Now Iris, on the other hand, she still hadn't brought him his drink.

"On second thought, Iris," Jack said, "maybe I'll have a cup of tea."

Iris asked Sadie to pass her a cup from the tray, and Freddie asked Jack if he intended to go back to Windsor when the war was over.

"Only if we win it."

"Really?" Iris said, handing Jack his tea. "All the way back there?"

"Oh, well, you know," Jack said. "I haven't decided yet." He looked at Vivian. Something had startled her. "Who knows," he said, "maybe I'll stay here."

Iris looked at Vivian. Jack smiled at the twins. No one said a word.

WILLIAM HENRY

The house William Henry and Benny were working on was in Walkerville, owned by a man who worked at Hiram Walker's, an accountant or something, something to do with money, anyway. It was a big yellow-brick house with ivy growing over it, looked like a jungle there on Willistead Crescent, attached garage, private backyard, must have cost a fortune to build, and Hiram Walker probably gave it to him. William Henry regarded working in the man's house not so much as an obligation as a kind of promise he was fulfilling that he wished he hadn't made. It was a small job, anyway: take out a stud wall between two rooms on the ground floor to make a larger room. William Henry had told Jackson to quote high so they wouldn't get it, a hundred dollars, but the owner went for it anyway. Money meant nothing to some people. It was their second morning at it. William Henry and Benny did the grunt work in the mornings while Jackson got his beauty rest, and then Jackson did the easy work after lunch.

Benny had already taken a crowbar to the wall and had most of the plaster on the floor, and William Henry was pulling the exposed laths off carefully because they were hand-split cedar, not machine-made, and he would reuse them somewhere else, maybe in the dream home they kept talking about building for themselves. Maybe out River Canard way. Two dream homes, one for him and Josie and one for Benny and whoever he settled down with. Alvina could have their current house in town. Jackson wouldn't be wanting a home in River Canard. That wasn't his dream.

Which was too bad, thought William Henry, as he worked the lath nails loose. Jackson always seen himself as destined for better things. Well, who didn't? Didn't Benny want better? Didn't William Henry want better for both his sons? Just that for Jackson, better meant whiter.

"When I get my own place," Benny said, "I'm going to have faucets like the ones they have in their bathroom upstairs. You seen 'em? Some kind of polished copper or maybe brass, looks like gold, anyway. And a stand-up shower. And they got closets in each room big enough you could turn one of them into a bedroom. These people were not brought low by the Depression, like we was."

"Some people do well in hard times," William Henry said.

William Henry and Benny agreed on most things. These days, anyway. Wasn't always the case. Benny had been wild in his youth. Drinking and fighting, shoplifting, minor offences but they added up. William Henry had been down to the police station more than once to bring him home. For a while there he thought he was going to lose both his sons.

"Why he ain't in the Army?" the cop asked the last time. "The Army'd straighten him out soon enough."

But it wasn't Benny who needed straightening out, it was Jackson. The damn fool couldn't even wait until he turned eighteen, tried to join when he was sixteen, lied about his age. His mama had to go down to the recruiting office herself to show them his birth certificate and get him out of it. What he want to go and do a thing like that for, give his mama a heart attack? What did that war have to do with him anyway?

William Henry had known there was a chip on that boy's shoulder since the day he was born, as soon as the women wouldn't let him into the bedroom to see his newborn son. They were living on Tuscarora then, in that small house with no basement and water heating on the oil stove, and the walls so thin he could hear everything going on in the next room, Josie forgetting she'd turned Baptist and calling on her Catholic saints to help her, the women wringing out towels in the basin and telling her to push, that's right, darlin', push a little more, that's it, while he sat in the front room with Alvina and little Benny wondering what in God's name he was going to do to pay the bills.

The Chrysler plant had just opened at the top of McDougall so it must have been 1925. He might be able to get a job there. They didn't hire coloureds for the assembly line, but they did for the foundry, which was dirtier work. He'd been plastering and doing odd jobs around the Settlement, hauling ashes, cleaning garages, anything he could do with a truck. They'd been getting by, it wasn't the Depression yet, but they didn't need another mouth, that was for sure. A big one, too, by the sound of it. And then everything went quiet in there, all at once, like an angel flew over, and he knew something gone wrong.

He couldn't hear Josie anymore. He remembered looking at Alvina and her looking at him. She was twelve, old enough to know what was going on, but Benny was only four, he was playing with some pieces of wood on the floor. They stopped moving, poised to listen, like they were in a forest, like they knew their future was about to become even harder than they thought it was going to be. He turned to look at the wall and saw the photograph of Josie's sister, Hazel, and thought someone would have to tell her, if they could find her, because she'd gone off to Chicago. And then he thought of Josie's father, the Reverend John S. Rickman, the AME pastor, who was somewhere in Indiana now, he'd have to be notified even though he was the one who gave Josie up for adoption. And then the baby started crying, maybe it had been sucking all that time, and he heard Josie's voice pleading, don't let him in, don't let him in. But he was so happy to hear her voice he got up and went in anyway.

William Henry stared down at the lath in his hands and realized he had drifted off. That was happening a lot lately.

"We need to cut that wire and re-run it through the ceiling," Benny said, lighting a cigarette and looking at him oddly.

William Henry nodded. "We're going to lose money on this job," he said. "Jackson should've known that wire was in there."

Benny shrugged. "Not even Jackson can see through walls," he said, and they both laughed.

In the truck, heading into the city for lunch at the British-American Hotel, William Henry's mood lifted. It was as though they were setting off on a vacation together, father and son, a limitless stretch of freedom, understanding each other perfectly, united in the work that lay behind them and the hours that stretched ahead. He never had that feeling with Jackson. But William Henry *had* got up from his chair in the front room the day Jackson was born, and he *had* gone into the bedroom to see his child, as what man wouldn't? "You kids stay here," he'd said to Alvina and Benny, who anyway made no move to join him. The women had changed the sheets on the bed and Josie was sitting propped up against the wall, holding the little bundle to her and looking at William Henry as though he was the Devil himself come to take the baby from her. Boy or girl? he asked. They already had one of each so it didn't matter to him. It was one of the women who said, "Boy." Josie didn't say anything, nor even lift the corner of the blanket to show him.

"Alive?" William Henry asked. Why else would they be acting so strange?

"Of course he alive," the other woman said. "Didn't you hear him hollerin' just now?"

William Henry leaned over his wife. "Josie?" he said. She was getting ready to cry, her chin wrinkled up and trembling.

"Oh, Willie," she said. "I never thought. All the time I was carryin' him I never thought . . . "

"Thought what? What you sayin', girl?"

She looked away from him, turning her head so far from him that the cords on the side of her neck stood out like tree roots. Then just as quickly she looked back to him. But this time she was defiant. With one hand she carefully unwrapped the bundle she'd been holding against her, exposing the child to him. By now he knew the baby had to be deformed in some way. He'd heard of babies born with extra toes, or tails, or with paddles for arms, or enormous heads with bulging eyes, every sort of affliction on this earth. He prepared himself for a shock. The light in the room was not good, but this baby looked all right to him. He could see two arms and legs, a little body curled up like a crawdad in the crook of Josie's arm.

Relief washed over him. "I don't see nothin' wrong with him."

Josie looked down at the baby. "Open the curtain, will you, Ephie, dear."

Light streamed in. William Henry saw immediately what was wrong. He saw the baby's pink cheek working to release the milk from Josie's dark breast. The baby's pink fingers, tightly closed with the effort of kneading Josie's stomach. Its little pink legs gently kicking.

"This here's a white baby," he said, horror-struck. Deformed after all.

"No, it's not," Josie said, pleading. "It can't be, Willie. It's just real light, is all."

"It's not. It's a white baby."

"I want you to love this baby, Willie."

"I can't, Josie. It ain't mine."

"Willie, it is. It surely is."

"How can that be so?" he said, louder than he intended.

"I don't know," she said. "But I swear it is."

He could see her wretchedness and it pained him, but his eyes kept going back to the child, a pale blemish against her beautiful skin.

"This," William Henry thundered, "is a white man's baby!"

"No!" Josie shrieked. "No, Willie, it's yours."

But William Henry was beyond listening. He felt his chest tighten as he realized what must have happened. He stood in his fury, his mind racing with the face of every white man he had ever known who she could have done this with. There were white men in the Settlement, plenty of them, workers who come up for the war jobs and the high wages but found them all taken, salesmen down on their luck, factory men between factories, he saw them every day when he went out for his shave. Did one come in here and make this baby when . . . ? Oh God, he'd made it so easy for them! He looked down at her now, her face streaked with misery, clutching the child to her breast. How could she have done this? And how could he stay here, how could he ever be seen with them? Might as well hang a sign around his neck!

He must have turned towards the door, because he heard Josie begging him, "Don't go, Willie," when not two minutes before she'd been saying don't let him in. He was at the bedroom door, then he was at the front door. He would not turn back. His hand was on the latch. Little Benny looked up from his wood scraps. He was wearing the green-and-blue-striped shirt that Hazel had sent him from Chicago. Alvina stared at him sombrely from the sofa, a little adult. They'd be all right without him. His hat was on the peg beside the door and he put it on.

"Where you going, Daddy?" Benny asked. "Can I come?"

"You stay here with your Mama and—" But he couldn't say "your new little brother." Couldn't get the words out. "And be good."

He went straight down to the British-American, Josie's wailing still in his ears, let the whole neighbourhood hear it, he didn't care, it had nothing to do with him. And he didn't step foot outside the hotel for a whole month.

VIVIAN

Jack was right: within months of his coming back from the Derry Run, the talk in St. John's was all about how soon the war would end. No more mines turned up in the harbour, the U-boats were all but cleared from Cabot Strait, and most of the convoys were getting across the Atlantic without being attacked at all. Allied troops in Europe and North Africa were being well supplied; it was the Germans who were starving and ill equipped, their morale low, so low, all the papers said, that any day now Hitler would capitulate or be relieved of command. People began to forget to close their blackout curtains at night and were talking about what they would do when rationing was over. Her father even mentioned going to England on one of the merchantmen. Mother told him not to be so dreadful daft, the Blitz could start up again at any time, but her father said his business was in Paignton, in Devonshire, where the family was from, and to his certain knowledge Paignton had not been targeted in a single air attack. Besides, the Luftwaffe was totally destroyed. Vivian told him she hoped he wouldn't go, but if he did she would like to go with him, to which her mother responded by taking to her bed and not reappearing for a week.

Freddie joked over dinner one Sunday that if her father went to England he'd have to join one of the convoys, and Jack could accompany him as an escort. "At least as far as Iceland," he said. But Jack, who was having dinner with them most Sundays now, only laughed and said he couldn't go if he wanted to. The medical officer on his last ship had filled out papers restricting him to shore duty.

"Worst case of seasickness he's ever seen." Jack seemed almost proud of it, as though he were Polynesian.

Of course Iris was appalled. Everything about Jack appalled her. "You mean to say that because you get a little seasick you don't have to go to sea anymore? You can just futter around here playing at dances and having gobs of fun?"

"I don't get just a little sick," Jack said. "I get *really* sick, all the time."

"He gets the dry heaves," Sadie announced proudly.

Vivian looked at him, trying to read his thoughts, but his face was a blank.

"Then you'll never make a Newfoundlander," Iris said.

Vivian glared across the table at her sister. "You join the Navy to see the world, Iris," she said. "Not the backside of some stuck-up little island."

"Oh, is that so?" Iris replied. "I would have thought seeing the world required a person to be able to set foot on a *ship* from time to time."

Freddie evidently felt it a good point at which to intervene. "Given any more thought as to what you intend to do after the war, Jack?" he asked.

Now Vivian glared at Freddie. It was her question to ask, not his. And it was one she'd been afraid to ask. Whatever he answered would mean a huge but ambiguous change in her life. She desperately wanted something; she couldn't say exactly what it was, but she felt it could only come from Jack. She liked things to come upon her suddenly, so she wouldn't have time to think and get confused and possibly make the wrong decision. She believed the best time to make a decision was when it was too late to make a different one.

"I don't know what I'll do," he said. "Go back to working for my father, I guess."

There was an awkward silence around the table. Even the twins went quiet. Vivian concentrated on her plate. The potatoes were mealy and the meat was tough. Freddie called Sunday their "day of roast," but lately the cuts were so bad Iris said she would set out steak knives if it wouldn't be so embarrassing. Everyone was waiting for Jack to speak, but he seemed unaware of the fact. He filled his mouth with mashed potato and took a rather loud sip of tea to wash it down. Iris winced, set down her knife and fork and told the twins they could be excused.

He left soon after dinner, looking angry or hurt, Vivian couldn't tell which. But when she saw him to the door, he said he would see her at the K of C on Friday. A whole week away, she thought. After he was gone, Vivian put the twins to bed and then helped Iris clean up. They washed and tidied together in silence, then Iris put the kettle on and they sat at the kitchen table drinking tea and smoking cigarettes. Lucky Strikes, Vivian noted, left behind by Jack.

"You can't seriously be thinking of marrying that . . . " As usual, she had already had most of the conversation in her head and was now favouring Vivian with highlights.

"Who said anything about marriage?"

"Come on, Viv. You should have seen your face when he said he was going back to Canada after the war. He didn't say anything about taking you along, did he?"

"Why should he have, after the way you attacked him? You practically called him a coward, and then you as much as told him to get off the island. I wouldn't be surprised if I never saw him again."

"He seemed to have taken it pretty well."

"He was being gracious."

"Gracious? He said what he said to hurt you. That man isn't gracious, he's just smooth. And he slurps his tea!"

"If you don't want him coming here anymore, we can have our Sunday dinners somewhere else."

"Don't be a pill, Viv. I don't mind him coming here. Well, I do, but Freddie seems to like him and the twins think he's the donkey's waistcoat." It was true: they would stand behind him on the chesterfield and comb his wavy, black hair like he was a gigantic doll. "I just think you could do better, that's all," Iris said. "There's something mean about Jack Lewis. I don't want to see you getting hurt. Besides, you don't know anything about him, not the slightest thing."

"He's sweet when we're alone together. And he's going back to Windsor to work in the family business. What's wrong with that?"

"Vivian, admit it. You only think you're in love with him because he's your ticket off the island."

But that wasn't true. Anyone could take her off the island; she wanted to go with Jack, if he asked her. Iris was a snob and didn't like Jack because he took his boots off at the door and used his fish fork for the salad. She didn't care what Iris thought. All Vivian wanted was to lose herself in work, then hurry home to lie on the sofa pretending to read but thinking about Jack, impatient for armistice so they could get on with their lives. Mrs. Jack Lewis. Vivian Lewis. Vivian Clift Fanshawe Lewis. She would have calling cards made up. He would be a good husband. He could be a soft, sensitive, caring person. Iris hadn't seen the musician in him. He heard music everywhere. If they were walking along the street and a bird was singing, he would whistle its song and the bird would answer. He showed her what a bosun's whistle sounded like. The other night he'd listened to her heart beating and made a song out of it: "*A little piece of heaven / has come down to where I live, / an angel with a halo / and her name is Viv.*" The chief question wasn't whether or not she would marry him if he asked her. Of course she would. The question was whether she would sleep with him first if he continued to press her to, and she was very much afraid that the answer to that was yes, too.

Oh, how he made her blood race. She'd been letting him get a little bolder each time they were together, fiddling with her buttons, touching her through her clothes. She now dressed with such sessions in mind. Layers, but not too many. And silk, not cotton or wool. Every time she put on her stockings she wondered if Jack would be able to manage the fasteners. She didn't see how she could suddenly call a halt to his adventurousness. If she were going to stop him, she would surely have done so by now.

It happened in Ferryland, of all places. She and Jack went down for a weekend in March, when the sky was as grey as an old blanket and the sea glimpsed between trees looked like quicksilver. Daddy came downstairs to meet him, looking like he'd just been awakened from a nap. His hair was wild and his vest buttons were askew. She went up to him and kissed him and said, "Daddy, this is Jack." The two men shook hands, but her father didn't take a liking to Jack, she could tell. He couldn't think of anything to say. Jack wasn't interested in birds or stamps or fish, and her father wasn't interested in the war. Not long afterwards, he went down to the store, saying he had inventory to check on, and she'd never known him to work in the store on a Saturday. She felt as though she'd lost an ally.

Lunch was a quiet affair, a Jigg's dinner. Wat wanted Jack to talk about the war. How many U-boats did the Germans have left, did he think? How many rockets? Jack replied like a propaganda newsreel, with authority but not much detail. Jerry was on the run, the Navy was cutting off German supplies, England was standing firm.

Her mother pumped him about Windsor as though she suspected he had made the place up. How big was it? What church did he go to? Was there rationing there, too? Had he heard from his people? Jack evaded questions about his family. They were fine. They were Lutherans, which made Iris's brows shoot up. Yes, there was rationing, but a person could get just about anything if he knew where to look, implying that he knew where to look.

"And you say your father builds houses," her mother said. "That sounds awfully difficult. Vivian's great-grandfather built this house, but he had help. You're fortunate to have something to return to after the war. So many won't."

"I know it," Jack said, looking at Vivian, and her heart lifted. "I feel very lucky."

After the dishes, she and Jack went for a stroll down past the store to the wharf. Saddlebacks and blueys squawked impatiently overhead: the fishing boats were still out and the splitting shed at the end of the dock was empty. Jack looked at the gurry buckets and held his nose. They climbed down and walked along the beach below the bluff, where they couldn't be seen from the house. When they rounded the headland, they were out of sight from the store, too. The tide was out and the harbour still except for bubbles on the beach pebbles when the waves receded. Farther out, the water seemed heavy and sullen.

"I'm sorry about the third-degree in there."

"I don't mind," Jack said, looking out over the harbour. "I've got nothing to hide."

"Will you really go back to Windsor when this is over?" she asked him.

"When what's over?"

"Oh, stop, Jack."

He took her another hundred yards up the beach, to where an old fishing boat had been washed or run onto the beach and abandoned. It had been there for ages; she'd played on it as a girl, clambering over its half-buried gunwale and up its sloped deck to the weathered wheelhouse. She used to bring books there, to read where no one would disturb her, forbidden books like *Lady Chatterley's Lover*. She remembered the way her eyes had danced over the pages, dwelling on the most delicious words, like *pulsating* and *tumescent*, and the way at the end she would look up and imagine her lover standing at the wheel, the wind pulling at her skirt as they churned through the uncharted sea. Away.

"Whose boat?" Jack asked.

"No one's."

"Then we can claim it," he said, pulling her towards it. "Law of the sea."

It was smaller than she remembered, maybe it had sunk deeper into the gravelly beach. They stepped over the gunwale and into the open cabin, her heart pulsating, there was no other word. There were rusted fish hooks scattered about, so they had to be careful where they put their hands. He inspected the bench, then sat on it and pulled her down onto his lap, pressing his face against her breast. *"A little piece of heaven has come down to where I live."* She cozied down into him, out of the wind. The sound of the waves would mask anyone's arrival; she looked through the open porthole but there was no one, and no one standing at the top of the bluff.

Jack was undoing her buttons, his fingers trembling so much that she brushed them away and undid them herself. Hadn't they been rehearsing this? Hadn't she gone to sleep every night for months imagining herself undoing his buttons, what his bare chest would look like, feel like, sound like? She would undo his flies. No, she wouldn't. But she did. He was tumescent! He leaned back along the bench and pulled her onto him. She lifted her skirt. She had no idea what she was doing, what was guiding her, how she managed her knees, how she could possibly fit him inside her. She knew there would be some pain, but she didn't think it would be in her thighs. He held both her arms and rose into her, gently at first, then harder. She moved with him, then against him, her thighs screaming, and then he arched his back and stopped, suddenly, as though he'd just remembered something. She was afraid she'd hurt him.

"Viv," he said.

She put her fingers to the side of his mouth and said, "Shh."

"No, I want to tell you about my—"

"Shh." If he had been about to say he loved her, she wouldn't have shushed him. But she didn't want to hear that he had a girl back in Windsor, or that he was being transferred the next day to Halifax.

They rearranged themselves and sat side by side on the thwart, looking out over the harbour. Her heart was still pounding. She took a deep breath and composed herself for hearing the worst.

"What was it you wanted to tell me?"

But he, too, had changed his mind. She saw it in his eyes, a veil descending.

"Nothing," he said. "You'll see for yourself."

"See what?"

Whatever it was, she had missed it.

"What if we took this boat and sailed away in it," he said, "out of the harbour, way out to sea, anywhere you wanted to go. Wouldn't that be fine?"

Should she remind him of his chronic seasickness? No, she should not.

"That would be wonderful," she said, taking his hand and patting it.

Now that they were lovers—she had no word of her own for what they were, so she borrowed one from her books—she thought everything would be different. She looked for ways in which their lives had changed. She searched his eyes, watched his hands, listened for new inflections in his voice. When they were alone together, as they contrived to be, after a dance or when Iris and the twins were somewhere, he was eager enough. She loved him then, even though they did it hastily, not very satisfactorily for her, always in some impermanent and impersonal place—the front porch when she was sure everyone inside was asleep, against a parked car on Duckworth. Risking everything. My God, if Iris ever found out. Or anyone. But it was worth it to feel him forgetting his coldness and coming back to her, to bury himself in her, if only for those fleeting moments, and be once again that lost little boy at a table for two in the crowded train station, waiting for her with a cup of tea and a story about spies.

But when they weren't making love he was distant from her, reserved, as though their whole relationship, not just the sexual part of it, were a secret to be kept from everyone. He didn't look at her when he talked, he didn't put his arm around her when they walked down the street. We're not even married yet, she thought, and already we're acting like an old couple. What will it be like when we're actually married?

She worried how to tell him she loved him without it sounding like a line from some movie. She practised telling him, in front of her dresser mirror, in the bathroom while brushing her teeth, but it always came out corny or flat. "I love you, Jack." Should she say it before they made love, or after? Would she say it casually or dramatically? She couldn't decide. She stopped practising and waited to hear herself blurt it out, maybe during an air raid, with the city collapsing around them, after searching for each other through the ruined streets. But there never was an air raid, the war was all but over, and she couldn't bring herself to say it. And each time they made love he seemed to retreat from her a little further, each kiss feeling like a final concession before they came to their senses and went their separate ways when the final bugle sounded. She back to Baird's, a ruined woman, he back to Windsor after a wartime fling.

Was he holding himself back because he didn't want to take her to his parents' home? Whenever she talked about Windsor, he stiffened and changed the subject. Why? She began to feel distant from her own family. If she had thought that being what one of her novels called "a woman of experience" would somehow put her on an even footing with Iris and her mother, she'd been wrong about that, too. She couldn't tell them the truth, of course, but surely they could see the difference in her? The way she crossed her legs when she sat, or nodded know-ingly when they talked about needing new curtains, or frowned when Jack's name was mentioned, or sighed when it wasn't? Wasn't womanhood a code that she had cracked? But there was no change, and she felt more remote than ever, cut off not only from Jack but from them as well, from her father, from Freddie, even from the twins.

One night, after she and Jack had made love in an old van parked on one of the wynds running up from Water Street, Jack leaned against the back of the driver's seat and lit a cigarette. "We should get married," he said, as though they didn't really have much choice in the matter. It was as though all the air had been let out of the van. She took the cigarette from him and agreed. That is, she agreed they didn't have much choice, which Jack interpreted as agreeing to getting married. She didn't correct him. She wrote to her mother the next day, announcing their engagement and listing the reasons for getting married—the war ending, his leaving, her desire to see something of the world.

"Besides," she added, almost as an afterthought, "I love him."

They were married in the Navy Chapel on Victoria Day— May 24, 1945—seventeen days after the victory in Europe and twelve days after Jack's twentieth birthday. The Navy chaplain said a few words, but he didn't know them from Adam. Frank Sterling was best man and Iris the bridesmaid. The reception was held in the YWCA. Jack's Navy buddies had put bunting around the tables and one of the Navy photographers took some pictures, but they couldn't have alcohol, at least not officially, and they had to be out by seven. None of Jack's family was there. Vivian's mother came, and Freddie of course, and her uncle Billie, who'd been wounded in Italy and sent home, and his wife, Minnie. Her father said he was too busy to come. He offered to book them a suite in the Newfoundland Hotel for their honeymoon, a whole weekend, but Jack said the captain of HMCS *Avalon* and his chiefs of staff had their headquarters in the Newfoundland Hotel and he didn't want to run into them. So they took a room in a small motel on Merrymeeting Road, a place called Flynn's Tavern. Iris practically screeched when she heard: "A *tavern?* Vivian, you can't be serious!" But it wasn't so bad. And they spent most of the weekend in bed, even having their meals delivered from the tavern downstairs, which Vivian decided was romantic, except that Jack always insisted they get up and dress before the food arrived, which she thought defeated the purpose. He didn't seem to know what dressing gowns were for. And he never tipped the poor waiter, a gaunt, hollow-eyed man who lived in the room across the hall.

They moved into a small flat on Harvey Road, furnished, although with not much more than a bed, a table and two chairs and a hotplate. Iris lent them some bed linen and two paintings, one a good one by Goodridge Roberts. It was their first home together and she loved it. Jack said it reminded him of a motel room. She lost her job at Baird's because of the store's policy of hiring only single girls, so while Jack was on parade Vivian spent most of her day in the flat, tidying up after meals, making it cozy, daydreaming and reading books from the public library, most of which seemed to be about women like herself—war brides, women married to men they barely knew. Some of the books ended happily, and she read those carefully for clues, but the ones that looked like they were going to end sadly she put down halfway through, even though they seemed more realistic to her. Sometimes the men changed, but most often it was the women. The war had already altered the men. It was as though people were capable of handling only one big event in their lives, and for the men it was the war. For women it was marriage.

Iris rang, and sometimes Vivian would go to Admiralty Road for a visit, but her sister still hadn't accepted Jack as part of the family. She referred to him as though he were a temporary unpleasantness, like a blocked drain. There didn't seem to be any doubt that they would soon be moving to Canada, and she was bracing herself for it. There were things she would have liked to talk about with Iris before she left, aspects of married life that mystified or troubled her, but because of Jack they kept their conversations resolutely on other topics. How the war dragged on, their mother's health, which was failing, their father's increasing abstractedness—he was now talking of buying a house on St. Lucia and going there in the winters to do his birdwatching—and Vivian would return to the flat to fix Jack's supper feeling guilty and out of sorts.

When V-J Day came in August, she went to Baird's and watched the parade from an upper window, filled with something she called anticipation but which felt more like dread. Some of the girls she'd worked with were still there, unmarried and concerned about it, wanting to know what it was like having someone *there* all the time. She told them it was wonderful. Down on the street, flags and bunting lined the parade route, and for once the weather was dry. When she saw Jack marching by, looking so serious in the first row behind the drums, she waved and shouted and he looked up and swung his trombone towards her, grinning crookedly behind the mouthpiece. Afterwards she walked around the department store in a panic, as though she should start packing everything in it up in boxes and calling the movers.

It astonished her that she and Jack had been married almost four months and she hadn't heard from Jack's family. She didn't understand it at all. She didn't even know how to talk to Jack about it. She understood them not coming to the wedding, half a continent away, but they could have sent a gift, or a card, even a telegram. *Had* he told them they were married?

"Of course I told them, what do you think?"

"Then why haven't they written? Don't they want to meet me? Is there something wrong with me?"

"No. You're Lily White," he said.

"I'm not Lily White," she said, close to tears. "I'm your wife. I'm Vivian Lewis. *Say* it!"

"All right," he said, laughing. "You're Vivian Lewis."

She realized with almost a physical blow that that was the first time she'd heard her new name spoken out loud, even by her. In four months! Vivian Lewis. She'd signed it, but that was different. Sometimes she would sign her middle names as well: Vivian Garna Clift Lewis. Only one name out of four was new, she told herself, hardly any change at all. Jack didn't even have a middle name. He was just plain Jack Lewis. "You only need one," he'd said when she asked him about it. Which was true, she supposed, except that everyone else in the world had more than one whether they needed it or not.

"That's not true," Jack said. "Lots of people have only one name."

"Like who?" she said. She didn't know anyone.

"Humphrey Bogart," he said. "What's Humphrey Bogart's middle name, if you're so smart?"

"I don't know," she said, "but I'm sure he has one. Everyone does. What about your father? Doesn't he have a middle name?"

"Never mind my father," Jack said. "We're talking about me."

"Middle names honour the people in your family," she said. "Garna is for my mother's father, whose name was Garnet. Clift is my father's mother's maiden name, Rosella Clift. Not having a middle name is like not having a past."

"Yeah," he said. "That's me, kid. No past. And you'll always be Lily White to me."

He pulled her up from the bed and put his hands around her waist. "You're cherry pink and apple-blossom white," he crooned in her ear. "You're the white cliffs of Dover. You're the cream in my coffee, you're the milk in my tea." He spun her around the room. He really was a good dancer. She had to close her eyes to keep from getting dizzy. "You're Snow White," he said, stopping. "And you want to meet the Seven Dwarves."

"Jack!" she said, slapping his arm. "That's no way to talk about your family." But she laughed. "Yes, that's what I want."

"All right," said Jack, "we'll go to Windsor. I've got a couple of weeks' leave before I have to go to Toronto to be demobbed."

See? she could say to Iris. He does love me.

"Boy," he said, "wait till Windsor gets an eyeful of you."

They gave up the flat on Harvey Road and stored what little they owned with Freddie and Iris. Temporarily, Vivian assured them without really thinking about it. She assumed they'd be coming back to Newfoundland after Jack's demobilization. She hardly even said goodbye to her family. The Overland Limited took them across the island to Port-aux-Basques, and from there the ferry to Nova Scotia docked in North Sydney at six in the evening. She didn't find the crossing rough, but Jack was green-faced the whole time and stayed in the passenger lounge, stretched out on blankets between two rows of benches. She went out into the fresh air to smoke and to watch Newfoundland recede from her in the wake of the ferry. Hundreds of birds escorted the ship, hagdowns and bottle-noses, sea-pigeons and annetts, making her think her father had sent them to see her safely across the no man's land of Cabot Strait, now forever free of U-boats. Since the wedding there'd been a show of welcoming Jack into the family, but no one had actually found him a place. If Jack had noticed, he'd been too polite to say anything.

She was alone on deck when she caught her first sight of Canada, long, rolling, tree-topped hills that opened into a harbour lined with soot-blackened buildings and tall derricks. North Sydney was an industrial port. If this was Canada, she said to herself, she didn't like it much. God, was she going to be like Iris after all? The taxi wove them through the low town, black smoke hanging over it from the coke ovens, everyone looking haggard and drawn. The women in thick, dull sweaters, talking with their fingers touching their throats. They stayed in the New Belmont Hotel. In the morning she got up to open the window and found it painted shut. She wanted to see the ocean, but there wasn't even a view of the harbour. A huge saddleback

like he'd just seen a ghost. She realized how little she knew him.

"He's a performer," Iris had said. "He's meant to be looked at, not understood."

Was that true? Had he been performing for her all along, pretending to be something he wasn't?

"He's all surface," Iris said.

Iris had told her another thing that worried her. According to Iris, Freddie had offered to set Jack up in business in St. John's, some kind of construction project, and Jack had turned him down flat. Rather rudely, Iris had said, but of course she would say that. What bothered Vivian was that Jack hadn't mentioned it to her.

"Does it hurt?" he said to her.

She looked up at him, startled. "Does what hurt?"

"Having your nose stuck in a book like that."

She closed the book and put it on the seat beside her. "Sorry, darling."

She was trying to get used to calling him "darling," which was what Iris called Freddie, but it didn't seem to suit him. The only syllable that fit was *Jack*. She kept her eyes on him, smiling encouragingly, she thought, but he didn't say anything more. After a while he returned his gaze to the window, seemingly content that now he had gained her undivided attention he could pretend she wasn't there.

She looked at her watch, counted a hundred telephone poles and looked at her watch again. A minute and a half, golly. She hummed "In the Mood" to the rhythm of the train's wheels. She looked down at the book. They were passing through what seemed to be perpetual bush, farther from the sea than she had ever been in her life, nothing around her but trees and more trees rushing by like an endless school of startled fish. She took a sheet of New Belmont Hotel stationery from her purse and began writing a letter.

"Now what are you doing?" he asked her.

"Writing to my parents," she said.

"Let me see it when you're done, okay?"

"Why?"

"I might want to add something."

"Why not write your own letter?" she said.

He reached across and snatched the page from her lap.

"Jack!" she cried. "That's private."

"Oh-ho," he said, reading. "'Jack was really seasick on the ferry—some sailor! I guess he wasn't kidding about his time on the Derry Run.' Who said I was kidding about that?"

"No one. It was just something to say."

"Did someone think I was faking it, to get off active duty?"

"No, Jack. No one thought that."

"Iris?"

"No."

"I guess I should be flattered that Iris thinks I'm such a good actor I could fool a doctor."

"Jack, please. It was just something to say."

He tossed the letter back to her and laughed. She took it up and smoothed it. "Aren't you going to add something?" she asked.

"Naw, you go ahead." He resumed gazing out the window,

giving her the cameo shot, but now his eyes were hard and unseeing.

When the train stopped in Moncton they got off to walk on the platform and she dropped her letter into a postbox inside the station. She watched the envelope disappear through the slot and thought about crawling in after it, but that was silly. Wasn't this what she'd wanted, to be away? When they returned to their seats and the train was moving again she looked for her book, but it was gone. Jack called the steward and asked if he had seen it but the man shook his head. "No, *suh.*"

"You sure about that?" Jack asked him.

"Very sure, suh," the steward said evenly.

Jack told him to bring him a Coke and some ice.

"Anything for the lady?"

She shook her head. She was devastated by the loss of her book, the last thing she had received, might ever receive, from her sister. It was as though she had lost Newfoundland and any possibility of going back to it. She remembered seeing Jack standing by a dustbin on the platform while she was in the station. It was a terrible suspicion for her to have, but there it was. When the steward came with his drink, Jack picked up the magazine and became deeply absorbed in it, studying each page with exaggerated attention. Teaching her a lesson.

"Tell me about your parents, Jack," she said. "What kind of people are they?"

He shrugged. "They're nothing special."

"They're special to me, they're my parents-in-law."

"Maybe," he said, "but after this trip you won't be seeing much of them."

"Why not?"

He looked up. "Because they'll be in Windsor and we'll be somewhere else."

He had a way of making the most outlandish things sound logical, and then getting all riled up when she didn't go along with him. It frightened her.

"I'd still like to hear about them."

He turned another page of the magazine and spent some time looking at an advertisement for laundry soap.

"Are they nice people? Not so nice people?" she persisted. "What kind of house do they live in? What's your mother like?"

"You'll find out soon enough," he said.

"But I want you to tell me."

"All right," he said, sighing and closing the magazine. "They're like your folks. They live in a big house in a nice part of town, bigger than Iris and Freddie's. Brick, with a big front porch with a swing on it. There's a living room on the ground floor, but they only use it when they have guests, like that room in your parents' house. Their parlour's on the second floor, at the top of the stairs."

He paused. How odd, she thought, to have a parlour on the second floor. "Do you mean like a sitting room?"

"Not a room, really, more like a big space with some chairs

and a coffee table, but that's where they spend most of their time. Mom knits and listens to the radio. She's small but she's a real fighter, wears herself out doing charity work all day, belongs to lots of clubs. She likes listening to *Amos 'n' Andy* in the evenings, you don't get that in St. John's, and George Burns and Gracie Allen. I sit up there with her sometimes after dinner. Through the windows you can look down over the tops of the chestnut trees and see the Detroit River, and Detroit on the other side of it. Now that the war's over the barrage balloons will be gone and at night the skyline will be lit up like a Christmas tree. You never seen such tall buildings. I told you me and my sister Alvina used to go there to hear the big bands and watch movies in the Fox Theatre."

"What's your sister like?"

"Alvina?" he said, leaning back in his seat. "She's big, and blonde, like Dad and Benny. She's twelve years older than me. I take more after my mother."

"And Benny?"

This was what she wanted, this was the intimacy she craved. She didn't know why she'd practically had to force it, but once he started it was like music pouring out of him.

"He and my father don't get along, maybe because they're too much alike. Benny's taller than me, blond hair, blue eyes with brown flecks in them, never seen that in anyone else except my father. Women go crazy over him. He's got his own place now, just around the corner from my folks' house. They'll probably give us his old room at the back of the house on the ground floor. The sun pours into it in the morning and you can walk out of it into the backyard."

"What about your father?" she prompted.

"What about my father?"

He paused again, longer this time. "He wears expensive suits with a white handkerchief tucked in the breast pocket that he never uses, just for show, see? He always smells like talcum powder and aftershave. His father was a barber, but he's dead now, has been for years. Granddad used to take me to the Detroit Zoo and Tiger Stadium, and Belle Isle, where people go when it gets too hot in town. Windsor's the hottest place in Canada, did you know that? It's always summer, never snows, they got trees that never lose their leaves, and flowers growing in the middle of January."

"You were talking about your father," she said gently.

"Dad was already in the construction business when I came along. He started out with one truck, with 'W. H. Lewis and Son' painted on it. When I was born he added the 's' to make it 'Sons.'"

He looked out the window, and for a second she was afraid he was finished. Then he shrugged, as though a second conversation was going on in his head, one she couldn't be part of.

"When my father and Benny have a big job they have to be careful who they hire. Windsor's a working-class town and there's a huge coloured population. Coloureds'll steal the shirt off your back. They take things from my father, paint and plaster and stuff to fix up their own shacks with, and they steal from the house owners. Stupid things, like shampoo, or kids' toys, or that book of yours. There are some parts of the city you can't go into because of them."

"What do they do?"

"Are you kidding? They'd slit your throat as soon as look at you. Those people carry knives."

He retreated into silence after that, but she felt close to him. He had constructed a bridge between them. She reached across and took his hand and squeezed it, blinking back tears. He smiled at her tightly, but his eyes were soft.

When the train pulled into Toronto, it was nearly midnight and she couldn't see anything of the city. The connection to Windsor didn't leave until six in the morning. Jack didn't want to leave Union Station. She suggested they put their bags in a locker and go for a walk, get something to eat, see the city, have an adventure, but Jack insisted it was too late, that everything would be closed and the streets would be too dangerous so late at night. Station employees had copies of all the locker keys, he said, and they went through people's luggage looking for valuables.

"This is the real world, kid, not some Fairy Land."

"We don't have any valuables," she said, but they sat on a wooden bench, curled up under their coats, for the whole six hours. This isn't the real world, she thought. In front of them was a kiosk that sold books and magazines, but it was closed and wouldn't open until nine. She leaned her head on her husband's shoulder and gazed through the wire grille at the titles—there was *The Razor's Edge*, its pitch-black spine with white lettering perched just out of reach behind the iron screen.

On the train in the morning he barely spoke to her. Something terrible seemed to be going on in his head, but what it was she couldn't fathom. They were in a coach, the tight, red plush seats like those in a theatre rubbing the backs of her legs. Twice they were shunted onto sidings while cargo trains roared by importantly in the opposite direction. Jack barely seemed to notice them.

"Jack, you *will* show me the tunnel when we get there?" she said, trying to cheer him up. "The one that goes under the river to the United States?"

"Sure, doll," he said without enthusiasm. "All the old haunts."

Just before noon the conductor hurried down the aisle calling "Windsor!" as though the city's name were a warning. Five minutes later the train began passing scrap-metal yards, the backs of unpainted houses with their weathered stoops and sooty windowpanes, grey laundry sagging in the yards. Windsor was so much duller than the other cities they had seen, duller even than Sydney, not at all the balmy metropolis Jack had described to her. A physical pall hung over everything, the station, the streets, the river, even the people, all of whom seemed to have come down to the station to meet someone they didn't like.

She looked at Jack. He was staring out at the faces in the crowd, looking terrified.

My poor, poor darling, she thought. What have I done to you?

PART II

WILLIAM HENRY

After driving into town from Walkerville, Benny parked the truck near the corner of Sandwich East and Ouellette, not exactly in front of the British-American Hotel but close enough by. The sidewalks were unusually busy for a Monday, especially down by the ferry dock, where people were pushing and shoving like something was being handed out for free. Coloureds and whites. William Henry always felt uneasy when he saw a crowd acting agitated. Benny noticed it, too.

"What's goin' on down there?"

"Nothin' good," William Henry said.

They entered the hotel through the side door off Ouellette, which would take them past the barbershop. Harlan was cutting a customer's hair and William Henry waved at him through the glass, *come and have a drink*, and Harlan raised his scissors and comb, *soon as I'm done here*. William Henry and Benny continued across the lobby towards the open tavern door.

"Morning, Betsy," William Henry said to the coloured clerk at the front desk.

"Afternoon, Mr. Lewis," she said. "Benny."

Fast Eddy must have seen them coming, because he had four glasses of draught on their table before they even sat down. Benny went to the bar and bought a pack of Buckinghams. There were three or four other men in the place, all sitting at different tables, but none of them looked up as William Henry took his work hat off and hung it on a hook on the wall. He was never one to drink with his hat on, it seemed too impermanent.

William Henry loved this room, settled into it like a tired foot into an old shoe. In his dream house, the entire ground floor would be this tavern, with the same terrazzo floor and a dozen round tables, each with four captain's chairs around it, a bar running along one wall and Fast Eddy in constant attendance. In this dream tavern, the beer was always cold, the salt flowed freely from the shaker, and nothing ever changed. Friends dropped in for drinks and sat silently at their tables, each absorbed in his own thoughts or not, as the case might be. There were no windows, or maybe windows made of hollow glass bricks. The air was thick with tobacco smoke. Most of the light in the room came from behind the bar, reflected off a long mirror like the one Harlan had in his barbershop. The sawdust on the floor was from sawn white pine or cedar. No distinctions were made between night and day, winter and summer, these dark days of the war and the glory days of the Depression. The war was not a constant topic of discussion, and being out of work was not a disgrace.

He would have his regular table in the corner, far from the door to the men's room and the radio above the bar. Only he and Harlan and Benny would sit at this table, and Jackson if he wanted to, but he wouldn't want to. Jackson would think he was too good to sit in a tavern with the likes of his father and brother and uncle. He would want to bring his white friends in. They would treat Fast Eddy like a servant. They would not like his insouciance, and Fast Eddy would not like their sass. And that would be the end of William Henry's dream home.

The British-American was where William Henry had lived for the month after Jackson was born, in the tavern during the day and on the floor of Harlan's room upstairs at night. He would sit here from opening to closing, drinking and nurturing his hatred for the world in general and for whoever had fathered Josie's bastard son in particular. It could have been that fat Polack who lived behind them in the brown house on Windsor Avenue; he would check the wooden fence between their yards for a hidden gate or signs of scaling. Or it could have been the sheeny who drove his horse and cart up and down the alleys, collecting junk. Christ, it could have been anyone, any white son of a bitch who liked his meat dark. Josie was a beautiful woman, white bastards were always snooping around the Settlement like the whole six blocks was their own private whorehouse. Not even Alvina was safe and she was only twelve years old.

At first he'd had to nurse his beers because he hadn't brought any money with him, but gradually friends would drop in, Harlan would pick up his tab, or the hotel would hire him to do odd jobs around the building in exchange for room and board. Someone kicked in a wall upstairs, William Henry would fix it. A toilet started leaking, or a shingle blew off the roof, William Henry to the rescue. For the whole month he never ate anything but sausages and mashed potatoes or pickled eggs washed down with beer. He had his morning shave every day across the lobby, as usual, although sometimes it wouldn't be until noon and only then because Harlan kept that bottle of Kentucky sour mash in his cupboard. Jack Daniel's at first, but William Henry got him to switch to Jim Beam because the name Jack Daniel's reminded him of Jackson. That was another thing, her naming him Jackson.

"You name that bastard after my father?" he said to her on one of her many attempts to get him to come home. She'd come down to the hotel with the baby wrapped up in a shawl so no one would see his shame, and Harlan let them have the barbershop to talk in while he invented some errand he had to run uptown.

"I named your son after his grandfather," she said, a fire in her eye he hadn't noticed before.

She sat and nursed the child in Andrew Jackson's barber chair and he perched himself in the other one, staring at them in the mirror, mother and child, unable to avert his eyes or look directly at her. He wanted to believe the baby was his, he could feel himself leaning towards it, but every time he laid eyes on the child sucking at her breast he shook his head. How could it be? How else could it be?

"How you gettin' by?" he asked her reflection, putting as much meanness in the question as he could muster.

"We gettin' by," she said. "Alvina and Benny, they miss you. They keep askin' when you comin' home. What am I supposed to tell them?"

"Tell them they want to see me they can come down here. This where I live now."

"They too young to understand that."

"Then tell them any damn thing you want," he said. "Tell them the truth."

"I do tell them the truth. I tell them that you're their daddy, and you're Jackson's daddy, too, and someday you'll wake up and come home where you belong."

William Henry never had nothing but trouble from white people, and now here he was with a white son. That was it in a nutshell. He'd heard tell of a coloured couple in Detroit had a white baby but it turned dark after a while, and by the time it was a year old it was the same colour as its mama, dark dark. William Henry kept his eye on Jackson for the whole month he lived in the British-American, every time Josie brought him down to tempt him, but he never saw any sign that the boy was turning colour. That baby stayed resolutely white. If anything it got whiter. Now Jackson was almost eighteen and he was still white as a Klansman's bedsheet.

As a child Jackson never fit in. William Henry would watch him trying to play with other kids, coloured kids on the block, and they always kept away from him. They'd be in a circle playing marbles or something, and Jackson would want to join them, and they'd move aside to let him in, but they always moved a little too far, William Henry could see it from the house, how they'd shuffle over without actually letting him in. Jackson felt it, too, he wasn't no dummy. He'd come back to the house, and the circle would close up again as if he'd never been in it, like water.

"What's wrong with them?" he'd ask William Henry, tears filling his little eyes. But there wasn't nothing wrong with them.

When he got older and started going to mixed schools, Jackson would steal coins from William Henry's pants pockets to give to white kids so they'd let him into their gangs. William Henry caught him at it several times and whupped him pretty good for it, but it cut him to see his wife's son so desperate to be liked. One day when Jackson was ten or eleven he got invited to a birthday party in another part of town, God only knew how much that cost William Henry. Alvina was supposed to pick him up when it was over, but William Henry had to go get him early for some reason, and when he got to the house and knocked on the front door, the woman who answered it stepped back like she'd been struck. William Henry was used to that, he barely noticed anymore.

"Hello, ma'am. Would you tell Jackson that his daddy come to take him home?"

The woman looked over William Henry's shoulder, and he knew she was looking for Jackson's white father sitting in the back seat of a big, shiny car, and he didn't say nothing but just looked at the woman with that blank expression he'd learned to use, and when she finally caught on she sucked in her breath and her face set and she went and got Jackson and that was the last birthday party he was ever invited to outside the Settlement. So it wasn't like William Henry didn't *understand* Jackson.

Let him go, thought William Henry. Boy wants to go, let him go.

A month after Jackson was born, Harlan come into the tavern, sat down across from William Henry at this very table and give him a disgusted look.

"What wrong with you?" William Henry asked him.

"What wrong with *you*, is the question," Harlan replied.

"You know what's wrong with me."

"I been watchin' you drag yourself around this here hotel for a month now, wonderin' when you was going to get down off your high horse and go home where you are wanted and needed."

"Harlan, my wife had a child by another man. A white man. What you think I'm going to do? Get down on my knees and thank her?"

"Did Josie never tell you what happened?"

"No. What happened?"

"I don't know what happened. But I know what you *think* happened."

"I know how people make babies, if that's what you're talkin' about."

Harlan played with William Henry's box of matches. He took out a match and snapped it in half, then took out another and snapped that in half. Barbering had given him strong fingers.

"You think Josie been seein' some other fella. Some white fella," he said.

William Henry snorted. "That's how it's done. You'd know that if you was married."

Harlan shook his head. "This ain't no joke, little brother," he said, still toying with the matchbox. "Didn't you ever consider that maybe she was forced?"

William Henry narrowed his eyes. "What you mean, forced?"

"I mean maybe she wasn't seein' some other man. Maybe some other man jump her. Maybe a car full of other men. It happens, Will, you know that."

William Henry's ears started ringing, like some new pressure building up in his head.

"History of our race," said Harlan, taking out a third match, lighting it and blowing it out. William Henry never seen him so nervous. "Maybe you think too bad of your wife, and too good of other people."

William Henry stared at his brother for a long time, waiting for the ringing to stop. All this time sitting here, and the thought had never crossed his mind. When the ringing didn't stop, he pushed his chair back from the table and walked home. He went in the front door and saw Josie sitting in the rocking chair, nursing her baby. When he told her what Harlan had said, she put the baby down in its crib and stood up to him.

"William Henry Lewis," she said in his eye, "I wasn't raped, and I wasn't seein' someone else. I never in my life been with any man but you, stupid-assed woman that I am. I told you, this is your child. Your flesh and blood."

William Henry didn't understand the woman. Here he was, trying to comfort her, trying to forgive her, trying to make up with her, and she was just getting madder and madder. There was no sense to it. But he made up his mind to come back to her, and when he made up his mind about a thing it was as good as done. He kissed her and told her he believed her and that their life could go back to normal. But deep down he never did bring himself to believe that Jackson was his, just like he never stopped thinking of the British-American as his real home. Maybe he was wrong on both counts and maybe he wasn't, but that was what he believed. In his mind, even now, he and Benny lived at the hotel and occasionally visited the house where his wife and her son lived.

A few minutes later, Harlan came in and sat in the chair between William Henry and Benny, full of news. Harlan was always full of news about something bad. William Henry raised three fingers and Fast Eddy brought six beers. Then William Henry tapped the salt shaker on the tabletop, sprinkled salt into his beer and followed the grains as they dropped slowly to the bottom of the glass like tiny white men sinking to the bottom of an ocean of piss.

"What's all that commotion down by the ferry?" he asked Harlan. He'd know if anyone would.

"You didn't hear what happened on Belle Isle?"

"No, I didn't," William Henry said. "Someone get ants in one of their chicken sandwiches?"

"Somebody got throwed off the Belle Isle Bridge."

Benny leaned forward in his chair. "What's that?"

William Henry looked up and saw Jackson coming in the lobby door.

"White woman and her baby," Harlan said. "Crowd of coloured boys from Detroit chased her down and throwed them both off the bridge."

"What they go and do that for?" Benny said.

When Jackson came over to the table William Henry asked him, "You finish that Walkerville job?"

"No," said Jackson. "Couple more days, maybe."

Then why was he here? "We done our part," said William Henry, maybe a little sharper than he intended. "You need help?"

"I'll take care of it," Jackson said. "Anyway, he paid me." And he tossed a white envelope onto the table.

"Give that to your mother. Whyn't you sit down and have a beer first," William Henry said, but Jackson was already headed back to the door. Goddamn, that boy was hard to figure out.

"Take the truck," he called after him. "There's gas coupons in the glovebox."

But he was gone. William Henry looked after the boy for a moment, shaking his head, then Harlan's voice came back to him. "Some coloured boys said they got throwed out of Eastwood Park and was gettin' their own back."

"On a white woman and her child?" William Henry was suddenly angry. "That's just stupid."

"Damn right it is. Whites in Detroit ain't going to stand for that."

"Shit," said Benny, standing up. "I gotta get over there."

"What for?" William Henry said.

"If there's somethin' goin' on, I got friends over there," Benny said.

"Finish your beer first," William Henry said. "I better come with you, keep your dumb ass out of trouble."

JACK

Jack had just turned eighteen, the cut-off age for the Windsor
Sea Cadet Marching Band, also known as the Windsor All-
Whites. When the bandleader found that out, and that he had
quit high school, he would tell Jack it was time to move on.
Jack was waiting for the tap on the shoulder, and then what?
Meanwhile, he concentrated on learning as much as he could,
thinking he might join the Navy Band. When the All-Whites
wheeled left, he marched in place for six paces, knees high,
left foot turning fifteen points of the compass with each step.
On right wheels he marched double time, twelve long paces,
eyes right, keeping the line straight. Try doing that without
moving the trombone or blowing air through the side of your

mouth. Try moving the slide out to seventh position without hitting the marcher in front of you. You had to concentrate. You couldn't do it if you were thinking about being kicked out of the band, so he didn't.

They were called the All-Whites because of their white uniforms: hats, tunics, trousers, even their shoes. Privately, they called themselves the All-Whites because there were no coloureds in the band, not exactly by design or decree, it just turned out that way, as everything always did in Windsor. No one blinked when Jack joined the band, which meant no one knew anything about him or his family. Another test passed.

The band practised drills in the Armouries on Saturdays and Thursdays, taking over the polished floor from the Army cadets, groups of sullen schoolboys in oversized woollen uniforms the colour of baby shit. The cadets would come up from the basement rifle range smelling of cordite and idle on the sidelines, drinking Cokes from the machine and, having just fired real rifles, eyeing the band in their white uniforms as though they were so many moving targets. They had that look of aggressive disdain in their eyes, the way all Army men eyed the other forces, which was also the way all whites looked at coloureds. Army cadets were the kind of smug assholes he'd quit Patterson Collegiate to get away from.

There'd been other tests, girlfriends, lunch-counter waitresses, the high-school baseball team, and so far he'd passed them all. His nonresident alien's card for getting across the border said he was white. He'd hung around with white kids all his life. They'd made him do things for them because he was younger, not because he wasn't like them. He was. At the movie theatre, where coloureds had to sit in the balcony, he always sat downstairs, right up at the front, sometimes with a girl, sometimes with his buddies from school. If anyone had suspected anything, they'd have asked to see his card, they were always checking for stuff like that. Even the old man knew he was white. His father didn't understand it any more than Jack did, and he didn't like it, but he never stood in his way.

But all that could change with a moment's inattention. Some slip, some fluke, somebody sticking their nose where it didn't belong. Someone hearing the old man call him Jackson instead of Jack. One false step and he'd be shining shoes down at the train station, or breathing in plaster dust all day with Benny and the old man.

So he was glad when his squad wheeled away from the sidelines and the Army cadets were behind him. His arms felt like lead from holding the trombone up while the fifes and drums fought it out behind him. The All-Whites knew seventeen field drills, twenty-six marches. They even had a symphony section that played in Riverside Park on civic holidays, a band within a band, although Jack wasn't part of it.

Peter Barnes, first trumpet, two over on Jack's right, was in the symphony. Peter was white, a doctor's son, had the world fed to him on a silver spoon. But he was all right. Jack usually went to Peter's house after band practice, which wouldn't happen if he thought Jack was coloured. It was the fourth year of the war that was supposed to have lasted only a few months, a year at most. People were still saying it would be over any day now that the Yanks were in it, but the Yanks had been in it for nearly two years and the war was getting worse, if anything. Jack was glad of it. The war was the future waiting for him, his ticket out.

At Peter's house they sat in an open area on the second floor, at the top of the stairs, usually with Della, Peter's mother, who talked to him in a way no white woman ever had before. No woman, come to think of it. She seemed to actually like having him around. He never got the look from her, she never talked as though there were things she knew that he would never know. Whatever she knew, she shared with him and with Peter. There was a fireplace, two soft chairs and heavy red curtains held open during the day by braided gold cords, closed at night because of the blackout; he could stand at one of the windows, pull aside the curtain a fraction and look out over the deserted street, above the tips of the chestnut trees, and she would not say, Come away from there.

It felt safe, but it was dangerous for Jack in this house. He was pretty sure Peter and his mother didn't know anything about his family, but he couldn't be certain. Peter probably wouldn't rat on him if he did know, but he couldn't be sure of that, either. The Barneses were white and they were rich, and he didn't really understand such people, didn't know what they were capable of, how fiercely they would protect their own. Coming to Peter's house, talking to Peter's mother, even calling her Della, was like putting his hand on a hot stove to see how long he could stand the heat. Even if he could stand it, he'd end up with a burned hand. But if he wanted to join the Navy, he had to pass all the tests, and so far he had.

Doc Barnes had been away with the Navy for a year and a half. The surgery, when he was home, took up half the ground floor, but it was closed for the duration. Passing the pocket doors on the way to the stairs, Jack hardly noticed the antiseptic smell anymore. On the second floor, Peter and Jack and Della drank tea and listened to jazz on the radio, which stood on a low, mahogany table between the windows, beside a photograph of Peter's father: the doc in his white Navy uniform, his collar insignia that looked like a walking stick with two snakes twisted around it. The radio was tuned to a Detroit station, Detroit bands. Jack liked the big swing bands, it was like being in the All-Whites, the same feeling of belonging, an all-encompassing, tightly controlled sound, each lick, even the improvised solos, strictly choreographed. Harry James ran his band like the ringleader of a circus. Once you were in a band like that, you were set for life. You'd passed. He'd heard that Calloway was making fifty thousand a year in New York before the war. Not that he wanted to play trombone in Calloway's band. Calloway was coloured, all his band members were coloured. There were plenty of better bands around.

Parting the curtains on one of the windows and squinting through the chestnut trees, he could see the Detroit River and the anti-aircraft barrage blimps anchored to the shore. Detroit was a prime target. If German bombers came up the river, they would hit the chains holding the blimps and crash into the river, or maybe into Detroit. But how would German airplanes get this far inland? They'd have to have flown up the St. Lawrence River all the way from Newfoundland, and then over Lake Ontario and Lake Erie, without being detected. Such a thing was impossible, but every time anyone heard a plane overhead, or train cars shunting together down on the tracks, they looked nervously up at the sky. Jack imagined what a hundred Junkers Ju 88s would sound like as they flew in—a long, steady, low E minor, the first note of a symphony with no end.

"How did you become interested in music, Jack?" Della asked him. She was wearing a cream-coloured blouse with a collar that knotted at her throat and hung down like a tie over the mother-of-pearl buttons that gleamed in the weak light. She seemed young to be Peter's mother, more like an older sister, like Alvina. Her blouse and skin, their paleness accentuated by bright red lipstick, made her look as though she'd been carved from a kind of stone, alabaster or marble, something that if you rubbed became soft and warm in your hands. She looked like one of those women in the magazines who wore party dresses and high heels while doing housework, or while pouring a cup of Maxwell House coffee for her husband. Jack had never seen her doing any sort of housework. She was the kind of woman who would hire someone like his mother to do it for her.

"My grandfather was a bandleader," Jack said. "On my mother's side."

"Is that why you joined the All-Whites, because your grandfather was a bandleader?" Her knitting needles clicked in time with the music. "Socks," she'd said on one of his first nights there, "for the boys in the trenches."

"Foxholes, Mother, not trenches," Peter had corrected her, and she had smiled.

"My mother says it's in the blood," Jack said.

"What is?"

"Music."

"Is she musical?"

"No, not very."

"Martin Luther called the trombone 'the voice of God,'" Della said, brushing her blonde hair back over her ear. He didn't know who Martin Luther was, but he remembered standing beside his mother in First Baptist, watching her sing with her head thrown back, swaying on her feet, mouth open, eyes closed, the pages of her hymnal flapping in her gloved hands like the wings of a frightened pigeon. The voice of God. He'd never felt comfortable in that church; people gave him too wide a berth.

Della paused in her knitting to look up at Jack. "But perhaps musicality skips a generation."

"It didn't with us," Peter said.

"Gracious, look at the time." Della pressed what she had knitted against her thigh. "There's one finished. One sock a day, that's my limit. Time for a drink."

Peter, still at the window, turned to Jack. "We're thinking of going over to Detroit. Want to come?"

"Oh, yeah," Jack said. "Long time ago. Cut myself shaving."

They cruised along Woodward and stopped in front of the Paradise Theatre. The streets were dark but busy with traffic, trolley cars on Woodward and pedestrians on both sidewalks. A long line of people snaked from under the Paradise's unlit marquee up Woodward and around a corner. Peter drove north as far as East Adams, then turned right and parked in front of the Horse Shoe jazz club, a long, narrow tavern with octagonal windows on either side of a deeply recessed door. Jack had been to the Horse Shoe before, with Alvina. It was a black-and-tan, open to both coloureds and whites, but few whites ventured this far into Detroit's Black Bottom district. Most went to places on Hastings. Why were they coming here? he wondered, but didn't ask. Peter dropped Jack and Della off in front of the club and went to find a parking space. Jack held the lounge's heavy wooden door open for Della, trying not to look like a doorman, and when they were inside Della breezed past the bar and found them a table near a small platform on which three dark-skinned men were sitting on chairs, blowing horns that had cigarette smoke coming out through the bells. Another man, wreathed in smoke, was playing a banged-up set of drums, bass, snare, hi-hat and two toms. The alto sax and clarinet deferred to the tall, lighter man with the trumpet. The tune was fast and jittery, a lick that might have started as one song but long ago had lost its train of thought. At the tables around them, coloured men and women engaged in conversations that had, with the noise and the smoke and the booze, become improvised shouting matches, as though the music were there not to give them something to listen to but to rise above.

When Peter joined them, Della smiled a welcome. Jack thought she looked more at ease here, in this place where the three of them stood out like beacons, than she had in her own house, and it made a kind of perverse sense to him, because he felt more at home in her house than he did at his own. He was faintly jealous of Peter; Peter lived with her all the time, not just on Thursday nights. Peter saw her in daylight.

"Who's at the Paradise?" Peter asked the waiter, who leaned over to wipe the table and say something close to Peter's ear that sounded like *Billy Eckstine*.

"Big crowd," Peter said. The waiter nodded and left.

Jack didn't care who was at the Paradise, or here either, he didn't like this jungle music, this tribal jiggaboo jazz. They really should be over on Hastings, at the Three Star or the Flame Show Bar, where it was busier, better lit, safer. He liked his music smooth and mellow, flowing like a deep, continuous river. There was nothing mellow about these boys, their cheeks and eyes bulging out of their heads, sweat shining on their faces. They looked as though they'd been carved out of hard, wet coal. This music wasn't the voice of God.

But Della was watching the trumpet player like she was trying to get inside the man's skin. Her head was turned slightly away so that he could see, in the bluish light coming from the Pabst sign above the bar, the pulse in her throat keeping time with the music. He allowed his eyes to caress the contours of her blouse in the smoky darkness. Everything around her was in motion, moving waves of sound, yet she was calm and still, fearless. He marvelled at her, a white woman in a room full of coloureds, a doctor's wife surrounded by assembly linemen, machine-shop workers, drill-pressers, tool-and-die punchers, men who made tanks and bombs for a living, who swept floors and cleaned toilets, who eyed white women in ways that could get them arrested if a white man caught them at it. They were eyeing her now, looking her over between outbursts of laughter, calculating, sizing up him and Peter. What's she doing here? they were thinking. What does she want? When she picked up her glass and put it to her lips they followed the liquid as it slid down her throat. Jack knew she could feel them watching her because she never took her eyes off the stage, not even to look at him.

"They're good tonight," she said when the waiter brought their drinks.

"They picked up when you come in," the waiter said.

Peter was watching the trumpet player. Jack leaned forward, elbows on the table, aware of the men watching him from under soft caps pulled down tight on their foreheads, loose shirts with greasy collars, sleeves rolled up over glistening biceps. The women were bolder, better dressed, probably office workers. They sat with their legs crossed and their sweaters draped over their shoulders, buttoned at the throat, dark skin showing through white blouses. The men met his eyes before looking away. The women held his gaze coolly, like they were reading his thoughts.

The set ended in a long, sinking chord, a train whistle running out of steam, and Peter laughed, picked up his beer and drained it.

"Man!" he said, looking at Jack, eyes glowing. "That has *guts*!"

"You like guts?" Jack asked.

"Damn right I do."

"Not really something you could dance to, is it?" Jack said, turning to Della.

"Would you like to dance, Jack?" she asked, smiling at him.

For a second he thought she was serious. "No, not really."

"Well, then."

Before leaving, she went up and said something to the trumpet player, who nodded and said something back, looking over at their table. Peter waved at him. Jack saw Della hold the coloured man's hand for too long, and squeeze it before letting go. He thought, she must have been giving him a tip.

Jack told Peter to drop him off at the tunnel exit and he would walk home. Della turned in her seat to look at him.

"What about your trombone?" she asked him. "Didn't you leave it at our house?"

"I'll come and get it tomorrow."

"Are you sure, Jack?" Peter said. "We can pick it up now and drive you home."

"No," Jack said, then added, "Thanks, but I'd rather walk."

It was after midnight and the Settlement's streets were quiet, the air still and heavy and sweet-smelling from the

Hiram Walker's distillery in Walkerville. Men and women sat out on their porches, smoking and drinking beer, arguing in low voices about whether or not it was warm for June. The Depression was over, the factories were operating again. There was money to be made. Hiram Walker's was hiring, Chrysler's was making Jeeps and personnel carriers, people were migrating up from Georgia and Alabama for the high-paying wartime jobs. A person could make sixty dollars a week at Packard, assembling airplane engines. Jack could hear their lazy drawls floating down from the porches: *Detroy-it, Will-It-Run, Forward Motors, Harm Walker.* His father could have been making a fortune building houses for the veterans who would be returning any day now, but instead he made petty cash turning Settlement houses into tenements and apartments for the factory workers, who'd be happy living in packing crates as long as they were cheap.

Jack stopped in front of his house. The old man's Dodge was parked at the side, *W. H. Lewis & Sons, Plasterers.* Hoe handles and sawhorses stuck out of the box as if they'd been thrown in. The row of whitewashed stones dividing the driveway from the bare front yard glowed like skulls in the light from the house, his mother's pathetic stab at elegance.

He thought about going inside. His father would be down at the British-American, his mother in the kitchen playing solitaire or baking something for a church supper. Benny would be home with one of his coloured girlfriends. They would be drinking and slapping one another, running up and down the stairs. The saying in the Settlement was, coloured women all wanted to sleep up, and white women all wanted to sleep down.

He didn't want to go in there. He walked over to the truck and tried the handle, found it unlocked, climbed into the cab and stretched out on the seat. He lay on his back, smoking, looking up through the windshield at the hazy night sky. All he wanted to think about was Della. It frightened him, the way he thought about her, but he gave in to it. When he went to her house to get his trombone in the morning, in the daylight, he half hoped she'd invite him in. He wasn't sure what he would say to her, and he imagined several ways it could go, each one ending with him kissing her and her letting him. And then her kissing him back. His heart raced with the thought of it, the sweet, shared danger. There would be no test he couldn't pass after that.

But when he drove the Merc to her house the next day, only Peter was there.

"Mother's in Detroit," he said. "She's buying something there, don't know what. You coming in?"

"Naw," Jack said. "I just came for the trombone."

He set his horn in the back of the Merc and drove out to Walkerville, to the Schuler house. Mr. Schuler was a Jew, an executive at Hiram Walker's, drove a brand-new Packard with fake whitewalls and automatic transmission. He wanted a wall knocked out and the resulting room plastered and repainted. Jack had done most of the work himself, as usual, while the old man and Benny drank beer down at the British-American Hotel. Della would like this house, he thought as he worked. He imagined her behind him, curled up on the sofa in the living room, listening to *Tales of the Texas Rangers* on the expensive floor-model radio in the corner. "Come and join me, Jack," she would say, patting the cushion beside her, and he would put down whatever he was doing. This would be their life, their perfect home.

"You're doing a fine job in there," Mr. Schuler said while Jack was cleaning his tools at the end of the day. "Not like those darkies you had working for you these past two mornings." And he handed Jack an envelope with money in it, a hundred dollars.

His father and Benny had made a mess taking out the wall, hauling out debris in burlap bags through the living room instead of passing them through a window. That morning they'd worked for a couple of hours, then left. Jack knew they'd be in the British-American, celebrating having work.

"They stole from me," Mr. Schuler said.

"Who did?" Jack turned towards him.

"Just some shampoo from the bathroom. My wife noticed it. Stupid, eh?"

"I don't think—"

Mr. Schuler interrupted him, clapping Jack on the back. "Niggers," he said. "What can you do?"

Jack drove the Merc slowly along Wyandotte with the window down. Shampoo, for Christ's sake. Why would Benny steal shampoo? When Wyandotte hit Ouellette, he turned towards the river and looked for a parking space outside the

British-American. The truck was parked a block up from the hotel on Sandwich, as if that would fool anyone. As he turned down Ouellette to the B-A's tavern entrance, he noticed that the ferry terminal was livelier than usual. Factory workers let out early? Maybe the war was over. He walked through the lobby, past his uncle's barbershop, which was closed, and opened the door to the tavern, to be hit with the reek of stale beer and air that had already been breathed a dozen times. He hated the place. A dozen sullen men slouched around black-topped tables, smoking and nursing glasses of warm beer. Benny and Uncle Harley could usually be found at the old man's table, drinking beer, smoking, reading newspapers, eating pickled eggs, talking occasionally, watching the waiter move around the room emptying ashtrays and wiping tables. Uncle Harley came and went according to a schedule known only to him. His entire life revolved around the corner of Ouellette Avenue and Sandwich Street, the hub of Windsor. He was older than the old man, smaller and darker and, when it suited him, livelier. Jack thought of him as a black widow spider and did his best to avoid him.

Jack approached their table and took Mr. Schuler's envelope out of his jacket pocket. No one looked up. ". . . You hear about what's going on over at Belle Isle?" Uncle Harley was saying.

"You finish that Walkerville job yet?" the old man asked, interrupting Uncle Harley. His voice had more gravel in it than usual.

"No," Jack said. "Couple more days, maybe."

"Couple more days? What's the holdup?"

Jack shrugged. The holdup was that he was the only one working on it. "I'll take care of it," he said. "Schuler paid me." He tossed the envelope on the table. His father looked at it but didn't pick it up.

"White woman and her baby," Uncle Harley went on. "Crowd of coloured boys from Detroit . . ."

"Sit down and have a beer," the old man said.

"No, thanks."

"They sayin' there's a crowd of coloureds gatherin' in Detroit right now, goin' teach whitey a lesson. They throwed a white woman off the Belle Isle Bridge."

"What's that?" Benny said, looking up from his paper.

"Jesus Christ," Jack's father said, slapping his palm on the table. "Doesn't nobody ever come in here with good news?" Then he turned to Jack and pushed the envelope back at him. "You go on home and give that to your mother. Tell her we'll be along. Take the truck and leave the Merc for us."

Jack tossed the keys to the Merc on the table, picked up the truck keys and headed towards the door.

"And put some gas in the truck," the Old Man called when Jack was nearly out. "There's coupons in the glovebox." Always wanting the last word.

Jack drove the truck home without putting gas in it. He gave the money to his mother, changed his clothes and ate some supper, then walked to band practice carrying his trombone.

A stream of cars was coming out of the tunnel, unusual for a weekday, and each city bus he saw was filled. Someone big playing at the Top Hat, Count Basie, maybe, or Cab Calloway. The people looked out their car windows, at him with his trombone, and maybe thought he was with the band. Calloway played at the Graystone Ballroom on Mondays, which was coloured night, and the story was that white musicians climbed up the telephone poles outside the hall to listen so they could copy his licks.

After band practice, he and Peter walked back to Peter's house. Peter didn't know if his mother would be home or not, and Jack was hoping that she would be. It was nine o'clock and just beginning to get dark, two days from the summer solstice. Ouellette Avenue and Chatham and Pitt streets were still swarming with people. He could tell they were from Detroit because they didn't seem to know where to go or what to do with themselves. They milled about on the sidewalks, some leaning against the storefronts, others stepping off the curb to let Peter and Jack pass.

When they got to Peter's house, there were no lights on and the front door was locked. Peter felt through his pockets for his key, then said he'd have to go around back and come through the house to let Jack in. Jack waited on the porch swing, looking down towards the river. It was still daylight over the water, but there were plumes of smoke rising from the vicinity of Black Bottom. It looked like a house had caught fire or someone was burning tires. Then he felt something in the pit of his stomach, but he didn't know what it was.

"Mother's not here and the car's gone," Peter said when he opened the front door.

Jack stepped into the house and stood in the front hall. Something was wrong. He hadn't been here before when Della wasn't home, and without her the house seemed empty. His mother always said that a house without a woman was like a body without a soul. The trombone case echoed loudly when he set it down on the hardwood floor. Suddenly, the house reminded him of somewhere he'd been before. He took in the push-button light switches, the faint whiff of carbolic, even his long, black horn case: it was a funeral home. His aunt Maisie, Uncle Harley's wife, died when Jack was ten, and there had been this same chemical smell at her viewing. He remembered envying the people who could afford to live in such a fine house, they must have been rich people, he'd said, and Benny had laughed at him. "The only people live in this house are dead people," he said.

"Want a beer?" Peter called from upstairs.

"Sure." He climbed the carpeted stairs slowly. "Where do you think she is?"

"Who?"

"Del— Your mother."

"Search me," said Peter. "She's been acting pretty scattered lately, always rushing off somewhere."

Peter was standing by the radio, tuning in a Chicago station. Della's knitting was on her chair; she hadn't finished her day's sock. "I think she said something about meeting a friend on

Belle Isle after finishing her business in Detroit. Didn't think she'd be this late, though. You hungry?"

Belle Isle. What was it Uncle Harley had said about Belle Isle?

Peter made ham sandwiches in the kitchen and brought them into the family room. They ate and drank beer, listening to the radio, Louis Armstrong singing "Shine." Peter, eyes closed, long legs crossed at the ankles, was soon lost in the music, barely aware of where he was, but Jack couldn't listen to Armstrong. He thought about the smoke he'd seen hovering over Detroit, and what his Uncle Harley had said about a woman being thrown off the bridge. He looked at the clock and saw it was after eleven.

"I think we should go out and look for your mother," he said.

"Why?" Peter asked, and Jack told him.

"We'll have to go to Detroit," Jack said.

"Mother has the car."

"I'll go get my father's truck. You call around while I'm gone, see if she's at some friend's house."

The street lamps were off, of course, but there was enough moonlight to see by. He ran down Victoria to Chatham Street and across Ouellette, which was still awash with people. It was a mob now. Had they come to Windsor looking for more whites to throw into the Detroit River? He darted through them, hoping that the truck was where he had left it, parked beside the house. It was. It didn't start right away, it never did when the weather was humid. Goddamned Dodges. He sat for a moment, catching his breath, then pulled out the choke, pumped the gas pedal and tried again. It caught, and he backed sharply out of the driveway, between the line of skulls poking up through the grass.

Peter was waiting for him on the porch. He came down to the sidewalk, flung open the passenger door and got in.

"Any luck?" Jack asked him.

Peter shook his head. "She's not with any friends that I know of. And none of the clubs in Detroit are picking up."

"You think she'd be at a club?"

"I'd say so, wouldn't you," he said flatly, "this late at night?"

Jack swung the truck around a corner. A bottle rolled behind the seat.

"I listened to the news on the radio," Peter said. "Crowds of coloureds fighting crowds of whites, fire trucks blocked, police wading in. We may not be able to get across the river. There's a full-blown riot going on over there."

At the border, coloureds were being held up and their vehicles searched, but Jack barely had to slow down to be waved through. He drove to Woodward Avenue and stopped in the middle of the street. What he saw was bigger than anything he had thought about before. There were fires everywhere. Hundreds of people running in every direction, disappearing into the darkness between buildings. Gunshots and explosions punctuated the night. Every store along Woodward had had its doors and windows broken, and people were running out with armloads of goods, clothing, radios, shoes. Some were lying on the sidewalks and in the gutters, not moving. The smoke he had seen from Peter's window was coming from stores and over-turned cars. A trolley had been tipped on its side. The street was awash with flames from burning gasoline and water sluicing from the few fire trucks that had made it through the crowd.

"Jesus," he said. "We'll never find her in this."

He pulled the truck onto a side street and parked, and when he got out he saw a group of white men and women surround a car driven by a coloured man and begin to rock it. He and Peter hid behind the truck. The driver of the car tried to open his door but the crowd pushed against it, keeping him trapped inside. Then they tipped the car over, first onto its side, then onto its roof. There were cheers from the crowd and screams from inside the car, and the sound of collapsing metal. Gasoline spilled from the tank and someone lit a match.

"They're going to kill him!" Jack shouted, and felt Peter's hand clamp over his mouth.

There was a tremendous outcry as a large crowd of coloureds, brandishing baseball bats and hammers, a few with hunting rifles and handguns, rushed the upturned car, releasing the man from the vehicle and pushing the white rioters back into the alleys and side streets. Some of the whites fought back, but most ran off, looking for battles with better odds. When the street was clear, Jack and Peter ran down Woodward, away from the fight-ing. Peter was the first to spot Della's car in the next block, also flipped onto its side. There was no sign of Della.

"We should split up," Peter said. "I'll stay on Woodward, you go over to East Adams. Try the Horse Shoe first."

"Why?"

"Just a hunch. I'll go along Hastings."

Jack turned to go but Peter grabbed his arm. "If you find her, don't come looking for me," he said. "Get her to the truck and take her home."

Jack nodded and watched Peter run off up Woodward.

Before Jack could move, a coloured man came up to him and grabbed him by the shirt, a big man with a thick B of flesh at the back of his neck. His eyes were wide open and unfocused, as though he were staring at smoke, and he smelled of booze. Jack tried to push him away, but the man held on like he was drowning and started yelling into Jack's face.

"Get your truck down there, man!" He pointed down a darkened alley. Then he laughed. "We got us a liquor store to unload."

"What?" Jack shouted back at him.

"The truck, friend. Drive it down that alley behind the liquor store."

"No, I've got to find someone."

"Hey, boy, whassa matter wif you?" He shook Jack, but gently. "You can't hear what I'm sayin' or somethin'?"

Jack cursed and broke away from the man. He continued running down Woodward towards East Adams. He heard the man yelling after him: "Hey! Hey, boy! Come back here! Where's your head at?"

Jack turned down a side street, ran a hundred feet from

Woodward and stopped to catch his breath. He was in front of a shop with the word "Spirits" scrawled above its window in white paint. Most of the window was in shards on the sidewalk, and the door hung open, half off its hinges. A mob of maybe thirty white people brandishing sticks and baseball bats stood watching the shop and shouting. He tried to cross the street to avoid them but skidded on the broken glass and went down. The crowd surrounded him, and he curled into a ball, thinking they were going to beat him senseless, but instead they helped him up. A woman looked at his hands and a blond man brushed shards of glass from the front of his clothing.

"You okay?"

"Goddamn niggers're emptying the place out," another white man said. "Run and find us a cop!"

"I can't." Jack tried to pull away.

"We'll stay and keep them inside. You go now."

Jack started backing away, then someone in the crowd yelled, "Hey! They're gettin' out the back!" and the surge dragged Jack around the side of the building into the alley. In the dim light, he saw two men run from the back door of the liquor store, chased by the posse of whites down the alley to the next street. When the fugitives saw Jack's truck they veered towards it, and Jack realized with a jolt that the two men were Benny and his father. What the hell were they doing here? People crashed into him from behind, and he started running towards the truck. His brother and father reached the truck just before the mob got to them. Benny tried to open the doors but they were locked. Jack felt the weight of the keys in his pants pocket. He watched as the mob grabbed Benny and his father and shoved them against the side of the truck.

"Goddamn niggers!"

"Get 'em, boys!"

Jack's mind flew between the mob and his father, but his body was frozen on the spot. He shouted, "No!" but the sound was lost in the uproar. Three men started beating Benny and his father with their fists. The rest of the mob closed in around them, shouting encouragement and obscenities, poking bats and rake handles blindly through the press of bodies. One woman was so excited she began beating on the back of a white man in front of her. Jack lost sight of his brother and father. Then, as though an electric shock had been applied to his limbs, he rushed into the mob, trying to pull people out of his way. Others clawed him from behind. From where he was now he could see Benny again, his arms up around his head, his eyes wide with terror, but the mob was too tightly packed for Jack to reach him.

He saw Benny go down, big as he was, and then the old man, still on his feet, arms flailing, fending off blows. Jack tried to get closer, but could make no headway. He saw his father search through the sea of white faces, saw his eyes find his own, light up momentarily and then turn away. Jack watched as his father went slack, dropping his arms and letting himself be pummelled by the crowd.

He searched for an opening. When he couldn't find one, he grabbed the shirt of the man in front of him and yelled, "Stop them!"

"Don't you worry, son," the man said gleefully. "We're stoppin' 'em all right. They'll be lucky we don't string 'em up on that telephone pole!"

Just then two policemen came charging down the street on horseback, the sound of their police whistles rising above the clatter of the horses' hooves on the pavement. The crowd turned and wavered, then broke. Jack caught sight of his father on his hands and knees, Benny lying flat on his face under the truck. A river of fire was flowing along the curb from Woodward, heading directly for the truck and Benny. He saw the old man's body fall in front of it, engulfed by water and flames. Then his view was blocked by one of the horses, the policemen's truncheons rose and fell in the moonlight, and he heard the crowd's blood cries turn to shouts of pain and panic. Gunfire, like a drum roll of firecrackers, reached him from a distance, and then the keening of a siren. He turned from the horror and ran.

He didn't stop until he reached East Adams, where he collapsed in the alcove at the door of the Horse Shoe Club, curled in the corner like a frightened animal, his eyes squeezed shut. Had he done what he could? Hadn't there been something in the old man's look that said, Get the hell out of here, son? Sure there was. What else could he have done, alone against so many?

After a while he straightened and entered the Horse Shoe, half expecting to hear a blast of trumpet music, a lick of jazz, as though what had happened behind him belonged to someone else's history, a realm of chaos he could simply step out of. Della. He would find her and bring her home. If she wasn't here, in the familiar headiness of beer and cigarettes and people drinking and talking as if news of the riot hadn't reached them, then she'd be in the next bar or the one after that. He would search them all until he found her.

Drinkers glanced up at him with incurious faces before going back to their sullen conversations. On the nickelodeon, Billie Holiday was singing "Strange Fruit." He staggered and gripped the bar, leaving a smear of blood on the polished wood. It wasn't enough, but it was something.

When he saw Della sitting at a table in the back, he almost wept with relief.

"Della," he said. She looked up and he hurried to her. She was with a group of men and a young woman, all of them coloured. The woman had been injured in the riot. Her eyes were closed and she was sobbing. Della was dabbing with a towel at a cut on the girl's forehead. Her own dress was torn and there was a smudge of dirt on her cheek. A large glass of gin sat on the table in front of her; he could smell it. It had a reddish tinge because Della was dipping the towel in it. Jack recognized one of the men as the trumpet player whose hand Della had held that night. When he saw Jack, the man started to get up, and Jack clenched his fists and braced himself, but Della put her hand on the man's arm and said, "He's one of us," and the man sat down, eyeing Jack uncertainly.

"There's a war going on out there," Jack said, sitting down beside Della.

"Haven't you heard?" she said. "There's a war going on everywhere."

He started to tell her what he had seen, what he had been through, but he had no words. There was too much he had to leave out, and nothing he could invent. The look on the face of the coloured man in the burning car. The drunk who had called him boy. The telephone pole rising like a cross in the darkness above the alley. His father and Benny as the flames floated towards them. When he told her about falling in front of the liquor store, she took his hands and swabbed them with gin.

"Where's Peter?" she asked quietly.

Jack looked down at his bleeding hands in hers. "I don't know."

She handed the towel to the trumpet player, stood up and walked behind the bar, where there was a phone. She dialled a number and Jack heard her voice, low and soothing, like the sound of a cat purring. They all listened. It seemed incredible to Jack that anything out there was still working.

Jack looked at the others around him. The trumpet player was now holding the towel against the girl's forehead. One of the other men said that no white woman had been thrown off the Belle Isle Bridge. "That's a lie started by whites." He said a black woman had been raped and killed on the island the day before by a group of U.S. Navy men. "Crackers from the South—Georgia, Virginia, and the Carolinas. They go round lookin' for heads to crack."

"Peter's home," Della said, returning to the table. "He was

frantic, poor thing. I told him you were here and that you'll bring me back safe and sound. You will, won't you, Jack?"

"Yes," he said, almost starting to cry. He had failed his father and his brother, but he would not fail her. "Of course I will."

She turned to the trumpet player. "I'm going now," she said. "Will you look after Dee-Dee?"

The man nodded. Della walked towards the front of the club. Jack took a last look at the trumpet player, then followed Della out.

Woodward Avenue was in ruins, smouldering and deserted. Jack hurried Della along, but she insisted on stopping to help another woman who was lying on the ground outside a burned-out clothing store. The woman's coat was still smoking, and she clasped a rolled-up ball of cloth in her arms. Her hands were charred black.

"We've got to get a move on," Jack said, looking around nervously.

"She's dead."

Della stood and backed away from the body. She slipped her arm through his and together they hurried on, stepping over lead pipes, shovels and other makeshift weapons abandoned on the sidewalk. The truck was where he'd left it. His father and Benny were nowhere to be seen. Jack bent to examine dark spots on the pavement where they had lain, spots that may have been anything, brake fluid or spilled liquor.

"What is it, Jack?"

"Nothing," he said. Straightening, he took the keys from his pocket, unlocked her side and helped her in, then turned to see a riderless police horse cantering past the smoking hulks of cars, stirrups flapping, eyes widened with terror. When he climbed in the cab, he let Della wrap his right hand in a handkerchief, but when she reached for the left he pulled it away.

"We've got to get out of here."

For once, the truck started on the first try. He put it in gear and decided against the tunnel. "If we can get over a few blocks west, we can take the Ambassador Bridge. It'll be safer the farther we get from downtown."

Della didn't answer. She was leaning back on the seat, her knees pulled up, staring ahead through the windshield. He shifted gears carefully. "That poor woman," she said. "All she wanted was a nice dress."

He drove up Woodward, weaving around wrecked cars and broken glass and patches of burning oil. Firemen directed him past a parked ambulance, its panel doors open and its roof light flashing, but he saw few people, and no one told him to stop so he kept going. At Vernor he turned left, taking a longer route to the bridge but one that would keep them above where the worst of the rioting had been. But even here there were smashed windows and downed power lines, shadows moving between houses. At West Grand the streets were almost normal, and he began working his way towards the river and the bridge. He looked at his watch. One o'clock in the morning.

Just as they turned onto Fort Street, still a few blocks from the bridge, the truck's engine coughed twice and then stopped. "Shit," he said softly. He should have bought gas when the old man told him to. "Shit, shit, shit." They coasted for another half a block until they came to a gas station. Closed, of course, but he managed to pull the truck into the lot before it came to a final stop. Della brought her knees down and looked around.

"Well, this is a fine how-do-ye-do," she said.

After the ruckus downtown, the night was disconcertingly quiet. He lowered his window and heard crickets and the hum of traffic on the bridge.

"Out of gas," he said.

"Out of booze," she replied.

He looked at her and smiled. "This truck is never out of booze." He fished behind the seat for the bottle he'd heard rolling around earlier. Rye, mostly full. He opened it, handed it to her, and she took a sip.

"Is your hand still bleeding?"

"Probably." The steering wheel had felt sticky but he hadn't thought about what was causing it.

She exhaled and reached for his left hand. This time he let her. "You need to clean it and I need to pee," she said. She looked about the truck. They were half a mile from the bridge, miles from home, too far to walk. "What's that?"

"What?"

"Down the road a bit."

The Ambassador Motel, the sign unlit but legible in the moonlight. He thought they would spend the night in the truck, but she opened her door and got out. Her light-coloured hair and white skin glowed angelically in the dark. He watched as she walked down the road. He thought about joining the Navy. He imagined his uniformed arm around Della's waist, their picture on the table beside the radio, wouldn't that be something? After a time he saw movement down at the motel, and in a few minutes she was standing next to his window, holding up a key attached to a miniature replica of the Ambassador Bridge.

"Cranky old bugger," she said, "but I explained the circumstances and he gave us a room. I called Peter again and told him to go to bed."

Jack climbed out of the truck, locked both doors and followed her to the motel. While he'd been waiting, the cut on his hand had stopped throbbing, but now it started again. He tried to stay behind her but she waited for him, took his arm when he caught up to her. A room. Was she going to let him stay in the room? Or had she taken two rooms? "We're in number six," she said.

He had never seen a motel room before except in movies. When she opened the door and turned on the ceiling light he was amazed at the tidiness, how everything was reduced to only what you'd need if all you ever did in this room was sleep and wash, or maybe sit and smoke. A bed, neatly made, a sink with a mirror, two towels, a small bar of soap wrapped in paper to show it hadn't been used, a dresser with nothing on it but an empty ashtray, a single chair. Through an open door he saw a toilet and the corner of a metal shower stall. Della told him to take off his shirt and ran lukewarm water into the sink. He watched her in the mirror above it, but she didn't look up. His pants were cut through at the knees, he hadn't noticed that, and the blood on them had begun to dry. He took his shirt off and put it on the bed, then went over to the sink. Della took his wrist and put his hand in the basin and kept it there. Their eyes met in the mirror. Then she looked closely at his palm. "You're a mess," she said, as though what happened had been a bad decision on his part. She looked up at him again through the mirror: "Now you'll have a scar on your hand as well as on your cheek."

He said he was all right, it didn't hurt, but it did. She cleaned the cut with a corner of a washcloth. He smelled her hair. He watched her breathing.

"Your dress is torn."

"It doesn't matter. It's just a dress." She started to cry and he put his arms around her, but she moved away and dried her eyes with the washcloth.

"You shouldn't have come here," he said. "Couldn't you see it was dangerous?"

"Someone tipped my car over."

"Were you in it?"

"No, I was about to be. So I turned and ran to the Horse Shoe."

"But why——?"

"Shush, now," she said. "I was there on business."

"What kind of business?"

"My business."

She seemed to be staring at his bare shoulder. He thought

if he made the wrong move she would leave the room and go outside to phone Peter. She might even call the police, although she'd have a hard time explaining what she was doing in a motel room with him. No, she wouldn't. He's my son's friend. He was hurt. They'd look at her torn dress. Doctor's wife, white. They'd look at him. She leaned forward slightly and pressed her cheek against his shoulder, her body brushing against his arm. Jack saw her in the mirror above the sink, the tear in her dress revealing one strap of her slip. They wouldn't believe me, he thought. She smelled of soap and smoke and faintly of rye, and his skin where she touched it sang out.

The bed was unforgiving. They made love with the light on, him arching above her and a red flush spreading slowly up from her breasts to her throat, her eyes shut and then suddenly wide open in a sort of amazement, as though she were seeing something incredibly beautiful taking shape somewhere behind his back. When his release came, her nerveless gaze fixed on his and held him in a state of suspension until at last he collapsed, unable to breathe. After a while he got up to turn off the light, still half erect, and she watched him with a puzzled look that disturbed him. What was she seeing? But when he got back into bed she took him into her mouth, then ran her tongue up his chest until he was in her again, even more urgently than before.

After, they remained clasped together in the dark. He had never actually slept with a woman before. The girls who had come into his room at home, Benny's castoffs, had climbed on him, had their revenge on his brother, and then slipped back to

Benny in the dark. In the morning they'd be gone, or he would see them stumble out of Benny's room looking for their shoes. Now he realized that it wasn't sex but sleeping together that completed the act of love. You didn't have to trust a woman to have sex with her, but you did to sleep with her. Della slept with her back towards him, curled away from him, breathing as naturally as if she were alone, while he lay on his back watching the morning flood around the curtains into the strangely familiar room, the shadow of the light fixture circling the ceiling like an hour hand. Keys on the nightstand, her clothes on the chair by the bathroom door. He strained to make them out until he, too, finally fell asleep.

But the day was a disappointment from the moment he opened his eyes. Della was already awake, already up and dressed. He wanted to talk about their future. He would take her away. They could take the Merc, maybe drive west to Chicago, then on to the Pacific. She was in the bathroom, putting on lipstick.

"Come on, Jack," she said. She strode out of the bathroom, she even had her shoes on, for Christ's sake. She opened the curtains. Bright sunlight exploded into the room.

"What's the big hurry?" He felt awkward about getting out of bed naked when she was watching him, fully dressed. "It's Sunday, isn't it?"

"I've got to get home," she said. "Peter will be worried."

The gas station opened at eight. Della gave him five dollars and he bought gas, then drove the truck around to the motel office. She came out, climbed into the truck and sat facing straight ahead. He didn't know what he had done wrong.

He drove down Fort towards the bridge and the Windsor skyline. She sat stiffly, rubbing her bare arms. What were they going to do after they got home? He could take her for a picnic out near Amherstburg. He wanted to feel the sun burning his back as they made love, and see again that look of amazed ecstasy on her face, the flush spread up from her breasts to her throat. Just before the bridge they stopped at an intersection to let a line of Army tanks file by, heading downtown. The mayor must have called in the troops. When the tanks were gone Della looked at him sadly, as though she thought the Army had been searching for them and eventually they would be found out. Jack put the truck in gear and drove across the bridge.

When he pulled up outside her house, Peter was sitting on the porch steps. Jack turned off the engine, rolled down the window and waved. Peter waved back, not warmly.

"Better stay here," she said.

"Why?"

"Let's give it some time."

"How much time? When?"

"I don't know, Jack." She looked past him and waved at Peter. Then she put her hand on his arm, a gesture he suddenly hated. "There'll be police reports, insurance people to call about the car."

"Is it because of Peter?" He looked up at the house. Peter was coming towards them. He would want answers. He would be writing to his father. Would he tell him about this?

Della got out of the truck. Jack watched her embrace her son, wondering what she would say to him. The thought of her lying about him hit Jack like a blow to the chest. There would be no picnic in Amherstburg, no more nights after band practice. No more band practice. In a rage, he started the truck and drove off, slapping the steering wheel with the palm of his right hand until it bled again.

He followed the river, turned up Walker Road, drove along Tecumseh to Ouellette and back down to the river, though not as far as the dock, then made the loop again until he was certain he could trust himself. He calmed down as the city came to life. Smoke or mist still drifted across the river from Detroit. He hoped the city had burned to the ground. He drove home. There was no one there. He changed his clothes and put a fresh bandage on his hand, then went back downtown, parked in front of the Recruiting Office and turned off the ignition. Then he went inside and joined the Navy.

Only then did he remember Benny and his father.

PART III

VIVIAN

Vivian stepped down from the train onto the conductor's stool and searched the throng for Jack's brother, Benny, who was supposed to be picking them up at the station. She was sure she would recognize him from Jack's description: tall and blond, brown eyes with blue flecks in them. Looking into them, she imagined, would be like gazing up at the sky through a canopy of trees. When Jack joined her he looked grim, as though he'd had a fight with the conductor. He took her arm and pulled her through the crowd, almost to the exit. She should have worn lower heels. Near the door, a tall man in splattered work clothes was grinning widely at Jack. So this was Benny. His hair was blond and wavy, just as Jack had described it, but his complexion was like tanned deer hide, like that of someone who'd been working outside all summer. There were large brown freckles on the backs of his hands. Vivian hadn't seen anyone before who looked quite like Benny, but she couldn't put her finger on what was different about him. Jack introduced her, and Benny gave her a brief, appraising look, but instead of reaching out to shake her hand he clapped Jack on the back and said, "Well done, little brother." What was that supposed to mean?

"Where's the others?" Jack asked.

"Mom's at home," said Benny.

He took their two suitcases and led them through the station to the street. He still hadn't said a word to her. She thought they would get into a taxi or a car, but they turned left and walked along a sidewalk, down a dreary street that smelled of dust and sewer, with shuffling pedestrians going into and out of cheap hotels, diners and pawnshops. Jack and Benny walked ahead, talking. She strode doggedly on, glad, now that she thought about it, to be moving after the long, tense train ride with Jack. This was her first real walk in Canada, a surprising thought given that she was almost two thousand miles into it. She let the distance between her and the men increase. With the wind coming from the south, it was warmer than it would have been back home, but people were walking with their hands in their pockets and their heads down, as though trudging through driving sleet. In St. John's so warm a day would have had them taking their coats off and smiling up at the sky.

She studied the men ahead of her, her husband and his brother—her brother-in-law, although that title still seemed to belong to Freddie. Benny walked in a loose-jointed lope, so unlike Jack, whose gait was more swagger than stride. Jack's uniform was out of place here, his widened cuffs even slightly ridiculous. Windsor wasn't the natural home of sailors. She felt sorry for him, though she knew it was disloyal for a woman to feel sorry for her husband. Benny and Jack hadn't seen each other for more than two years, yet they'd greeted each other like grudging acquaintances, without touching except for that disconcerting clap on the back. *Well done, little brother.* As if Jack had won her at a fair.

At last they turned down a side street, and when she reached the corner, Benny was lifting the suitcases onto the bed of an old, dented pickup truck.

"We can all squeeze in the front," he drawled. "If I'd known you was bringing a lady friend, I'd've brought the Merc."

She looked at Jack in alarm. Had he not told his family she was coming? It seemed impossible to believe, and yet what else could those words have meant? Surely he'd written to his mother; in fact, he'd told her he had.

If Jack noticed her dismay, he said nothing. He motioned her into the truck's cab. She sat between them, her heart pounding. The floor was littered with oily rags and papers and small cardboard boxes. She didn't know where to put her feet.

"Are they still living on Dougall Avenue?" Jack asked. After much gear shifting, Benny finally had the truck in motion.

"Dougall? They never lived on Dougall."

Keeping his voice low, Jack said, "How's Dad?"

Benny grunted. "Back to normal." Jack turned his head and looked out the window, as though he were still on the train.

McDougall Street was only a few blocks from the train station. It was a narrow, treeless street of small clapboard houses built shoulder to shoulder and close to the sidewalk. The majority were rough and neglected, their shiplap siding weathered, porches aslant, windowpanes cracked, lawns bare or overgrown. She had seen ramshackle houses before, some of the shanties on Springdale and Carter's Hill in St. John's made you wonder what kept them standing, but these were worse. Surely his parents didn't live here? Benny parked in front of the most dilapidated of them all.

"Christ!" Jack exclaimed. "They didn't move up, they moved down."

"Uh-huh."

The house looked as though it had never known paint. Its patched roof sagged in the middle. The open porch was cluttered with sawhorses and pails, metal troughs, long-handled hoes and shovels, everything spattered and smeared with what Vivian took at first to be birdlime—making her think of the rocks off Ferryland—but which, when she was at the door, turned out to be caked plaster. Where was the big house with the guest room overlooking the river, the one Jack had described on the train?

Despite her own mounting alarm, she thought it best to keep him calm. He looked at her with such panic in his eyes that she put her hand on his arm. "It'll only be for a few days," she said, patting him. But when he turned away from her, she realized she had pushed him back into his shell.

Before she could say anything else, Benny opened the front door. Jack squeezed past him into the house and she followed. There came a shriek from the far end of a narrow hall, and a small, delicate woman wearing an apron bustled towards them. She was tiny but spritely, as tiny creatures often are. Her wavy, dark hair, so much like Jack's, was brushed over one eye, and her face was pale. When she reached them at the front of the hall, Vivian detected the soft perfume of rose-scented facial powder.

"Jackson, my baby!"

Jackson? It hadn't occurred to her that his name was short for anything. She sensed Jack recoiling slightly, but he allowed his mother to embrace him, and when she was finished she turned to Vivian. "And who's this?" she cried in delight. "Who have you brought us?"

"Ma, this is Vivian."

"Oh, my," she said. "How do you do, Vivian?"

"It's so nice to meet you finally, Mrs. Lewis."

There was an awkward silence while they watched Benny come in with the luggage. "You two aren't sleeping here," he said, "but I thought I'd better bring these in from the truck before somebody stole them."

"Where are they staying, then?" Jack's mother asked in surprise.

"At my place," Benny said, winking at Jack. "There's more privacy there. I'll sleep here on the chesterfield."

"Oh, well," Jack's mother said vaguely. "I'll just go and set another place at the table. Oh, it's no trouble. We have plenty of plates."

Vivian very nearly sagged against the wall. The situation was so utterly beyond her comprehension she couldn't even form a thought about it. Jack *must* have told them she was coming. They had forgotten, that was all. Forgotten that their *son* was bringing his *wife* home to meet them. Almost worse than everything else was the ease with which they accepted his bringing a strange woman home and expecting to share a room with her. It was humiliating in the extreme. What did they think she was? She wanted to run from the house, out into the menacing street, but she couldn't. She wanted to take Jack aside and ask him what he had told them, but she couldn't do that either. Benny was behind her, so she couldn't even shoot Jack a meaningful glance. She followed him down the hall to the kitchen. She would have to wait until later. Maybe everything would be clearer by then.

In the kitchen, Jack's mother looked at her and exclaimed again: "So, you're Vivian."

"Yes, Mrs. Lewis," she said, as though speaking to a child. "I'm Vivian Lewis, Jack's wife."

A baffled look came over Jack's mother's face, but she recovered and said, "Oh, you must be exhausted after your long trip. Would you like some tea?"

"I would love some, thank you."

Jack cut in. "Where's Dad?"

"He's upstairs lying down." She turned to Vivian. "He's feeling under the weather today. He said he might come down for a bite of supper later on. He'll be so happy to meet you."

Jack's mother opened a cupboard door and began removing dishes, the offer of tea evidently forgotten. Perhaps Jack had written to her after all, and it had simply gone out of her head, like the tea. She tried to catch Jack's eye again, but he was talking to Benny and Jack's mother suggested Vivian help her reset the table in the small dining room.

"The war has spared my son," Jack's mother said happily, handing Vivian a water glass with yellow polka dots painted on it, "and given him a bride!"

"We were so sorry you couldn't come to the wedding," Vivian said.

"Oh, was there a wedding?"

Vivian nearly dropped the glass. "Yes, of course there was," she said. "In May."

"May is such a lovely month."

The table was heavy and dark, too big for the room. Everything was. A large, glass-fronted cabinet in one corner held glassware and serving dishes, and next to it was a big matching sideboard. An upright piano on the opposite wall was festooned with at least a dozen silver-framed, pre-war photographs, and she wondered why Jack had never shown her a photograph of anyone in his family. Jack's mother laid the table for six. Who was the sixth guest? She knew only of an Uncle Harley, and she thought Jack had said he lived in a hotel.

"There," Jack's mother said when they were finished. She herded Vivian through an arched doorway into the living room and bade her put her feet up while she put on the kettle. She hadn't forgotten the tea after all. "We'll let the boys talk," she said. "Dinner won't be too long."

She left Vivian alone in the room, which, like the dining room, contained more furniture than it could comfortably hold. They had evidently moved from a larger house, perhaps the one Jack had described to her on the train. Had business been bad during the war? Yes, that was almost certainly it. The war had shrunk everything. Except, apparently, the furniture. On the wall was a faded print of Jesus in pastel robes, kneeling at a rock with his hands folded in prayer, eyes lifted imploringly towards Heaven. No one she knew would have had such a thing in their house, not even the Catholics. She sat in a red plush armchair that reminded her of the seats on the train, and put her head back, trying to clear it of worry and suspicion. Jack would never lie to her about something this important, how could he hope to get away with it?

A short while later, Jack's mother called the three of them, Vivian, Jack and Benny, to sit at the table while she served from the kitchen, scurrying back and forth carrying food in pots and mixing bowls but never actually sitting down herself. Jack's father did not come down for his bite of dinner, nor did another guest arrive. No one mentioned the two empty chairs. There was a pot roast, cooked to within an inch of its life, and mashed potatoes, boiled cabbage, a cooked green that looked like spinach but somehow was not. The only condiment was salt. There never was any tea, and Vivian did not have the heart to ask for it. By the end of the meal, Jack's mother still had not sat down to her own empty plate.

"Shouldn't we save something for Dad?" Jack asked when there did not appear to be anything left to save.

"Let's let him sleep," said his mother brightly, perching on one of the unoccupied chairs. "I don't like to wake him," she said to Vivian. "But you can go up and take a look at him if you like."

"Oh," said Vivian, taken aback. "Won't we be seeing him tomorrow?"

"Of course you will," Jack's mother said.

"Jack," she said when they had left the house to walk the short distance to Benny's apartment—Benny would bring their luggage around later in the truck—"what is going on? There is something very odd about . . . about your family." There, she'd said it. What would Jack say in response? But he surprised her.

"I know," he said. "I tried to warn you."

"You did? When?"

"Lots of times." Then he looked at her. "You'll get used to it."

She walked beside him, sensing a kind of relief in his voice. Something she'd said had made him feel better. But when had he tried to warn her about his family? He'd barely mentioned them.

Jack had given the Navy Benny's apartment as a contact address to which to send his demob notice, so she knew it was on a street called Tuscarora. "An Indian tribe," Jack had joked. "Don't worry, long gone." The street was better lit, and there was a bit of grass in the yard. Jack had a key for the main door and another for the apartment. She felt almost regal entering it, it was so much bigger than their little flat in St. John's, which had seemed as big as the world to her. Benny had said he lived alone, but there was a small hand mirror and tubes of lipstick in the bathroom, a percale housedress hanging from a hook behind the bedroom door.

In bed that night, their first real bed in days, she decided to risk being more direct in her questioning.

"Did you or did you not tell your parents about our wedding?" she asked him, although now that she'd said it, it sounded more absurd than ever.

"I told you, I wrote to them," Jack said.

But he had told her so many things that weren't quite true; that his parents lived in a big house, that his father owned a construction company.

"What exactly did you tell them?"

"I told them I was getting married," he said, "to an angel from Fairy Land. A wonderful girl named Lily White."

"Jack, your mother had no idea who I was."

"I can't help what she knows and what she doesn't know," Jack said. "She says whatever comes into her head."

"Did you tell her I was coming to Windsor?"

"Yes, I told them you were coming to Windsor."

"Benny didn't seem to know, either," she persisted.

"Benny!" he said. "He knew, all right, he was just pulling your leg."

Why did so little of what Jack said make sense to her? He was staring up at the ceiling, gone from her again.

"Jack," she said slowly, "why does your mother use so much face powder?"

"What?" he said, turning on her. "What are you talking about? She doesn't."

"She does, Jack."

"Well, how would I know? Maybe she likes face powder." He reached across her, and for a moment she thought he was going to embrace her, to reassure her, to tell her something she could believe and trust, but he was just turning out the little lamp on the bedside table. "If you don't have any more dumb questions," he said into the darkness, "I'd like to go to sleep."

In the morning, as she unpacked and was deciding what to wear, she said to Jack, "Am I to meet your father today?"

"No, not today. He and Benny have a rush job in Leamington. They won't get back until after midnight."

How did he know that? "We could wait up," she offered. The thought of Jack's father being kept from her by his family had kept her awake most of the night.

"That's if nothing goes wrong," Jack said.

The next day there was a different excuse. His father had to go to Detroit for supplies, then take them out to Ann Arbor where Uncle Harley was working on a nursing home. But wasn't Uncle Harley a barber? He was, but he helped out with the plastering when they were busy. And he was an American citizen, so he could work in Ann Arbor without a work permit. How was Uncle Harley an American citizen? Didn't he own a barbershop in Windsor? He did. It was all so confusing and so inconceivable that she would not meet her father-in-law that she stopped questioning anything at all. She let herself believe it was simply a matter of waiting. She did have the unkind thought that if they were so busy with work then why were they still living in such a dingy little house, but she put that away from her, too, not wanting to invite another angry response. She had no idea how much a house in Windsor cost, or how much plasterers were paid. She contented herself with the mornings in Benny's apartment, sleeping late, reading for a bit while Jack slept, then getting up to make coffee and toast and fried eggs and bringing them back to bed for Jack, who jumped like a disturbed cat when she gently shook him awake.

After dressing—Jack had brought some civilian clothes from his mother's house—they would walk to Ouellette Avenue, Windsor's elm-lined main street, and turn up towards the river, looking into shop windows and wandering through dime stores, killing time before going to Jack's mother's for lunch. She forced herself to move lingeringly. They were on holiday, a kind of honeymoon, and she wanted to enjoy it. She would pick up some small item in a shop, a scarf or a comb, and he would stand beside her jiggling coins in his pocket.

"Do you want to buy it?" he'd ask her. "Go ahead."

"No, thank you, darling," she would say, putting it down,

trying to keep her voice light and her spirits up. "Maybe we should send Iris a scarf?"

"Why, is it her birthday?"

"No. Never mind."

Close to the river the shops became smaller and cheaper and the streets more congested. It reminded her of the St. John's waterfront, only here the sidewalks were filled with coloured people instead of dockworkers, people with varying degrees of the Windsor tan, as Jack had once called it. She had seen Negroes in St. John's, of course, merchant mariners from cargo ships. They came ashore for a day or two and then left. Coloured people in Windsor behaved more like they belonged to the place. And here the waterfront was a river. Rivers were unfriendly, she thought. She was used to water coming towards her like a greeting; here it swept past as though it hadn't noticed her at all, dismissing her the way Jack did.

There was a dirt lane at the bottom of Ouellette, leading down to the ferry dock, and a path running east with the flow of the river, with a wooden railing to keep people from falling over. When they reached it, she leaned against the top rail and closed her eyes, breathing in the wind and the rusty cries of gulls and the warm autumn sun pressing against her bare skin. When she opened her eyes again, she was surprised to see a city shimmering like a mirage on the other side: Detroit, it must be, the Arsenal of America.

Jack took her hand and they walked back up Ouellette on the east side. In one of the shops she bought him a fedora, and he wore it pushed back on his head, looking more like Frank Sinatra than ever: people turned to look at him, and as the afternoon passed his mood improved.

Eventually they came to a large park, with a low, black-painted chain fence dividing it from the sidewalk. Paths ran among shade trees, bordered by neatly tended flower beds and wooden benches. It looked cool and safe.

"What park is this?" she asked.

"Jackson Park."

"Can we sit for a minute?"

"Sure," he said, "if you want to be mugged."

A shadow had crept into Jack's voice. Why? Why did something as innocent as walking in a park cause him to scowl? He was the touchiest person alive. Maybe if she jollied him enough, said the right things, avoided saying the wrong things—like mentioning his father, or his mother's use of face powder—the old Jack would return and they would get on with their real lives. But she never knew when the next crash would come, and the strain on her nerves was wearing her down.

Soon he'd be out of the Navy, though. This visit would end, Jack would be demobilized, and she'd be on her way back home to her family in St. John's.

"But we won't be mugged if you're with me, darling," she said. "You'll protect me, won't you?" And she drew him into the park.

JACK

The grass was trampled at the Ouellette end, nobody stayed on the paths, probably because they were muddy and traced with bicycle tire marks. And why did dogs always shit on paths? Vivian didn't seem to notice, even though she was the one wearing white shoes. He guessed she also didn't see the squares of waxed paper caught in the shrubbery, or the coloured couples entwined on the benches in broad daylight. She walked with her arm through his, looking up at the trees as though they were on a country lane.

"Isn't it amazing," she said, "how one tree can be perfectly still and the tree right beside it is trembling in the wind?"

"Just like you and me," he said.

They sat beside the fountain, downwind of the spray so the freshened air blew over them, and then they walked again. They could hear traffic from Tecumseh Boulevard. When they reached the sunken garden without being mugged, she led him down the steps. Flower beds lined the paved walkways and she stopped at each one, stooping to sniff or to cradle a bloom in her cupped fingers. Masses of rose petals fell off into her hands, and she lifted them to him. "Just smell their bouquet," she said, but they reminded him of his mother's face powder and he turned his head away. Through the trees they could see Kennedy Collegiate, which backed onto the park from McDougall Street.

"My old high school," he said, nodding at the back of the turreted, red-brick building. "We used to call it the Castle."

"Were you a good student?" she asked him.

"Oh, sure, straight As. Captain of the baseball team, all that." He stared at the deserted diamond behind the school.

"Actually," he said, "I didn't finish grade nine."

"Why not?"

"I had to help my father."

"Building houses?"

"The war was on, the Depression was over. Anyone who didn't have a job had joined up, so wages were high. Dad couldn't afford to hire anyone except coloureds, so I quit school and worked for him as a plasterer for next to nothing, room and board. Didn't you ever work in your father's store in Ferryland?"

"No," she said. No, of course she wouldn't have.

"That's why I joined the Navy," he said. "I got tired of working for nothing."

He could see this information puzzled her. He had told her his father owned a big company and could have afforded to hire lots of workers, but now she'd seen enough to know that that hadn't been entirely true, and he had to give some other reason for his leaving Windsor. What he'd told her might have been true. Just as it might have been true that he had gone to Kennedy Collegiate, which was an all-white school, instead of Patterson, which was mixed. He should have gone to Kennedy, so what was the harm in saying he did? He knew his family didn't believe he was white, but he believed he was, and that was all that mattered. He didn't know how it had happened and he didn't care, but he knew it was true. You only had to look at him to see it was true.

He hadn't thought about Jackson Park in years. When he was a kid he'd believed the park had been named, like him, after his grandfather, Andrew Jackson Lewis, and that, although the park didn't exactly belong to him, he had a special right to be there. As he grew up, Jackson Park had been one of the few places where he felt he belonged. In the summer, when the other kids on his street gathered there to play baseball, he used to wander to the pavilion, climb up to the grandstand and look out over the gardens, imagining himself conducting an orchestra or singing into a microphone. He preferred singing because a singer stood before both the orchestra and the crowd, and both sides looked up to him. People strolling along the paths would wave at him, coloured couples in their Sunday clothes, unaware that they were waving goodbye.

The big celebration in Jackson Park was always August the first, Emancipation Day, the anniversary of the end of slavery in the British Empire. When he was little, he'd thought slavery was illegal only on that day, and that the rest of the year people could treat coloureds any way they liked, since they did. His parents would dress him up and give him a nickel. The park, his park, would smell of horseshit and barbecued pork, and there would be gambling tents and watermelon tables and more coloured people than he'd ever seen in one place before. His father would park their car on the grass just off Tecumseh Boulevard, next to other cars with licence plates from all over the northern States, from Indiana and Ohio, Michigan and Illinois. By nightfall everyone would be drunk just to show how free they were, and Benny and his friends would swig stolen beer and check car doors and watch out for the police, who mostly weren't around. He remembered his father singing in the grandstand with the Garden City Quartet, and Alvina, who was barely into her teens, wearing high heels and lipstick and smoking cigarettes given to her by men in tan suits and wingtips, men with southern drawls and skin so dark that if they shut their eyes at night Jack was sure they'd disappear.

In the morning there would be blood on the pathways, torn shirts in the garbage cans, men and women sprawled under picnic tables. Before going to First Baptist, he and Benny would collect as many bottles as they could fit into their wagon and take them down to the sheeny man, who gave them a dime a load. That was during the Depression, when you could still buy something with a dime. He'd always felt as though the dime, earned only once a year, was a gift from his grandfather. At First Baptist the pastor would preach about Sodom and Gomorrah, two cities on the banks of the Jordan River, as near to one another as Windsor was to Detroit, destroyed by Jehovah in a shower of fire and brimstone for the wickedness of their ways. What that wickedness consisted of was never spelled out, but the reference to Emancipation Day was clear and the congregation squirmed in their seats.

When he turned eight and found out that Jackson Park had been named for an old mayor, he felt as though he'd been kicked out of it. The knowledge had lowered his grandfather in his eyes. Of course, he'd thought, why would anyone name a park after a barber?

WILLIAM HENRY

"How's things at home?" William Henry asked Benny. Benny was sitting across from him in the tavern, reading a newspaper. If you saw a person reading, it meant he was bored, and William Henry didn't want Benny to get bored and leave just yet. He raised two fingers to Fast Eddy and four draughts appeared on the table. Benny took a drink from one of them and lit a cigarette. William Henry relaxed.

"Okay, I guess," Benny said. "Jackson brung home his new wife. She's a bit confused, though, if you ask me. First time she took a look at me I could hear the gears whirrin' away in her head. I don't think Jackson told her a thing about anything."

"White girl?"

"White as a mushroom."

"They must not get any sun in Newfoundland."

William Henry took a long pull. Jackson didn't just want to be white, he thought he *was* white. How he explained that to himself or to his new bride William Henry didn't know. Maybe he didn't explain it, maybe he just brassed it out. Weren't many other ways he could do it. William Henry remembered the time when Jackson was fifteen or sixteen, working summers at that mattress factory on Walker Road, where they didn't hire coloureds. Jackson just walked in and applied like he was white, like he had the right to work wherever the hell he wanted, and they hired him just like that. One day, William Henry was walking down the street and he seen Jackson and his boss talking on the sidewalk in front of the factory, smoking and laughing like they was old friends, and William Henry had had a good mind to go up to Jackson and say something like, "Yo' mama wants you to buy her some cracked corn on your way home, we gonna have us some fried mash for supper." That would've been the end of that job. But he didn't do it. Jackson seen him coming and his face froze, like he was expecting something like that, and his eyes drifted off, and William Henry just kept walking by, didn't say nothing, didn't even nod to his own son. Pretended he didn't know him. Did him a favour, just like William Henry done during that riot in Detroit. Let him go. How many times in his life had he said that about Jackson? Just let the boy go.

"Look at this," Benny said, pushing the *Free Press* across to his father. "Says they doin' some work on the old Fox."

William Henry loved talking about the Fox Theatre, his moment of glory. It pleased him that Benny had brought it up. He had a big outfit then, six people working for him, took them a week just to put up the scaffolding. That was 1925, the year Jackson was born. He shook his head. Whenever there's sun there has to be shadow somewhere.

"Let me see that," he said.

Detroit was safer in them days, he could give Benny a nickel and let him walk down the street without thinking twice about it. He always come back with something different, a twist of licorice, a balsa-wood airplane, a stick of gum. Jackson stayed at home with his mother and Alvina. That was maybe the trouble with Jackson, he'd been raised by women. They let him keep his attitude, let him think too highly of himself.

When the Fox opened things were good for a while. Lots of contracts, new truck from Labadie's. They even almost moved out of the Settlement, had their eye on a house on Church Street, their first dream home, which they could've got someone white to buy for them and when they moved in probably nobody would've said anything about them being coloured because Josie and Benny were almost light enough to pass and they had Jackson, who was lighter than all of them. Anybody started asking questions they could just stick Jackson out on the front porch in his carriage. Jackson would've felt right at home growing up in that neighbourhood. Things would surely have been different. When the crash came in '29, all the offers dried up and Labadie repossessed the truck and the house on Church Street got sold to somebody else for under five hundred dollars. Like he said, no sun without shadow.

"They should get you to do that work," Benny said, pointing at the article.

"I couldn't do that kind of work today," William Henry said. "I'm too old."

"You ain't that old," said Benny.

"What's that mean? How old ain't I?"

"You ain't too old to put up gypsum board."

"Maybe not. But I'm too old to want to."

William Henry's father hadn't wanted to cut hair anymore, either, that was probably what killed him. When the old man died, William Henry was Jackson's age, it just struck him. The old man hadn't been living at home, either, spent most of his time down here at the British-American. Something to think about. That man sure cut a lot of hair in his day, though. First he had a place on McDougall, then a place on Albert, then he got a chair in a big barbershop in the basement of City Hall, mirrors on all four walls, six chairs going all the time. When Harlan turned eighteen and said he wanted to be a barber, too, they took this place in the British-American. That's when something went south, he didn't know what it was, his father just got tired of cutting hair. Maybe it was the people who come into the shop wanting their hair cut just so, not the way he done it last time. Even customers Harlan had had for thirty years started bringing in pictures of movie stars from magazines, wanting their hair to look like this one or that one. And when they got home and looked in a mirror and didn't see a movie star, the next time they went somewhere else to get their hair cut. It was the same with plastering. You spent your life getting good at something, you thought people appreciated what you did for them, and then some new way come along that looks like hell but is easier and cheaper and suddenly it's *so long, old man, we don't need you anymore.* Gypsumboard, he wouldn't touch it. Don't talk to me about loyalty, William Henry thought. My own son taught me all I need to know about loyalty.

"Why'd he bring his wife here, d'you think?" William Henry asked, more to himself than to Benny.

"Wanted to show her off, more'n likely," said Benny, taking the paper back.

VIVIAN

On their fourth night in Windsor, Vivian and Jack crossed the river to hear some music.

"You wanted to see Detroit, didn't you, doll?" Jack said to her. What she wanted was to meet Jack's father, but she didn't dare bring that up again. And she did want to see Detroit. It would be her third country in a week. She was seeing the world, even if the world wasn't what she thought it would be. Maybe Iris was right, after all.

They ate supper in Benny's apartment, a nice stew she'd made on top of the stove, then she and Jack walked to his friend's house on Victoria Avenue, a couple of streets over from Ouellette. "A better part of town," Jack said as they walked, pointing out the houses and lawns and shade trees. It was starting to feel like fall, the days were shorter but still warm enough that she didn't need a sweater. "Peter's father's a doctor. We were in the cadet band together."

"Did he join the Navy, too?" she asked him.

"Who?"

"Peter."

"No." But he seemed uncertain about it.

They walked in silence for a while under the elms and chestnuts. Maybe he was afraid that the war had changed his friend as much as it had changed him.

Jack rang the bell and a woman came to the door.

"Hello, Della," Jack said when she opened it, and it took Vivian a moment to realize that this was Peter's mother. In a slightly flared skirt and silk blouse, she looked very pretty, and young enough to be an older sister. Still, Vivian wasn't sure if she should call her Della or Mrs. Barnes.

"Yes," Della said, "do come in. Peter will be down in a minute." She seemed flustered. She didn't appear to know what to do with her hands. They were standing in a large, open foyer, just inside the door, with stairs at one end and large, solid wooden doors taking up almost the whole of one wall. "You must be Vivian," Della said. "I'm Della. How do you do?" They shook hands rather vigorously. "How are you liking Windsor so far?"

"It's very different," she said.

"And what about you, Jack? How was the war?"

"I just caught the tail end of it," he said.

"Howie's still at it," Della said, brightening, then turned to Vivian. "My husband. He's in Cornwallis."

"Not back yet?" Vivian said sympathetically. "How awful for you."

"I've had good company," Della said. "Jack and Peter and I used to go to Detroit all the time, didn't we, Jack. My son plays trumpet, he's starting his own group."

"Ensemble, Mother," said a young man, obviously Peter, coming down the stairs. His hair was light brown, the same colour as Della's, and he was wearing heavy black glasses and an argyle vest. "The Peter Barnes Ensemble. What do you think, Jack? Sound classy enough for you?"

"Hello, Peter," said Jack, and the two men shook hands.

"Well," said Della, "we should be off."

They took Della's car, with the top down and the side windows rolled up to cut the wind. She was in the back with Jack. Della was half turned towards them, and saying something to Jack, who was leaning forward to hear her, but the wind made it impossible for Vivian to eavesdrop. She didn't mind, she was studying the tunnel. She had been expecting something narrow and gloomy, but this was four lanes wide and lit up like a ball-room. It was as though someone had built a brick sky over an airport. How had this feat been accomplished? A tunnel under a river! Halfway through, she leaned her head back and looked up at the ceiling, imagining the tons and tons of water above the yellow tiles, the fish and mud and sunken logs that would come rushing in if it cracked. Would she be able to swim up through the hole and be saved? She forced herself to think of something less frightening. Della had stopped talking to Jack and turned to face ahead. Vivian looked at Jack, who had given up conversing and was now leaning back, staring out the window. He'd probably prefer to be in the front with Peter, she thought. Surely they were nearing the end of the tunnel? She wanted to tell Jack she loved him before the roof caved in.

At the border, the uniformed guard looked quickly at their papers and motioned them through. Peter drove to a street called East Adams, and they went into a bar called the Horse Shoe Club. It was a long, narrow, smoke-filled room with a bar down one side and a low stage at the far end, painted black, with a piano and some chairs along one side and a Wurlitzer in the corner playing "Star Dust."

"That wasn't here before," Jack said as they found a table. Above the stage hung a black-and-white curtain, patterned like a zebra skin. The rest of the room was taken up by tables covered with beer glasses, cigarette packages and ashtrays, and between the tables people, most of them coloured, were all talking at once. Everyone seemed to know each other. There was an electric feeling in the room that she hadn't noticed in Windsor. Many of the men, even the coloured men, sported pencil-thin moustaches that had been popularized by fighter pilots during the war, even though none of them could ever have flown an airplane.

The song on the Wurlitzer ended and some men at one of the tables near the back stood up and took the stage. It surprised Vivian that they played fast but almost without moving. They played jazz versions of songs that had been popular in the thirties. They took a standard melody, the kind Jack and the King's Men had played in the K of C, and turned it into something new and outrageous, natural and lovely, like a tree that had grown up constantly buffeted by wind. The sound obliterated all that had happened between then and now.

"Ain't this grand?" Peter said, leaning towards her.

She nodded. She asked him what he had done in the war.

"Nothing. I was a conscientious objector. They made me join the Army, but they didn't send me to the front. I worked in the recruiting office. Isn't that rich? A conscientious objector sending hundreds of other men to their probable deaths? Sick bastards."

She didn't know what to say to this. It had never occurred to her that anyone could refuse to have anything to do with the war. What else could one refuse to do?

Peter returned his gaze to the musicians. "We saw Dizzy Gillespie here last March," he said. "He played with some local cats, Willie Anderson and Milt Jackson. Man, was that something." She smiled. "He wanted to take Milt and Willie A. back to New York with him, but Willie A. didn't want to leave his mama. What d'you think about that?"

"*You're* living with your mother, aren't you?" Vivian said.

He laughed. "I guess we're all mama's boys."

Was he including Jack? He hadn't wanted to come back to Windsor, but he had given in easily enough.

"And your father? Was he overseas?"

"No, he was down East, in the Navy. It was my father who saved Jack's bacon by signing those exemption papers."

"Your father was in Newfoundland?"

"Yeah, he was Jack's medical officer on the *Assiniboine*. Didn't Jack tell you?"

Another thing he hadn't told her. Had he really been chronically seasick on that trip, she wondered, or had his friend's father done him a favour? She looked across the table at Jack. He was talking with Della, their heads close together. She hadn't seen him so animated since they'd arrived in Windsor. Something stirred within her, and she turned back to Peter.

"When does your father come home?"

"Any day now," Peter said. She caught him looking uncertainly over at his mother, and then she heard Jack say something about Ireland and staying in a castle, and wondered what on earth he was talking about.

Then Peter's name was called by one of the men on the stage, and Peter stood up and made his way to the back. He gave a short bow to the house and accepted a trumpet from the man who had called him.

"He's not going to use that man's horn, is he?" Jack asked.

"Why not?" said Della, smiling at Vivian. But then Peter took his own mouthpiece from his jacket pocket and slid it onto the instrument.

Peter put the trumpet to his lips and blew a long, plaintive note that wavered towards the end, as though he had run out of wind, then folded it into a rippling cascade that ended in low, sobbing tones. The piano player joined in, playing fast when Peter played slowly and slowing down when Peter picked up. The drummer stirred his brushes on the snare, making a sound like rain hitting a sail, and held the cymbal with one hand while he scraped at it with the tip of the drumstick; a howling wind, a storm at sea. They weren't playing any particular song, rather they were relating to each other in a sort of commiseration, an impression that was bolstered by the audience, which was attentive, almost trancelike, some of the listeners calling out from time to time as though consoling Peter on some ordeal he had suffered and that the audience had suffered before him and now they were united in their recovery.

When she looked at Jack he was nodding, but his smile was frozen in place. Della was sitting on the edge of her chair, holding a cigarette halfway to her lips, transported by the music. She looked beautiful in the hazy, blue light, and Vivian wondered if she herself had looked like that when she'd first heard Jack play his trombone. She'd always thought of music as song, but this wasn't song, it was purer than that, it was above song, beyond the rules of song. She liked it. Then the drums picked up and the bass started in, and with the new tempo they were playing "I'm Getting Sentimental Over You," the song Jack had once played for her, but a version of it they seemed to be making up as they went along. When it was over, Peter returned the trumpet and made his way back to the table through the applause. The waiter brought them another round of drinks. "On the house," he said. Jack didn't say anything. Della leaned across the table and touched Peter's arm, then looked at Jack with an expression Vivian couldn't quite read.

Instead of taking them home through the tunnel, Peter drove across the Ambassador Bridge so they could see the skyline up and down the river. Jack and Vivian were again in the back, but Peter had put the top up and she felt encased in the car. Della was sitting half turned towards them, her bare arm along the back of her seat.

"It must be difficult for you," Vivian said to her, "with your husband away and all."

"Yes," Della said. "It has been."

"Whenever my father goes to England, my mother misses him terribly."

Della turned to look ahead. "The bridge is much prettier now with the lights on," she said. "They were off all during the war."

Peter added that the lights were yellow to discourage mayflies from landing on the bridge.

"What are mayflies?" she asked, and Peter told her they were huge winged insects that came up from the bottom of the river every spring in such vast numbers that they coated every surface in the two cities, so that the roads were slick with their crushed carcasses. That was what it was like being in this car with the top up, she thought, like being underwater in a canvas cocoon, waiting for spring.

"And they stink of fish," Peter said. "The city smells like a sardine can for weeks."

"It's amazing," Jack said, "how a harmless little insect can cause so much damage when you put enough of them together."

"Like an army," Peter added.

"Like lies," said Della.

Vivian and Jack spent the next afternoon by the river, sitting on one of Benny's blankets close enough to the water to hear the ducks squawking as they flew in tight formation above the wavelets. Her father would have loved watching the oldsquaws bobbing close to shore, their long tail feathers pointing at the sky. Jack's mother had packed them off with a picnic lunch of egg-salad sandwiches and iced tea. It the past five days she had come to like Jack's mother very much. She still hadn't met Jack's father. It was now something of a bitter joke.

"I don't believe you have a father." She was picking eggshell out of her sandwich. "I think you crawled up out of the river, like one of those horrid mayflies."

"You may be right," he said.

She sighed. "Where is he, Jack? And don't say, 'Where is who?'"

She didn't expect a straight answer, and she didn't get one. In the mail that day had been a letter from the Navy. Jack was to report to Toronto for demobilization when his leave was up. After that, she supposed they would go back to St. John's, and she would never meet his father at all.

"How long does it take to be demobbed?" she asked.

"I don't know," he said. "Not that long."

"And we still have our train ticket home?"

"Sure, doll. They have to send me back to where I came from."

But where he came from was Windsor.

After another attempt at supper in the apartment (meat loaf and boiled potatoes that Jack said were delicious), they walked to his parents' house for tea and dessert. His mother was sitting alone at the kitchen table, playing a form of solitaire Vivian didn't recognize. She looked worried. Benny was out and needed a ride home, and Jack's father was somewhere complicated, as usual. The truck had broken down and he'd spent the day waiting in a garage for it to be fixed, then a client had complained about a plastering job and he'd gone to see about it. Jack said he would fetch Benny in the Mercury, and hurried off, leaving her alone with his mother. They sat in the kitchen drinking orange pekoe tea, which had finally materialized. Jack's mother started talking about Jack as a little boy, always running off and getting into "situations."

"Was he a big baby?" Vivian asked. She was investigating her theory that Jack was adopted.

"No, he wasn't no trouble that way," Jack's mother said. "But he got difficult later on, oh my. His daddy was pretty hard on him. I remember the time he climbed over old Mr. Mandleson's fence and stole some green apples. His father was none too pleased about that."

Vivian seized on this opening, hoping it would lead to talking about Jack's father. But his mother veered in a different direction.

"That was in the Depression," she went on, "when apples was money. Old Mr. Mandleson lived on Windsor Avenue, across the alley from us. He come flying over to our house, Who took my apples? Did you take my apples? And Jackson lying on the couch, innocent as a lamb, half a dozen big green apples stuffed between the cushions. No, sir, I didn't take no apples. Musta been one of them coloured boys."

Jack's mother laughed. Vivian smiled but felt the warmth rise to her cheeks. She was still shocked by the way Windsorites talked about colour as often as Newfoundlanders talked about fish. According to what she'd overheard in the shops and lunch counters, soldiers coming home from the war were finding all the jobs taken by coloureds. Not only the jobs, but all the houses, the women, even the parking spaces. If there were no bananas in the grocery store, it was because the coloureds had bought them all up. They came over from Detroit. They came in from Chatham. Couldn't go to a movie. Couldn't sit in Jackson Park for all the coloureds taking it over.

"Jack and I were in Jackson Park the other day," Vivian ventured. "It's beautiful, isn't it?"

"A lovely park. All them trees and gardens. And the bandshell." Jack's mother took a sip of her tea. "That's where we have our Emancipation Day picnic every year."

"Emancipation Day?"

"First of August. It's a big day. People come from all over, and there's live music in the bandshell. We used to take Jackson to it when he was little, but he don't go no more, now."

Vivian felt she was getting close to something. "Why not?"

But once again, Jack's mother became evasive. "He just stopped. Would you like some more tea, dear?"

Vivian put her cup down. "Yes, please."

"Let me just read it first," Jack's mother said. She took Vivian's teacup and placed it upside down on its saucer, gave it a half turn, then picked it up by the handle and peered into it.

"When did you move into this house?" Vivian asked.

"Oh, we only been here a year."

"It's a nice house," she said.

"Maybe a bit rundown," Jack's mother admitted, looking around the kitchen. "Nothing that can't be fixed. The tap drips, the roof leaks and the basement stairs need tending to. I'm almost afraid to go down there. Benny says he's going to take care of it, but you know Benny." Vivian nodded. She didn't know Benny. "Benny's a lot like his daddy. So's Alvina."

"Does Jack take after his father?"

"I think there's a lot of me in Jackson."

"Alvina is Jack's older sister," Vivian said, "the one who took him dancing across the river." And someone else she hadn't met.

"She sure did. She wanted to be a singer, like her aunt Hazel was. Tried out with every band in Windsor and Detroit and as far away as Chicago. She sung jazz and the blues." Jack's mother shook her head. "There's always been music in this family. Jackson's daddy sang in a barbershop quartet, called themselves the Garden City Quartet, did Jackson tell you that?"

"Is 'Garden City' Windsor?"

"No, Detroit."

"What's Windsor, then?"

Jack's mother laughed. "I guess Windsor's where you come to when you're kicked out of the garden."

The remark reminded Vivian of the sense of comradeship she had felt in the jazz club the previous night.

"I gather Alvina and Jack don't get along?" she said.

"Alvina's always had a wild streak in her. When she started singing she took up with all kinds. Always coming home in a different car. She hasn't done any singing at all since getting married to Vernon. That's when the trouble with Jackson started."

"What kind of trouble?"

"Alvina married dark." Jack's mother cast her a conspiratorial look. "Vernon is brown as a old penny. Jackson says she married beneath herself."

"You mean her husband is a Negro?"

"Hmm, dark dark. Jackson says she disgraced the family, but that's just Jackson. Vernon's a very nice man, a good worker, hardly drinks anymore and he's never laid a finger on Alvina, not like her lighter boyfriends. And he got her out of all them dives she was singing in."

Vivian wanted to pursue this, but just then she heard Jack coming in the front door and down the hall towards the kitchen.

"Did you find Benny?" his mother asked him.

"No, he wasn't there. Let's go," he said to Vivian.

She stood up and said the tea was lovely but it was getting late and they'd had a full day. She promised she would come back the next morning, their last in Windsor. Her last chance.

"Come for breakfast," Jack's mother said, and glanced at the icebox.

"Maybe Mr. Lewis will be here," Vivian said pointedly.

"Oh, he'll be here, child," she said. "He just dying to meet you."

"Come on," Jack said to her. "We have to go."

"Tea leaves don't seem to be speaking to me tonight," Jack's mother said, replacing Vivian's teacup on its saucer.

The next day she still did not set eyes on Jack's father. Jack was keeping her away from him, the whole family was conspiring against her. The full weight of this struck her as they were walking up Ouellette Avenue, away from the river. She knew the names of each cross street by now: Sandwich, Pitt, Chatham, London.

They were about to turn down Pitt towards the apartment to start packing.

"I want to go home, Jack," she said.

"Why?" he asked her.

"Because I don't like Canada! And I don't believe you wrote to your parents to tell them I was coming here, or that you were married. And because I think it's horrid that your father won't meet me."

"I can explain," Jack said after a pause.

"Well?"

"He drinks."

"So? Lots of people drink. Do you think I haven't seen drinking in St. John's?"

"Not like Dad's." Jack sighed. "He goes on these binges, see. Real tears. Everything's fine for a while, sometimes for a whole year, he goes to work, builds up the business, they move to a nice neighbourhood, and then he starts drinking again and that's all he does. He doesn't work, he doesn't eat, he doesn't pay the bills, he hardly ever comes home, we don't see him for weeks at a time, we don't know where he is. He's been like that since the day I was born. You have no idea how many times me and Benny have gone into every saloon in Windsor looking for him. That's where I went last night. Sometimes we find him, sometimes we don't."

Surely he wouldn't lie about a thing like this. Was it naive of her to believe him?

"Your poor mother," she said, taking his arm.

"He was all right when I joined up."

"You can't blame yourself."

A weight lifted from her mind; it was like looking up from a gloomy book and seeing a cloudless sky. Tomorrow they'd be in Toronto, and soon after that they'd be in St. John's, and Jack would go back to being light and breezy, Frank Sinatra in a sailor suit, the man she'd fallen in love with. And when she got him back to St. John's she would talk to her father about finding him a job in the company. Everything would be fine.

PART IV

JACK

Jack had loved Toronto when he was there for his Navy training, two and a half years earlier. No family, no Della, no past. He'd spent all his time with his fellow recruits at the Armouries or with his closer mates who shared his boarding house a few blocks up on King Street. They had all been united in a single purpose: to bury the past and use the war to carve themselves out a new future. This time, however, with the war over, the streets crawled with ex-servicemen glaring at anyone who might have been a lower rank or seen less active duty, and Jack felt targeted on both fronts. Everywhere he looked he saw men who kept their hair short and wore hats and looked uncomfortable in civilian clothes, and women who'd been happy enough getting their monthly cheques in the mail during the war but looked less than thrilled at having home the men who'd sent them. But they all seemed to respect anyone who'd survived. No one had seen what they'd seen, been through what they'd been through, deserved what they deserved. After a week or two, Jack was beginning to feel that he belonged in Toronto.

Frank Sterling was there. They had met up again during their demobilization. Frank had a job in his father-in-law's construction company. When they ran into each other, Jack and Vivian were staying in a boarding house not far from Jack's old place on King. It was small but clean, and the rent included breakfast. Frank and Jeannie had an apartment in the city's west end, on Euclid Avenue—Easy Street, Frank called it—and Frank invited Jack and Vivian over for a drink the next night. When he and Vivian got there, they found that the so-called apartment was a second-storey walk-up that didn't even have its own door. They had to go into some wop family's house and walk up the stairs. Sure, when they got up there it was nice. Jeannie kept it clean, and they had a few sticks of good furniture. "Always buy the best," Frank said, "even if you can't afford it." Which made Jack feel good about living in Toronto. No one had ever let him buy something he couldn't afford.

And Jeannie and Vivian hit it off right away, nattering like a couple of magpies who'd known each other since Adam. It made sense, he guessed, they were both born with silver spoons in their mouths. But Jeannie was all right, a full-figured party with a nice face.

"You're staying in a boarding house in Parkdale?" Jeannie asked, making it sound like they were sharing a boxcar with a bunch of hobos. "We've got an extra bedroom here, why don't you move in with us for a while? That would be all right, wouldn't it, Frank?"

"Sure thing, old buddy," Frank said to Jack. "We'll string you up a couple of hammocks."

Jack looked at Vivian. She seemed pleased, and so he said okay. But he wasn't all that happy about the arrangement. Frank was still the easygoing, slap-happy guy he'd been in St. John's, ready to slip into any part of the good life that came his way. But he'd become a bit of a show-off, if you wanted to know the truth. What did he have to blow hard about? He was working for his wife's father, laying cement blocks. Big deal. A monkey with a piece of string could lay cement blocks. Things would be different for Jack. If he'd learned anything, it was that they couldn't go back to doing things the way they did them before the war. The way things were then was what had caused the war.

And sharing an apartment with Frank and Jeannie was awkward, no question about it. The walls were thin as paper. He and Vivian could hear everything that went on in the other couple's bedroom, which was plenty. Every frigging night, thump thump thump, *Oh Frankie!* as clear as if they were doing it on the radio. Jeannie was a squealer, you could tell that by looking at her. Compared to her, even compared to Della, Vivian was a mouse, afraid to let go. Most of the times when he wanted it she would turn away, or be reading a book, or say it was the wrong time of the month. And they only did it when Frank was at work and Jeannie was out shopping, like they were doing something dirty. Not dirty, Jack, private. Frank and Jeannie didn't seem to worry about private.

Still, the place was free. And he was glad to have Vivian out of Windsor. She'd stopped asking him all those questions about his family, and he was finally able to relax and think about what he was going to do. They had some money from his demob pay, and he'd cashed in their train tickets back to St. John's. They wouldn't be needing them, that much was for sure.

"So," Frank said at breakfast one morning. "What are your plans?"

"You mean for today?" Jack asked.

"Today, tomorrow, next month. Are you going to stay in Toronto?"

Ah, he wanted them out of his apartment. Jeannie was at the stove with her back to them, making coffee, still in her house-coat and slippers. Vivian was in the bedroom getting dressed. "I'll go where there's work, I guess," he said. "We'll get a place of our own."

"Lots of work here in Toronto."

"So I hear."

"What kind are you looking for?" Frank asked.

"Something in music," Vivian answered for him, coming into the kitchen. She was wearing a floral print dress with a wide, white-leather belt and white shoes. She always looked good in the morning.

"A band?" Frank asked.

"I've been thinking about it."

"You mean a dance band?" Frank asked, and Jack said, "Yeah, a combo."

"That would be nights, though, right?"

"Nights, weekends. You interested?"

"Me? Nah, the war's over, buddy. Besides, Jeannie keeps me pretty busy at night, don't you, Sugar?"

"Frank!" she said, slapping his arm.

No one spoke for a while, then Vivian, who never drank anything but tea in the mornings, said, "This coffee is delicious."

A week later they had their own place. Vivian found it. It was in the east end, south of Danforth, on a street off Gerrard called Hollywood Crescent. It had been advertised as an apartment, but it was really a small bedsit on the second floor of a private house, no kitchen or bath, but at least it wasn't a walk-up. It had its own door at the bottom of the stairs, its own mailbox on the front porch, and its own meter on the side of the house. They had to share the downstairs bathroom with the owners—a surly-looking truck driver and his thin, flimsy wife who looked afraid of her own shadow—and upstairs there was just a hotplate and a small icebox. But it would do until they could afford something better. Fifteen dollars a month.

Jack started going out to clubs at night, looking for musicians for his band, coming home late and a little drunk. He didn't want just anyone. Even putting a small band together wasn't something you did overnight. You didn't just call up the Musicians' Union and say, send me a piano player, a tenor sax, a drummer and a bass.

"Why not?" Vivian asked. "At least you'd get a list of names, hold auditions."

Auditions? Jesus, who did she think he was, Duke Ellington?

"Why don't you ask Peter to come up? He's a good trumpet player." She was full of bright ideas.

"You saw that club he was in," Jack said. "It was penny-ante stuff. I bet the musicians were playing for beer."

Besides, he thought to himself, there was no way he was going to play in some coloured dump.

He bought fifteen-cent sheet music and spent hours each day arranging songs for trombone and tenor sax. "You Made Me Love You (I Didn't Want to Do It)." "I'll Remember You (Always)." He'd hum them over and over until Vivian begged him to work on a new tune. He jazzed them up a bit, not much, just to give them some swing, something people could tap their feet to. After a few weeks he had enough songs ready that, when he had a band, they could play a whole evening of his own arrangements. The Jack Lewis Combo. That's what managers wanted, he told Vivian. Something distinctive. If people wanted to hear the Jack Lewis Combo, they'd have to go to such-and-such a club. That way the club could charge more to get in, have higher drink prices, pay the band more, maybe give them a cut of the take. That was how it worked, doll.

And before too long, he'd be playing the Royal York.

He had to have a signature tune, though, a song that the band would play every night that announced who they were, and then they'd play it again after each break. He chose "Blue Moon," and worked on it for days. He changed the tempo, added a few riffs, and worked especially hard on the trombone solo. He went over the song in his head, modulating his voice so that it was somewhere between a croon and a bark, a bit of Crosby, a bit of Sinatra. He even designed the plywood music stands that each band member would have, a huge quarter note in the form of a moon, painted blue, with "The Jack Lewis Combo" traced on top.

Meanwhile, they had to eat. He looked for jobs that would leave him enough time to work on his music. Something in sales, commission work, a white-collar position. He wasted a lot of time filling out forms and sitting outside the offices of people who never came out of them. He sat with his elbows on his knees, ruining the creases in his trousers, twirling his fedora in his hands, smiling at secretaries who kept shooting him looks. He read the posters on the walls a hundred times. "A clean workplace is a safe workplace." "Cooperative Economic Action— The Balance Wheel of a Free Economy."

"We need a car," he told Vivian after another day of fruitless trudging. It was humiliating, walking everywhere looking for work. He felt like a beggar.

"Cars cost money," she said.

"Look, two fellas apply for a job, one of them shows up all sweaty and wrinkled from riding on streetcars all day, the other guy pulls up in his car looking fresh, his suit nicely pressed, no dust on his shoes, who do you think gets the job?"

"I guess that depends," she said. "Are you talking about plastering or bricklaying?"

"I'm talking about a salesman's job. I didn't fight a war so I could come back home and do the same dirty work I was doing before. I'd be good in sales."

"That's true," she said, backing down. "You're a performer."

"Exactly. And ninety-nine percent of sales is pulling the wool over someone's eyes."

"You don't think an honest person can be a good salesman?"

"I didn't say that." There she went, twisting his words around. "I mean you have to convince the buyer that your product is better than anyone else's. And to do that, you have to honestly believe it, deep inside, even if it isn't true."

He bought a car the next day, a ten-year-old Hupmobile that he found at a sandlot dealership for thirty dollars. It was green and had a rumble seat in the back instead of a trunk, but it would do. "You can't beat these old Hups," he told Vivian when he drove it home and called her outside to look at it. She was less impressed than he'd hoped. Why couldn't she just pretend to like something he liked? She was worried about the price, two months' rent. Christ, the car would pay for itself in a week when he got a job. "How are you going to get ladders and hoes in a rumble seat?" she asked him, as though she already knew he'd be a failure as a salesman.

She was wrong, as usual. He got a salesman's job a week later, selling encyclopedias door to door, something called *The Funk & Wagnalls New Standard Encyclopedia Year Book for 1945*. Answered an ad in the paper, and he wouldn't have got it without the car. What did he tell her? Maybe now she'd have a little faith in him. "No home should be without a good encyclopedia," they told him at the training session in a big office building on Bloor Street. That was the pitch. "The accumulated wisdom of the ages."

"Don't worry, the books will sell themselves," the recruiter told him.

"So why do you need us?" he quipped. No one laughed.

The company divided the city into sectors, like on a war map, and he was given a territory in a new subdivision called Scarborough, in the east end north of the Danforth. He was to make his rounds on weekdays, when the husbands weren't home, because only women bought books. He got a dollar for every book he sold.

Scarborough turned out to be a mecca for returning veterans and their growing broods. A hundred and fifty bungalows, all built from the same plan on twenty-five-foot lots, no basements, no front yards to speak of, all of them looking across four streets surrounding the Pine Hills Cemetery.

He sold one year book the first week, to a woman whose husband was a schoolteacher, and two the second week, which was progress. At that rate, he calculated, by the end of three months he'd be selling two thousand books a week. When he managed to sell only ten books in his first month, he wasn't discouraged. The big numbers wouldn't start kicking in until month three.

When December came and went and he was still lucky if he sold a couple of books a week, he saw another ad in the paper, this time for people to sell Regal Greeting Cards door to door. He thought that having two reasons to let him in would double his chances of making a sale. People *had* to buy Christmas cards, didn't they? Vivian thought he was jeopardizing his job with Funk & Wagnalls, but how would they find out?

He was now making ten dollars a week, which covered the rent easy, and when he got his band going, he would double that. More important, for him, he was doing it on his own. No help from Vivian's family, no hindrance from his own. Nobody knew who he was, and nobody cared, which was Jack's idea of paradise.

He was still selling encyclopedias and cards when their first wedding anniversary came around. He'd wanted to have a quiet evening at home, turn on the radio, pull out the sofa bed, but Vivian had other ideas. Frank and Jeannie were taking them out for dinner. Well, that was okay by him, if it made Vivian happy. They exchanged their presents after breakfast. He gave her a bracelet with a heart engraved around the words *Jack and Vivian*.

"I love it," she said, slipping it over her wrist.

"It's not real gold," he said, "but you can't tell from a distance."

She gave him a book about music. As if he didn't handle enough books already. But he told her he loved it, too, and would read it as soon as he found time. What was it with her and books?

"You're supposed to get paper on your first anniversary," Jeannie said when they met them at the restaurant, a small place on Bloor West not far from Euclid. Tablecloths, real flowers, fancy waiters, a five-piece combo playing in a corner.

"I didn't know that," he said.

"Darling, I love the bracelet." She pulled back the sleeve of her sweater and showed it around the table. Jeannie murmured appreciatively.

Frank ordered a bottle of champagne. Vivian asked him if he could afford it.

"Always buy the best," said Jeannie. "Of course we can afford it, as long as we don't plan on eating until July." They all laughed.

"To long and happy marriages," Frank said when the champagne came. They clinked their glasses over the table. The champagne tasted like thin beer that had gone skunky, but he didn't say anything.

Then Jeannie gave Vivian a present, a tube wrapped in silver paper. When Vivian unwrapped it, it was a roll of wallpaper. "Aha!" said Vivian, unrolling it a ways to look at the pattern. "It's perfect!" But Jack didn't get it.

"Wallpaper?" he said.

"It's for your new house," Jeannie explained.

"What new house?" Jack said.

"Well," Frank said, "since it looks like you're staying in Toronto, we figured you're going to be looking around for a house."

"Who says we're staying in Toronto?" Jack turned to Vivian. He hadn't told her about cashing in the tickets. "Don't get me wrong," he said. "We could live here." A person could be anyone he wanted to be in Toronto.

"Actually, we're thinking of moving out," Jeannie said. "To Barrie or some other place up north."

"Maybe Barrie," Frank said. "Or Newmarket. Or Markham. Turn one of those one-horse towns into a big city." Frank said they had started their own construction company, F. Sterling & Sons. "The sons will come later," he said, winking at Jeannie. "Strictly new houses. There's no money in fixing up someone else's mistakes. You said so yourself, Jack."

Jack nodded. He'd had enough of that in Windsor.

"So, what do you say, Jack?" Frank asked him.

"What's that?" Jack said, startled. "Say to what?"

"To coming in with us," said Jeannie. "We're a construction company, you're a plasterer. How about it?"

"I'm not a plasterer anymore," he said. "But I'll think about it."

"It's a good offer, Jack," Vivian said.

"I said I'd think it over."

"Sure, you think about it," said Frank, leaning back in his chair. "You two lovebirds talk it over. Jeannie and I have made up our minds, though. Newmarket is the future, and we're going to be part of it. You could be, too."

Then the penny dropped. Talk it over with Vivian's family was what Frank meant. They were the ones with the money. Jack had never taken a cent from them, and he never would. This from Frank was a huge disappointment. The old Frank would have known better. He'd sooner sell books than ask for handouts, thank you very much. He'd sooner starve.

VIVIAN

Vivian didn't want Jack to be selling encyclopedias door to door. It was undignified work. Salesmen used to come to the store in Ferryland. They were a dusty, feckless lot, always on the go, on the make, lacking any kind of sincerity or industry, usually with a bottle stuck in their jacket pocket. Her father would look their wares over, order what he thought the village needed, then show the men out and come up to the house for a cup of tea. She didn't like the thought of Jack being treated like that.

But he seemed happy to do it, so she didn't say anything. Since coming to Toronto he was relaxed, more his old self, and she didn't want to do anything to cause him to feel that he wasn't a success. He had big plans, he said, he wouldn't be selling en-cyclopedias forever. She would keep her worries about Jack to herself, at least for now.

As the days shortened, she established a routine. She'd always thought that doing the same thing over and over would make time pass slowly, but in fact she found that knowing exactly what she had to do each morning freed her mind up for other things, so that each day held new meaning, even new adventures. First, after checking the newspaper to see what was on at the cinemas, she would turn to the grocery-store ads. Since she had only a tiny icebox she had to shop for perishables nearly every day. She didn't mind, it was fun, in a way, like the math problems she used to do in school. Grapefruit at Power's were six for twenty-nine cents; at Loblaws the big ones were three for twenty-five and those that were just "a good size" were five for twenty-nine. Where could she get the most grapefruit for fifteen cents? Carrots at both Power's and Dominion were two bunches for seventeen cents; Dominion had bigger bunches, but at Power's the rib roast was forty-five cents a pound and at Dominion it was forty-nine. She wrote down everything she had to buy and put the three totals at the bottom of the list. The sums were very close and always too high, but she calculated that if she walked to Power's, got a blade roast instead of a rib and made do without butter, then went to Dominion for vegetables, she could just about manage. The papers said the government was considering lifting the ban on margarine and she hoped it would do so soon. With margarine a third the cost of butter and sugar rationing almost over, she might be able to afford to make a cake for Thanksgiving dinner.

She kept up with her reading. There was a public library a few blocks east of Hollywood Crescent that was sort of on her way to the grocer's. It was small, but had most of the current popular books, and if she asked for a title they didn't have they would order it from the main branch. Jack grumbled about her books cluttering up the apartment, but she thought they added a certain interest to the place, proof that there was life beyond these four garishly papered walls. They were like letters from faraway places, and Lord knew she didn't get many of those. Iris was not a letter-writer. Her mother sent her brief notes in her eccentric handwriting and peacock-blue ink: crocuses up, peas picked, storm windows on, Wat gave a talk at the Junior Conservatives' Fall Convention. Her father wrote occasional long, sad, marginless letters laboriously typed on the office Underwood, probably after his secretary had gone home at the end of the day. She pictured him sitting at her rolltop desk in the little room behind the store, typing with two fingers as the evening light faded, reading everything over half a dozen times. He rarely mentioned himself. He wrote about her mother's health, the declining size of the catch, birds as they came and went in the harbour, the latest idiocies of Joseph Smallwood's confederate faction. "They think joining Canada will bring down the price of rum!" A roseate tern was spotted up the coast near Renews and he had considered going to see it, but the weather had turned mauzy and in the end he had stayed home and worked on his stamp collection. He had given up the idea of moving to St. Lucia. Wat was taking a car engine apart and putting it back together, and meanwhile the oily bits were scattered about the kitchen. Her father bet that Jack would like to help him with it, because being a Windsor man he would know about motors. Her breath caught at that, because it was the first time he had mentioned Jack. She wrote back saying yes, Jack would love to do that, he was so good with cars. She told her father about the Hupmobile, "our adorable old Hup," and the cute little rumble seat that Wat could ride in when they came to visit.

She saved Canadian stamps to send him. The eight-cent stamp showed a peaceful farm scene that she knew he would like. She told him about the two silken jays and the cardinal she'd seen in the ravine by their house. She wrote about her first ride in a streetcar and the unimaginable variety of goods in the shops along Danforth, as if she could afford them. She was beginning to like Toronto, she wrote. It was odd to think of herself living in a city that her father would find too big, too noisy, too dangerous, but she told him that where they lived was like a village, with the Towne Theatre at one end and Power's at the other. And it wasn't noisy at all. At night she could hear the crickets chirruping in the ravine, and the sound of heels on the pavement as far away as Gerrard. Being comfortable in Toronto made her feel older than her parents, and the distance she had felt from them since her marriage increased, despite her attempts to shrink it. She kept her letters gay so as not to cause her parents any anxiety, just as she was doing with her conversations with

that he worried about her, but she didn't want to start thinking like he did.

Sometimes after supper they would walk down to Gerrard, visit the shops and the soda fountains in the drugstores. Jack would buy cigarettes or get a haircut, and she would sit in the barbershop and watch the barber, an elderly man with glasses and a thin moustache who never smiled, never exhibited any emotion whatsoever except a smouldering hatred for cutting hair. Barbers were supposed to talk your ear off, Jack said, but here it was Jack who did all the talking. After he'd been getting his hair cut there for several months, Jack told him that his grandfather had been a barber in Windsor, had owned his own shop in the basement of City Hall before it burned down, and his uncle still had a barbershop in one of the biggest hotels in the city. This was only a slightly different version of the story she had heard before.

"That so?" the barber said.

Then Jack told him that his father, a successful businessman in Windsor, went to a barber every day for his morning shave, every single morning, never shaved himself. What did he think of that? The barber wasn't impressed. Jack frowned and asked the barber what he would say if he, Jack, came down every day for his morning shave. "That would be something, wouldn't it?"

"I don't open until eleven," the barber said.

She was amazed to see Jack getting angry about something so petty. She picked up a *Liberty* magazine and looked at the cover. It showed a smiling Navy rating holding an engagement ring and talking into a pay phone, proposing long-distance to his girl. She felt a catch in her throat, imagining the happy woman at the other end of the line, her mother and sister smiling in the background.

The summer passed. The bedsit no longer seemed impossibly tiny. Jack's trombone was behind the sofa bed, the case gathering dust. Their savings account held steady at thirty-four dollars, not enough for two train tickets to anywhere but enough to make them feel they could afford a movie or a dinner out now and then. She began looking at the Sears catalogues: the fall dresses had cinched waists and flared at the hips, she might be able to afford one. The newspapers had ads for wringer washers and cookstoves and she found herself looking around the bedsit, wondering where on earth she would put such things.

One afternoon towards the end of October, as she was reading the *Toronto Star*, her eye caught on a headline: "New Novel Flays Anti-Negro Prejudice." The book under review was *Kingsblood Royal*, by Sinclair Lewis, a writer she had read and enjoyed. This new one was about a man named Neil Kingsblood, who lived in a small Minnesota city called Grand Republic. Kingsblood started checking into his family history because, according to family legend, he was distantly related to one of the kings of England. "People have been warned before now about examining family trees too closely," the reviewer wrote, "owing to the number which have miscreants hanging from them. In this case it is not a miscreant that Neil finds, but a Negro."

She coughed and put her cigarette down in the ashtray. She looked around the apartment, making sure Jack wasn't there even though she knew he was at work. When her breathing settled, she got up from the table, found her scissors in her sewing basket, and cut the review out of the paper. Then she set it in the ashtray and burned it, stubbing out the ash with the remains of her cigarette.

Thank God they were out of Windsor.

By the second week of November she began to feel her body changing, though not in ways Jack was likely to notice. She found it more comfortable sleeping on her back; her breasts hurt when she lay on her stomach, or when Jack felt for her in the mornings. She noticed a metallic taste in her mouth when she drank tea. She tried it with less milk, but it was worse. She cut down on smoking; no effect, except that she felt irritable. There was a mild tightening in her lower abdomen, she wouldn't call it cramps, exactly. She didn't connect any of these sensations for a week or more, and then one night she sat bolt upright in bed, her eyes wide in the darkness. She was pregnant.

Her first thought was that she wouldn't tell Jack until she was sure, until she had seen a doctor. She didn't know any doctors in Toronto. She didn't know any doctors anywhere except back home. Should she write to Iris and her mother? No, not yet. She might tell Jeannie. You lucky devil, Jeannie would say. You must be so happy. Was she? She and Jack had been married for two and a half years, so it shouldn't come as a surprise. They hadn't been trying, but they hadn't been trying not to, either.

She realized with a tinge of guilt that every time her period had come she'd felt relieved.

She should be overjoyed, so why wasn't she? Their bedsit was much too small; they'd have to move. That wasn't so bad; she liked this place but she didn't love it, as she had loved their tiny apartment in St. John's. So that wasn't what was worrying her.

It was Jack. As she'd seen with the barber, it didn't take much to make his blood boil. He liked his job, he said, but he'd come home complaining about his territory and his customers, the hills and the snow, and he usually fell asleep on the couch after supper before they could even pull out the bed. She would sit up and read while he slept, smoking and drinking cold tea left over from supper. Was this to be their life from now on, both of them filled with secrets they couldn't share with each other? It wasn't just her body that was changing: the world was spinning around them, too. New styles. New countries. New gadgets. Televisions, vacuum cleaners, automatic washing machines. Jack kept talking about buying all of them on credit.

"Where would we put them?"

"You don't think we're going to live in one room all our lives, do you?"

Well, that was true, not with a baby on the way. She counted on her fingers: they wouldn't need to move until July or August. But they wouldn't be able to think of buying a house, not on Jack's commissions. Veterans Affairs might give them a mortgage, but where would they find the down payment?

"I should make supervisor in another couple of months,"

Jack said one night at dinner, when she'd broached the idea of moving. "All they do is drive around all day making sure joes like me are doing their jobs. Piece of cake. A year or two as a super and I'll be up for promotion to manager."

He made a year or two sound like no time at all. She couldn't think that far ahead. She made a mental list of things she couldn't think about. The baby after it was born. Jack's quick temper. The fact that she still hadn't met his father, or his sister. Jack's mother wrote from time to time, but they hadn't been back to Windsor since coming to Toronto, and she could hardly expect Jack's family to come all this way just for a visit. But then again, why not? If her own family lived only a few hours away, they'd be here every month, and she and Jack would go there at least on holidays. Wat would have put his motor back together and driven to Toronto every Sunday for dinner. Jack's family never even phoned. Making the list had only made her think about the things that were on it.

"What's wrong, Viv?" Jack asked that evening after dinner. "You're very quiet tonight."

"I'm sorry, darling. I was thinking that we haven't heard from your family for a while."

"That's because they don't need anything yet. Let's talk about something else."

But they didn't talk about anything else. They went back to not talking at all except about unimportant things. Would they listen to the radio or go out to a movie? Did she think he needed a haircut? How long could she put off telling him she was expecting? A month? Two months? She would tell him when she'd seen a doctor, when she started showing, when she had a due date. When it was safe.

By Christmas she still hadn't been to a doctor. She thought about telling Jack as a Christmas present, giving him something a father might need. A box of cigars, maybe: Surprise, darling, we're going to have a baby! She practised different ways of saying it. "Jack, I'm pregnant." No, too abrupt. "Jack, darling, we're in the family way." "There's a little bundle of joy in our future." None of them sounded right. In the end, she gave him a tie clip in the shape of a trombone, and he gave her some perfume in a really nice bottle.

On Christmas Day they brushed the snow off the Hup and drove all the way to Newmarket to see the Sterlings. The Danforth was bright with Christmas lights hanging from the hydro poles and in the shop windows. The snow was so deep that Jack drove behind a streetcar until they reached the edge of the city, the windshield wipers on and the wheels riding on the metal trolley tracks. She was afraid he would not be able to stop if the trolley suddenly stopped, but she knew better than to say anything about his driving.

Frank and Jeannie lived in a new house that Frank had built in the fall, a split-level bungalow with a gently sloping roof and grey brick siding below a bay window that looked out onto a tall blue spruce with Christmas lights strung on it and a wooden cut-out reindeer grazing in the snow next to the front porch. They had come up in the world, and Vivian was happy for them. She couldn't help thinking that if Jack had accepted Frank's offer, they might be living in such a house now, too.

"Looks cheap, doesn't it?" Jack said as they parked in the drive behind a new truck that had *F. Sterling and Sons, Contractors* painted on the side.

Inside, the house smelled of roasted turkey and floor wax. Frank kissed Vivian's cheek and Jeannie took their coats. She'd brought a jar of bakeapple jam, one of three that her mother had sent from Ferryland, all of which had survived the journey, and she had spent part of the morning baking oatmeal cookies. Jack handed Frank what was left of a bottle of Canadian Club. Frank took it and poured the drinks and Jeannie put the bakeapple jam and cookies under a tree in a corner of the living room. The tree was almost as tall as the one outside.

They spent a few minutes admiring the house. Jack knocked on one of the walls with his knuckles. "Drywall?"

"Five-eighths-inch," Frank said. "Nothing but the best."

"My parents had a house like this in Windsor," Jack said. "Had a fireplace in every bedroom. They lost it during the Depression."

"How's the encyclopedia business?" Frank asked.

"Can't complain. I'm in line for a manager's job."

"That's great, Jack," Frank said. "How long have you been there? Two years now?"

"About that. You going to sell this house when you build another one?"

"That's the idea. Why? You want this one?" Frank laughed.

"Naw," Jack said, "there's just the two of us. We'd be lost in a place this big, eh, Viv?"

"Come and help me in the kitchen, Viv," Jeannie said.

Jeannie's kitchen was done entirely in white and fire-engine red. White walls, white ceiling, red countertop, white cupboard doors with little red Scottie dogs on them, a new white icebox and a matching stove, and a white sink with two sections, one for washing and the other for rinsing. Even the tea towels were red-and-white striped.

"Are you all right, Viv?" Jeannie asked.

"Yes, I'm fine. Why?"

"You look kind of pale."

"I do?"

"You're not . . . ?"

Vivian nodded. Jeannie gave a whoop and Vivian shushed her. "I haven't told Jack yet!"

"Why not?"

"I'm not sure yet. I've only missed twice."

"Oh, Viv, I wondered how long you two were going to take. It's been over two years."

"What about you? Are you trying?"

"Yeah, we're trying all right, but so far nothing doing."

"Sorry," Vivian said quietly.

"Yeah, well. Still, it's fun trying."

They laughed, but Vivian felt uneasy about having confided in Jeannie before she'd told Jack.

"When are you going to tell him?"

"When I've seen a doctor."

"I'll give you the name of mine. He's an old sourpuss, but he's good. And he'll be happy to have a patient with ovaries that do what they're supposed to."

Vivian put off calling. Having a Toronto doctor would commit her to having the baby in Toronto, and she still had thoughts of going back to Newfoundland, to having her mother and Iris with her. There was plenty of time to make plans. Jack was still talking about starting a band, and on New Year's Eve he surprised her by taking a job with a small combo that was playing at the Rex Hotel on Queen Street. He spent most of the afternoon polishing his trombone, coating the slide with Pond's cold cream and humming "Blue Moon" to himself. When he finished, he tested his lip by playing "I'm Getting Sentimental Over You." There were a few sour notes, but he got through it, and she clapped appreciatively from the sofa.

Instead of going to hear him play, however, she spent the night in the bedsit, reading. At midnight she listened to Guy Lombardo and his Royal Canadians on the radio, and after the countdown she sang "Auld Lang Syne" under her breath, staring out the window at the ravine and fighting back tears. Old acquaintances back home would be doing the rounds of the houses dressed up as jannies, frightening the children and getting a drink of rum. The villagers called her father the Lord of the Hill because he owned the store, a title both of respect and resentment. During the war, the men from Ferryland who had joined the Newfoundland Regiment had sent their pay packets home to Vivian's father, rather than to their wives. Her father would put a little money on the families' accounts, enough to keep the store running, and give the rest to the families. When the men came back they'd been mean about the little he had held back, but why else had they sent him their pay? And how else could he have kept the store going and the village fed? But all was forgotten on New Year's Eve. There would be laughter and hijinks and rum, and any rifts there had been in the outport would be set aside. Whatever you did on New Year's Day set the tone for the rest of the year.

Later that night, actually early on January 1, 1948, after Jack had come home and they were lying in bed, she thought: I'll tell him now. But what if he got angry? She wouldn't tell him now. Maybe tomorrow.

JACK

One night after supper, Jack told Vivian he was going out to see a band. He whistled "I've Got You Under My Skin" as he buttoned his yellow sports jacket and put his trombone tie clip on his blue-and-yellow tie.

He drove down to the Royal York Hotel to hear Moxie Whitney's band in the Imperial Ballroom. He didn't pay the cover charge, just stood at the door pretending he was looking for someone. The bandsmen were all wearing tuxedos. They looked like Bay Street bankers, but he knew that up close, their suits would be shiny and smell of sweat and cigarette smoke, and he felt a silent bond with them, the fellowship of spit on brass. They weren't Guy Lombardo, maybe, but they weren't bad.

They already had people up and dancing and it wasn't even nine o'clock. He watched the trombone players when they stood up to take their turn. He could see himself as one of them, maybe not lead trombone, that guy looked as old as Whitney himself, but second or third, maybe alto. He wondered how much Whitney paid them. They were playing "Chattanooga Choo Choo," one of the songs he'd arranged back when he was planning his own band. He scanned the couples on the dance floor; they probably were bankers, in good tuxedos and ball gowns, and not a coloured face among them. The head waiter was standing behind a little lectern with a light on it, pretending not to notice Jack.

"I guess my party isn't here yet," Jack said to him on his way out.

"Perhaps she's in another part of the hotel, sir," the waiter said.

Bastard, Jack thought. But he had seen what he'd come to see, and went out through the lobby to where he'd parked the Hup. It had started to snow. Coloured bellhops were loading suitcases into the car behind his, and a coloured redcap was pushing a heavy wagonload of luggage across Front Street from Union Station, having trouble with the trolley tracks.

Jack drove slowly up University Avenue, fat snowflakes eddying in his headlights. What would it be like to have a room at the Royal York? To leave the Imperial Ballroom and take an elevator up to the tenth floor, no one giving him the evil eye, wondering what he was doing there. The room would have good furniture, a thick carpet that felt like you were in your stocking feet even when you had shoes on, and a well-stocked bar, anything you wanted, gin, whiskey, bourbon. He'd just have a beer, thanks. Trombone was thirsty work. He turned right at Bloor and headed for the viaduct, the coal-black Don River flowing somewhere far below. Who would be in the room with him after the rest of them had gone home? Would it be like their honeymoon room in Flynn's, or would it be like the Ambassador?

When he got home, Vivian was sitting on the sofa. She wasn't smoking much these days, and she'd asked him to stop smoking in the apartment, said it made her feel queasy. When she looked up at him he could tell she had more bad news. She wasn't exactly crying, but she wasn't far from it.

"What is it?" he asked.

She took a ragged breath. "Your mother rang while you were out."

Alarm bells sounded in his head. "What did she want?"

"Your father's in hospital," she said, coming even closer to tears. "I couldn't quite make out what happened, she wasn't very coherent. I think he might have fallen down some stairs."

Jack had a vision of his father on the ground, on his hands and knees, fire edging towards him. He almost cried out, but instead he put his hands over his eyes to erase the image. It didn't work.

"Jesus," he said. "What stairs?"

"I don't know."

Jack lowered his hands and took a deep breath. "He was probably drunk. What am I supposed to do, go down there and hold his hand?"

"Yes, Jack, that's exactly what you're supposed to do. He's your father."

"Jesus, Viv, Benny'll be with him." Benny.

"But what if he's seriously hurt?"

"That's what hospitals are for."

"Jack!" This time she did start crying. "Don't you care about your family? Don't you love them? How can you love me if you don't love your own family?" She stopped talking and looked at him wildly. "How can you not love the people who brought you into this world?"

"All they want is someone to pay the goddamn hospital bills." But even as he said it he knew it wasn't true.

"Can't we at least ring them back, find out how badly your father's hurt? Make sure Benny is looking after your mother? Jack, that's the least we can do."

"Yeah, yeah, I guess so. Sure, go ahead."

Vivian got up and went to the phone, which was on the wall beside the door. His mother must have given her the number.

"Hello?" she said into the phone. "Is Mrs. Lewis there, please? Who's this? Alvina?" She looked at Jack. He shook his head. He didn't want to talk to her. "Hello, Alvina. We haven't met. I'm Vivian, Jack's wife. Yes, the one from Newfoundland. We just heard about your father. Can you tell us more about what happened . . . ?" She was still looking at Jack, and now she mouthed the words: *Your mother's at the hospital*. "Jack and I were wondering how he's doing. Is he badly hurt?"

There was a long pause while she listened to what was

evidently a tale of unending woe. He felt constriction in his chest. What did she need to read books for? If she wanted a real tear-jerker, all she had to do was talk to his family. Her eyes widened, and at one point her hand went to her mouth. "Oh!" Then she said, "Oh dear," and repeated it two more times. Then she said: "Well, thank you, Alvina. I'll tell all this to Jack and we'll call back. Will someone be home tonight? Of course we want to help. Yes. Goodbye, Alvina. Give our love to everyone."

"Well?" he said when she'd hung up. "What'd he do, fall down at the British-American Hotel?" He hoped that was all it was.

"Jack, it's serious. He's in a coma. They don't know if he's going to come out of it."

"A coma. What the hell happened?"

"He came home in the middle of the night and had to go down into the basement for something . . ."

"That's where he keeps his whiskey bottle."

"And there weren't any stairs there."

"There *what*?"

"Benny had taken the old stairs out, and he hadn't put new ones in. And I guess it was dark, and—"

"Benny!" Jack said, pacing back and forth between the sofa and the counter with the kettle and the hotplate. "That idiot!"

"Your father landed on his back. They think his neck may be broken."

"Oh, that's just great, that is," Jack said. He was trying to think the matter through, and his mind was racing. He'd planned on going to talk to Moxie Whitney in the morning, see if he

PART V

VIVIAN

"Your sister didn't say which hospital your father is in," Vivian said to Jack when they reached the outskirts of Windsor.

"It'll be Hôtel-Dieu," Jack said.

"How do you know?"

He hesitated. "It always is."

New houses were going up in clusters between the highway and the lake, small, single-storey bungalows like the one Frank and Jeannie had built for themselves. She pictured the young couples who would live in them, imagining herself and Jack with a pram on the porch, the Hup parked in the driveway. But everything, she and Jack with a baby, Frank and Jeannie in Newmarket, Iris and Freddie back home, seemed so unreachably distant. These houses all looked empty and cold. She shivered. She was freezing. They'd been in the car for seven hours, since six o'clock that morning, stopping only for gas and more coffee when their Thermos was empty. The Hup had made it, somehow, but it had jettisoned a few parts along the way, a tail light, the windshield wiper on her side. Jack hadn't even stopped to retrieve them, saying something about not needing them anymore. The heater had quit just after London.

Hôtel-Dieu turned out to be a solid, red-brick hospital with rounded turrets at each corner, a bigger, square one above the main entrance, as though it had been modelled on a castle in France, a bastion against disease and suffering. Nuns worked at a wooden desk that stretched along one end of the foyer. As she waited for Jack to park the car she warmed her hands above a radiator and read a plaque on the wall. The hospital had been started sixty years before by the Hospitallers of St. Joseph. There was a photograph and a caption explaining that the hospital had at one time also run an orphanage for sick infants whose parents, too poor to look after them properly, had brought them here for treatment and then hadn't come back to pick them up. Vivian touched her belly through her coat. Many of the children, she read, were from coloured families.

Jack came through the heavy revolving doors, rubbing his hands together and looking around anxiously for her. Together they went up to the admissions desk. The nursing sister looked at them kindly, but she was firm. "Mr. Lewis can be visited only by family."

"We *are* family," said Vivian. She turned to Jack. "This is Jack Lewis, his son. And I'm Jack's wife."

The nursing sister looked at Jack for a long second. "Very well," she said. "Mr. Lewis is in Long-Term Care, third floor. The duty nurse, Sister Emmanuelle, will tell you which room."

"Thank you."

Jack didn't say a word as they rode up the elevator. He pushed the button marked 3 and watched the lights move glacially from floor to floor, fiddling with his hat, turning it around and around in his hands as though feeling for something hidden inside it.

When they got out, Sister Emmanuelle at the nursing station pointed down a long, wide corridor. "Third room on the right."

"Come, darling," Vivian said, taking his arm when he held back.

Most of the doors were closed, but the third room was open. Jack stopped at the door and Vivian stood beside him, looking around the room. The first thing she saw was Jack's mother sitting on the edge of a narrow bed, dressed in her Sunday clothes and looking calm and serene, as though nothing in the world could be wrong, and Vivian sighed with relief. Jack's father must still be alive. Benny was straddling a chair at the foot of the bed, staring at the floor, the very picture of dejection and guilt. A young woman wearing a black pillbox hat with a dark veil stood behind him, her back to the door, her gloved hand absently massaging his shoulder. A taller woman, who must have been Alvina, was pacing back and forth, looking angry, as though she'd lost something and wanted to know who took it.

No one spoke. Then Jack's mother noticed them at the threshold. She smiled, and everyone turned and looked at Vivian.

Perhaps it was their being all together like this, poised in a shaft of light coming through the window as though for a group photograph, that made Vivian see them objectively, even Jack's mother and Benny, as though for the first time. A thought struck her, a thought she had never quite formulated before but ought to have, she couldn't imagine why she hadn't: Jack's family was coloured. The realization made her forget about Jack's father and the reason they had come. As strange as it sounded, she knew in her heart that it wasn't because Jack's father was hurt that they had returned to Windsor. It was so she could see this.

She turned to Jack but he wouldn't look at her. She wanted to place his hand on her belly and tell him there was nothing to worry about, nothing that mattered, but of course it did matter. He was looking vague again, the lost little boy in a sailor's suit, and her heart went out to him. He had let her bring him to Windsor two years ago so she could see this, and she hadn't. Everything had been too new to her then, she hadn't been able to connect one oddity to another. But now, with everyone gathered in one room, she could finally see them for the first time.

Then she looked at the bed.

"Will," Jack's mother said to the figure lying under a blue sheet. "Will, Jack and his wife are here to see you, ain't that somethin'? They come all this way." The figure beneath the sheet did not stir. Jack's mother looked up at Vivian. "They say he can't hear us," she said, "but I don't believe them." She reached out her hand and Vivian stepped forward and took it, leaving Jack at the door. Vivian stared at the form under the sheet, avoiding the face on the pillow. She didn't know what to do. Was she supposed to say something?

"Hello, Mr. Lewis," Vivian said, leaning over Jack's father, still holding his mother's hand. He was lying on his back, legs and arms straight at his sides, looking like a long mound of fresh earth under a blanket of blue snow. She brought her eyes to his face. His eyelids were closed and the corners of his mouth turned down as though he'd been given a bitter pill, exactly like Jack when he was sleeping. A tube connected his right arm to a bottle of yellowish liquid suspended upside down on the wall beside his bed. The arm was puckered and wrinkled, covered in scar tissue as though from a severe burn. He wasn't dark dark, she saw, but he was dark enough, especially against the pillow. Jack's mother had said that Jack took after her, but Vivian could see Jack in his father; the father was like a photographic negative of his son. What surprised her most was that she wasn't surprised. She thought she would be, but when she looked at Jack's father she said to herself, yes, this makes as much sense as anything else Jack's told me. She placed her free hand on the man's shoulder, above the burn marks. He was cold to her touch. She wanted to say it was nice to meet him, but instead she started to cry. Jack's mother squeezed her hand, and Vivian let go and backed away to stand beside Jack in the doorway.

"The doctor says there been some damage done to his brain," Jack's mother said. "He says he'll probably never come out of this, or if he does he won't never talk again or probably know any of us. But we don't believe that, do we, dear?" she said, looking fondly at her husband. "I know he's here with us."

"That's from a gospel song, ain't it, Mama?" Benny's girlfriend said.

"I don't believe you met Dee-Dee before," Jack's mother said, and Vivian looked at Benny's girlfriend. The veil didn't obscure her face, but it was hard to tell where the veil ended and the bare throat began.

"Jackson," said Jack's mother, "you met Dee-Dee, didn't you?"

"No," Jack said. "Not that I know of."

To the tall, pacing woman Jack's mother said, "Alvina, dear, this here's Jack's wife, Vivian."

Alvina gave Vivian the once-over, curious and dismissive at the same time. "We talked on the telephone." Her hair was coarse and straw-coloured, and she'd had it permed into long waves that held firm when she walked. Like Benny's, it had a hint of red in it. But it was her skin that caught and held Vivian's attention. Where Benny's was pitted and unevenly tanned, Alvina's was a smooth, glowing, buttery brown.

Vivian moved Jack from the door into the room and they stood together by the window. It looked down on Ouellette Avenue. Vivian turned to Jack's father.

She had the feeling that everyone, especially Alvina, was looking at her expectantly, waiting for her to remark on what to them was unremarkable. She supposed they thought she would walk out of the room, out of the hospital, and not come back, but of course she wouldn't do that. For one thing, her knees were too weak, and she felt a tightness in her chest as from something long suppressed. But it wasn't anger or fear or even disappointment that was causing it, rather a kind of curiosity and a sense that now, at long last, things that she hadn't understood were finally out in the open. Benny's Windsor tan, Jack's mother's facial powder, the extraordinary efforts to keep her from meeting Jack's father, Jack's insistence that Alvina had married beneath her, all of it now fell into a pattern that she could piece together and understand.

She wasn't crazy, after all. Jack must have thought that if she couldn't see the truth for herself after he had laid it out for her like a hand of cards on a table, then there wasn't much to be gained by saying more. But now that she *had* seen it, suddenly, as though she'd been looking out to sea and seeing nothing and then suddenly discerned a flight of birds skimming inches above the surface, she could relax. Maybe now they could both get on with their lives. So she would not walk out of the room. The only unresolved question now was, if Jack's family was coloured, how was it that Jack was not? And that was important because, as she now realized so sharply that she had to lean back against the windowsill to remain upright, there was this baby inside her. Jack's baby.

When morning visiting hours were over, Jack and Vivian drove Alvina and Jack's mother back to the house, where they discussed

Jack's father's condition. Jack's mother insisted quietly that her husband would wake up at any moment, look about him, and ask grumpily what the hell everyone was doing in his room. Alvina protested less quietly that people didn't just wake up from comas like they did from naps. If the fall had damaged his brain, as the doctor said it had, he might never wake up at all. Vivian kept out of it. She took small bites of her egg-salad sandwich and asked if anyone would like her to make tea. Jack wouldn't meet her gaze.

As she waited for the kettle to boil, she studied each of them in turn, trying to see how Jack fit into the picture she'd carried from the hospital room. Between Jack's father at one end of the scale and Jack at the other, there was a bewildering array of combinations. Alvina had Jack's sharp tongue, his quick temper, his darkly suspicious nature. Jack's mother was very light, almost as light as Jack, and her hair had always intrigued Vivian; she'd wondered if she'd had it straightened, but then she realized that Jack's mother's hair and Jack's were similar if you took away the Brylcreem—soft and wavy, and they even parted it on the same side. Benny could be taken for white, especially beside Dee-Dee. Next to Jack, he looked like one of the Caribbean sailors who sometimes jumped ship in St. John's.

When lunch was finished and Alvina and Jack's mother went back to the hospital in Alvina's car, Vivian said she and Jack would stay behind to clean up and would join the others later. Vivian did the dishes, barely breathing, and then joined Jack in the living room. He was smoking a cigarette and sitting beneath the picture of Christ, in the same chair she had sat in the first time she'd been in this house.

"We have to talk, Jack," she said, and he looked up at her as though she had spoken a language he didn't understand, as perhaps she had.

"About what?"

"About your father."

"Aw, he'll be okay."

"Why didn't you tell me he's a Negro?"

"What do you mean, a Negro?" Jack said, as surprised and indignant as if she had told him his parents were codfish. "He's not. My father and Benny both have blond hair, Alvina has blonde hair. Have you ever seen a Negro with blue eyes and blond hair? Look at me. Do I look like a Negro to you? Does my mother? Stop talking nonsense."

She recoiled as though she'd been slapped in the face.

His response had evidently been prepared. And she *had* seen blond Negroes. In Windsor there was every conceivable combination of skin tone and hair.

"Jack, I have eyes, I can see."

"Your second time in Windsor and you're an expert?"

"It doesn't make any difference, you know," she said to placate him.

"It makes a big difference to me," he said, pounding his fist against his chest.

"How?" She was genuinely curious. Then she thought about that novel she'd read about in Toronto, *Kingsblood Royal*. Not all books were letters from faraway places.

"I wouldn't have anything to do with them, that's how," Jack said. "Whites and coloureds don't mix."

"But—"

"Look," he said. He stood up and began pacing back and forth in the room. Then he turned to her. "If people in Toronto ever thought I came from a coloured family, I'd lose my job. We'd be kicked out of our apartment. Is that what you want?"

"No, but—"

"Then stop talking foolishness."

"It's just that we have to be honest with each other," she said.

"I am being honest. I look in the mirror every morning and I see a white man. That's the only truth that matters. Anything else is just you seeing things that aren't there."

She realized she wasn't being entirely honest with him, although she longed to be. The time had come to tell him about the baby. "Jack," she said, "I'm pregnant."

He stared at her. He looked bewildered and terrified. She was relieved that she had delivered herself of her secret, she had rehearsed it often enough. But Jack's response wasn't what she had imagined it would be. He seemed not to have grasped what she'd said. Instead of his face lighting up with joy, he almost scowled at her. Had he even heard her?

"I'm pregnant," she said again, "with your child."

"So?" he said. "You're white, I'm white, so the baby will be white."

"But what if—?"

"What if what?" he said. He turned suddenly and went towards the front door. Then he stopped and spun around, and she almost covered her ears because she knew what he was going to say. "If that baby comes out coloured, I'll know it isn't mine!"

The door slammed behind him and she was alone.

JACK

He hadn't meant to slam the goddamned door, but he was having a hard time controlling himself. He got in the truck, slammed that door, too. If he took the Hup he'd have to go to the hospital with Vivian, and he didn't want to have anything to do with Vivian or his father. He was in no mood to sit around a hospital room wringing his hands with the doom-and-gloom patrol, the old man lying there like a corpse and everyone around him acting as though he was just resting his eyes.

He'd driven all the way from Toronto, and now here he was driving again. He sped down Ouellette towards the river, his mind seething, iron bands tightening around his chest. If Vivian thinks I'm coloured, he told himself, she'll leave me. She'll take her kid and go back to Newfoundland and tell her family they were right all along, the marriage didn't work out. He could just imagine what Iris would say. That was if the kid turned out white. Which of course it would. Assuming it was his.

He considered taking the tunnel across the river to Detroit, to clear his head, but he turned left on Sandwich instead and then left again on Pelissier, into Windsor's white district. He turned right onto Giles Boulevard and down Victoria, realizing where he'd been heading all along. He parked the truck in front of Della's house, thinking he might catch a glimpse of her, maybe at a window, or coming out to go shopping. He hadn't seen her in more than two years, but he had thought about her constantly, not only at night when Vivian was busy making herself unavailable to him but during the day, too, whenever he saw a gasoline gauge showing empty, and sometimes when he was knocking on doors, imagining her coming to open one in a loosely tied housecoat. "Like to buy a *Year Book*, ma'am?" "Oh, it's you," she'd say, and step aside to let him in. Damn it, he would speak to her. It's a free goddamned country, isn't it? Isn't that what they fought the war for?

As he sat, his breathing shallow, his heart thumping in his chest, the truck's engine running and the heater turned on high, the whole night at the motel came rushing back to him. It began with him walking into the Horse Shoe and seeing Della surrounded by refugees from the riot, their anxious faces looking up at him as he led her from that palace of darkness to the promised land, the Ambassador Motel. Della taking off her torn dress in that cold room. In his waking dream, this was where he usually shook himself awake, turned to Vivian or got a customer's order ready, but now he let his mind run its course. He laid Della back on the bed and slowly revealed, revelled in, her pale, beautiful body. He lay down on top of her and let her skin give way to his.

And it seemed to him that in the five years since that night he'd never wholly accepted the idea that she had rejected him the next morning. He couldn't believe that their night together had not constituted a beginning, because he had thought of himself as being in love with Della for much longer than that single night. Their love included all those nights after band practice, when he and she had sat side by side in her parlour, and he had watched her knitting and drinking tea and had had to dodge her questions about his family. And all the times he had thought about her since, lying in his narrow cot in the barracks in St. John's. The Ambassador, as it now shaped itself in his mind, had merely been an inevitable first step, not a consummation or completion. All the pain that came after that, her rejection, his joining the Navy, his not seeing or hearing from her, his marriage to Vivian, had been new episodes in his life, yes, but not breaks from his old life—the way a verse is not a new song but a continuation of the old song between repeated refrains. Della had always been the chorus.

And so he got out of the truck and, without any clear idea of what he would do once he got inside, knocked on Della's front door.

He'd been composing something to say to her husband, or to Peter, or maybe a receptionist, and then the door opened and she was standing there with a winter boot in her hand.

"I was just going out," she said when she saw him.

He didn't say anything, didn't trust himself to speak. She looked older. The new styles didn't suit a woman of her age and so she wasn't wearing them: a loose woollen coat with padded shoulders, her hair tied back with a babushka knotted at the throat, knitted scarf and gloves; she might have been an immigrant, a woman fleeing her homeland. She stood slightly bent over, one stockinged toe touching the floor and her boot in her hand. She looked into his eyes, then slowly straightened.

"I guess I'm not going anywhere. I guess you'd better come in."

If only she'd said that five years ago, that morning after the Ambassador. How different things would be now. He might not have joined the Navy, he might have stayed in Windsor, built up his father's business, be living in a big house now, with Della. Maybe even in this house. Six simple words.

While Della took off her other boot, he looked around the downstairs, took in the smell of disinfectant, the polio poster showing a child with a withered leg, the closed pocket doors leading to Dr. Barnes's practice, and he felt a kind of possessive pride in the grandness of it. As long as those doors remained closed, the rest was his. Della must have sensed the same thing because she glanced at them and then took Jack's arm and led him up the stairs to the parlour, which was just as he remembered it, the two soft chairs with the tall floor lamp between them, the radio against the wall in the bay window. Even the heavy curtains on the windows were the same, although pulled aside now to let the afternoon sunlight in. He had never been here during the day. After band practice it had always been night. "After band practice" sounded so juvenile now; this wasn't after band practice, this was after the riot, this was after the war.

He sat in one of the chairs and she sat in the other, facing him. She placed her purse and gloves on the little table between them and removed her babushka, letting her hair fall back over her shoulders, but she kept her coat on.

"What is it, Jack?" she asked, and still he could not find his voice.

He wanted to tell her to relax, see, there was nothing wrong with his being here, maybe she should take out her knitting and they could talk about music. More than anything he wanted this to feel normal, permanent.

"It's nice here," he said, looking past her at the leafless chestnut trees. The portrait of her husband in his Navy uniform was gone, in its place a photograph of Peter holding his trumpet to his lips. "You've kept it nice."

"Jack, what's this all about?"

"I wanted to see you again, that's all."

She sat back in her chair and looked at him. "How's Vivian?"

"Fine."

"Are you enjoying married life?"

"Are you enjoying yours?" he said.

She flinched, and he wished he hadn't said it. This wasn't how he wanted the conversation to go. His marriage was a closed door now, and he didn't want advice on how to open it. He wanted another door.

She leaned forward and opened her purse, took out a slim, silver cigarette case, extracted a cigarette and handed it to Jack like a peace offering, then took another for herself. One end of the case was a lighter. He found himself admiring the case, losing himself in its polished surface. He lit her cigarette and his. They would start over.

"Look, Jack," she said, "I don't know why you've come here now, after all this time, but really, darling, let's not pretend we can pick up where we left off."

"No, of course not," he said, and it was only a partial lie. Never tell them what you want. "I just wanted to sit in this room again. I like it here. I feel at home here. You know," he said, turning the cigarette around in his fingers, "I don't belong in my own family. It's like I was switched at the hospital or something. Do you know what I mean?"

"Jack, you're talking to a doctor's wife. That kind of thing doesn't happen. You are who you are."

"I'm not, that's just it. No one is."

He stood and went to the window and looked down the street towards the river.

"How can I help you, Jack?" It wasn't an offer.

He choked back a sob, as though one of the bands around his chest had snapped, and turned to her. "When I came here with Peter after band practice, it always felt like I was coming home, like this was my real home."

"Do you mean you thought of me as your real mother?" she asked, all but laughing at him.

But he was trying to be serious. "In a way. At first."

"I hope you don't look at your mother the way you looked at me."

"How did I look at you?"

"The way a man looks at something he wants. That's why you're here now, isn't it? Because I didn't give you what you wanted."

"I don't know what that is."

"I think you do."

"Vivian—" he began, as if Della had reminded him of an appointment he had missed.

Della set her cigarette in an ashtray on the table.

"How's your father, Jack?"

"My father?"

"I heard he was in the hospital."

Every time he thought he had his feet on solid ground, Della said something that pushed him back into the sea.

"He's all right. The doctors say he'll be fine."

Della looked at him sadly. "Jack," she said, "he won't be fine. He's in a coma he probably won't come out of. He's a very nice man, and you should be proud of being his son. I've known your father for a long time. He did the work on my husband's office downstairs."

Jack's breathing stopped, as though there was a tiny noise somewhere that he wanted to hear. She knew his father? "But I thought . . ." he started to say, but could not go on. "But . . ." He looked at Della helplessly, the shoreline receding. Then he said: "Vivian's pregnant."

"Oh." Della nodded slowly. "And she's worried that her baby will be coloured."

"No!" It had come out louder than he'd intended. "Of course she isn't!" Then his voice rose even more. "You don't know anything about me!"

"Jack," she said. "I've always known. You're the only one who didn't. It was one of the things I liked about you."

"But it's not true!"

"Keep your voice down," she said. "Sit here." She pointed to the second chair.

"Stop treating me like a kid!" he said. But he sat.

"I want to tell you something. A story. When I was your age, when I was eighteen, barely out of high school, Howard and I were engaged, sort of. There was an understanding. My father thought the fucking sun rose and fell on Howard Barnes, and I thought he was the biggest goofball anyone could possibly imagine. It was 1925. Everyone was wearing cloche hats and those skimpy dresses with long beads and elbow-length gloves, and the men slicked their hair back and went to the racetrack and drank Dom Pérignon with breakfast, and here was Howie with his tennis whites and his savings account. I panicked. I could see exactly what my life was going to be like. He'd have his medical practice and his roses and I'd have children and tea parties and a horse in the country, and we'd vacation in Florida where he'd play golf and I'd wear sundresses and drink too much gin."

She looked over at him. He tried to figure out where all this was going.

"It must have been the same for Vivian," she said.

He wasn't interested in Vivian's problems at the moment. He would have given his eye teeth for a rose garden and tea parties and a horse in the country. He'd have shovelled shit for the things Della had wanted to escape from.

"So I ran away," Della went on. "Well, I didn't run, I got a scholarship and went to Vassar, which wasn't in New York City but was close enough. It's a school, darling," she said when he looked at her blankly. "A very expensive private girls' school. If I thought I was getting away from tennis and bank accounts . . . But a bunch of us used to take the train into New York and haunt the cabarets in Harlem and listen to jazz. But you can't just listen to jazz, can you? Not the kind they played. You had to get up and join in the powwow. We got to be as good at doing the Charleston as the coloured girls, and the men would ask us to dance, and we'd get up and dance with them."

"You shouldn't have been there," Jack said, but he could see the lure of it, the thrill of being in a place where you didn't belong and were accepted anyway, no questions asked so long as you were careful. "What happened?"

"Disaster happened. One night I missed the last train to Poughkeepsie. I ran for it, I really did, and I got to Grand Central fifteen seconds too late. I remember standing on the platform watching it go, thinking, Well, girl, that's it, it's back to Windsor for you. Vassar girls didn't miss trains. You could miss a period, but you couldn't miss a train. I thought about my father, about telling him I'd been expelled and seeing the look on his face. I started to cry. I hadn't done anything wrong, really, but I knew I was going to be expelled. At the very least I would lose the scholarship, which would amount to the same thing. My life had been ruined over fifteen seconds."

"What did you do?"

"I stood on the platform watching my life pull away from me, and when I turned around, there was Jonesie."

"Jonesie?"

"A trumpet player. Hubert Jones. I'd seen him a few times in the cabaret. He was going to Chicago to play for a few nights and then come back to New York, but he missed his train, too. It didn't seem to bother him much. It hadn't changed his life, you see, or maybe it had and he was ready for a change. He had some money, so we took a cab back to the club and when the club closed I went back to Jonesie's place and spent the night with him."

"You *what?*"

"It seemed simple at the time, as if it was meant to happen. It was like we were following some kind of score. The next morning we both went our respective ways, and that was that."

"What happened when you got back to the school?"

"Oh, there was the usual weeping and wailing and gnashing of teeth. The dean of women, the scholarship committee, the registrar. But I no longer cared. I had grown up overnight. I'd become an adult—aged, grown old, withered and died, all in one night. If I'd told them I'd spent the night with a coloured man, they would have kicked me out, maybe even out of the country."

"Wait a minute," he said. "This guy was *coloured*?"

"Of course he was coloured. Anyway, I packed my trunk that afternoon and took a train to Albany and Detroit, considered going to Chicago to be with Jonesie. I even tried calling him at the club where he said he was playing, but he wasn't there and so in the end I took a taxi home. I told everyone I'd sat in Grand Central all night reading F. Scott Fitzgerald. A few days later I slept with Howard, and when I found out I was pregnant, we got married."

She sat back as though she had finally come to the point of her story.

"Do you mean you don't know who Peter's father is?"

"Jack," she said, "you of all people should know that you can't tell a damned thing about a person just by looking at him."

"You can tell what colour he is! And Peter isn't coloured."

"You can't know that. Do you remember the trumpet player at the Horse Shoe that night Peter played his solo? You were so disgusted when Peter borrowed his horn."

"That was Jonesie? That's impossible."

"Is it, though? Doesn't it make some kind of sense that after four hundred years of living on the same continent, in the same cities, in the same neighbourhoods, that no matter who our parents are, we're all having children that are neither one thing nor the other? Or both one thing and the other?"

"It doesn't make sense. It's crazy."

"It does make sense. And I think you're a perfect example of it. You spend so much energy trying to be white, trying not to be coloured, you can't just relax and be who you are. Jack, can't you see that it doesn't matter whether your baby is born white or coloured? That it doesn't matter anymore?"

"Stop it!" he shouted. He raised his hand to strike something, anything. She didn't move.

He jumped to his feet and rushed down the stairs. It was wrong, everything. Della, and the war and Vivian, and now Della again. He wanted to put his fist through the wall, the sliding door, see it splinter like straw before the might of his fury. He heard movement behind him and looked up to see Della standing at the top of the stairs, and when he turned to the pocket doors, Dr. Barnes was coming out of his clinic. He was wearing a white smock and carrying a clipboard and a silver pen. He looked past Jack and spoke to his wife.

"Del?" he said. "Everything all right?"

"Yes, Howie, everything's fine. You remember Jack, don't you? Peter's friend? He was on your ship."

Dr. Barnes looked at Jack. "Ah, yes! The young bandsman. Seasickness, wasn't it?"

"Yes, sir," Jack said.

"Well, you seem to have survived it."

"He was looking for Peter," Della explained.

"Right," the doctor said, turning. "Can't help you there, I'm afraid."

When Jack looked back up the stairs, Della was gone, and when he turned to the pocket doors again they were closed and the foyer was empty.

VIVIAN

Her misery and grief subsided, but they left a stain. When Jack came home after his outburst, he seemed to have forgotten everything, but she was wary of him. She didn't trust his moods. He always said he didn't mean the things he said when he was angry. Why didn't that stop him from saying them the next time? He asked about the baby, told her he was sure there would be no trouble with it, which she took to mean he cared only that it was healthy, and when she was alone with him she almost believed that everything would be fine. But when she was with his family, at the hospital or here at the house, she felt despair settle over her. She'd known women back home who had taken steps to rid themselves of babies whose fathers were gone or unsuitable, and she had never understood before how they could bring themselves to do it, how such monstrousness could be a comforting thought.

First they decided they would stay in Windsor until Jack's father came out of his coma. Then, when he was moved out of long-term care, or when he began to show signs of improvement, or at least until his condition became clearer. When none of those things happened, they found a furnished apartment on Janette Avenue, the second floor of a house that backed onto a railway yard. It had a living room, a small bedroom, a smaller kitchen and a tiny bathroom, and it filled with grit every time a train passed, raising dust from the cinders on the track beds. But Jack said it was on the right side of town and that they had moved up from the Settlement. The rent was eight dollars a week, and Jack took jobs playing with dance bands two or three nights a week. Alvina, who worked in a women's clothing shop on lower Windsor Avenue, was helping their mother with groceries, and Jack was paying his father's hospital bills. Benny wasn't working, but he didn't seem to need any help from them. Maybe Dee-Dee was supporting him.

They still visited the hospital most days, or Vivian did while Jack ran errands. He was keeping three households going, he said, theirs, his mother's and his brother's. Benny was always there, sometimes with Dee-Dee, sometimes alone, and Jack's mother and Alvina came as often as they could. The student nurse who looked after Jack's father was a young coloured woman named Marian Overton. She had gone to high school with Alvina, and every time she came into the room Alvina said, "Here she is, don't she look fine?" and Marian would smile shyly and tend to Jack's father, which, because there was never any improvement, consisted of taking his pulse and temperature, checking his saline solution, then shifting him to prevent him from getting bedsores. Marian was graduating in the spring. "She the first coloured nurse to graduate from this hospital," Alvina said, speaking proudly but bitterly. "Sixty years this been a teaching hospital, opened especially for coloureds, and in all them sixty years not one coloured nurse, not one, until Marian here. Now, you telling me not one coloured girl in all them years been smart enough to be a nurse? I don't believe it. I could've been a nurse. Dee-Dee here could've been a nurse. Lots of us could've been nurses. Mama, you could've been a nurse."

Jack's mother chuckled. "Alvina, dear, I couldn't have been no nurse. I wasn't good at shifting your grandmother when I was in service. I was too small. You got to be big and strong to move some of them patients around, ain't that right, Marian?"

"They're hard to shift sometimes," Marian said, "but not Mr. Lewis. I think he helps me turn himself over."

"There, you see?" Jack's mother beamed.

"You must've been some good at keepin' house, Ma," said Alvina, "otherwise Pop wouldn't have married you."

Once again, Vivian felt as though a curtain had been lifted between herself and Jack's family, but she couldn't say for sure whether she was in the audience or on the stage.

* * *

A week or two after she and Jack had moved to Janette Avenue, when Vivian was in her fourth month, Jack's mother invited her for tea. Jack's mother said she was having Alvina and Dee-Dee and another friend from the Emancipation Day organizing committee over on Sunday, and Vivian was touched that Jack's mother was making an effort to bring her into the family. The baby would likely be born in time for the picnic, and if it was coloured, she decided, she would take it to Jackson Park to show it the bandstand and the barbecue pits, let it hear the music and listen to the speeches. August would be hot and muggy. She'd need a carriage, and some cheesecloth to keep off the flies. Jack wouldn't be there, of course, he'd have hightailed it by then and she'd be alone with her child. But she no longer found that prospect as terrifying as she once did.

It was Dee-Dee who opened the door. Vivian knew that Dee-Dee and Benny were living together, and that they weren't married and didn't even pretend to be. Such a thing would not have been possible in St. John's, there would have been a dime-store ring at the very least, and the couple would conspicuously refer to each other as "my wife" and "my husband." Vivian liked Dee-Dee. She was pert and lively and her eyes sparkled with mischief. It was the first time she'd seen her without a veil or a kerchief on her head, and Vivian noticed a lighter-coloured scar on her forehead, just below the hairline, in the shape of a horseshoe.

Jack's mother was sitting on the red chair. She jumped to her feet when Vivian entered the room.

"You came!" she said. "I never thought you would."

"Of course I did," said Vivian, unsure how to take the welcome.

The other person in the room was a woman of Jack's mother's age, wearing a somewhat startling hat made of brightly coloured feathers and ribbons, like an inverted magpie's nest. The woman herself was birdlike, as tall and slender as a pheasant hen, and she glared at Vivian in so predatory a manner that Vivian was rattled and promptly forgot the woman's name.

"I call this meeting to order," said the bird woman when they were all seated in the living room. "All present and we have a guest, Mrs. Jackson Lewis. Miss Dee-Dee is taking the minutes."

"Dee-Dee knows shorthand," Alvina said to Vivian. "She works as a secretary down at the salt mines. But she a singer at night," she added. "They call her the Black Pearl on Hastings Street, don't they, darlin'?"

"Other places, too," Dee-Dee said shyly.

"What did they call you when you sang?" Vivian asked Alvina.

Alvina laughed. "They didn't call me nothin'."

"Do you know a trumpet player named Peter Barnes?" she asked Dee-Dee.

"Peter? Sure, I know him. He plays at a speakeasy his mother owns down at the bottom of Ouellette, the Flatted Fifth it's called. I sing there with him sometimes. He's good."

Della owned a speakeasy? But Vivian had long ago learned not to show when she was surprised. "Jack and I heard him at the Horse Shoe when we were there two years ago," Vivian said. "Do you ever go there?"

Dee-Dee looked down at her notepad. "Sometimes," she said.

"You went to the Horse Shoe?" the bird woman asked Vivian.

"Yes. With Peter and his mother."

"On East Adams?"

"Yes."

"In the Black Bottom?"

"Yes. Why?"

"Hmm." The woman sniffed. "That's a black-and-tan, and you don't look too tan to me."

"Would anyone like some tea?" Jack's mother said, and Vivian smiled at her gratefully.

Alvina spoke about a beauty contest they were planning for the Emancipation Day picnic, the Miss Sepia Pageant, the first of its kind in Windsor. They were trying to get Jackie Robinson, the baseball player, to come up and be a judge, but they might have to settle for Alf Hunter, a coloured boxer from Detroit.

"That's what we got to do on Emancipation Day," Alvina said. "We got to show people that coloureds've made a big contribution to this city, that we ain't just a bunch of housekeepers and barbers. And we got to show that to everyone, coloured or white. There's coloured businessmen, coloured lawyers, coloured nurses, coloured athletes."

"Coloured musicians," put in Jack's mother, nodding at Dee-Dee. She seemed to have forgotten her offer of tea.

"That's right," Alvina said. "We got the Black Pearl singing for us on Emancipation Day."

"You got a band for me yet?" Dee-Dee asked.

"We're talking to Jock Anderson and Brad and Wauneta Moxley," Alvina said. "We'll get you a band somehow." She looked at Vivian, who'd been wondering if she were a part of the meeting or just an onlooker.

"I could speak to Jack about it," she said, although she doubted that she would be able to speak to Jack about anything to do with his family.

"I already done that," Alvina replied. "Several times. He says, 'Why would you ask a white man to organize your picnic for you?' An' I says, 'I ain't, I'm asking you.'"

Alvina's forthrightness about Jack's colour both shocked and encouraged Vivian. If Alvina could speak to him so directly, perhaps Vivian would be able to as well. One day.

"Josephine tells us you're going to have his baby," said the bird woman, staring intently at Vivian as though she were a new species of worm.

"You'll need to see a doctor soon," Jack's mother said, looking at Vivian's waist.

"You'd be wanting a coloured doctor, then?" asked the bird woman.

"Please, call me Vivian."

"There's good coloured doctors in Windsor."

"We'll be in Toronto when the baby's born."

"Lots of coloured doctors in Toronto."

"But why would I go to a coloured doctor?" Vivian asked.

Dee-Dee stopped writing. There was a silence in the room. The bird woman stood up. "You stay there, Josephine," she said to Jack's mother. "I'll go get the tea, and I brought us a treat to go with it."

"You mustn't mind Ephie," Jack's mother said when the bird woman had gone into the kitchen. "She gets carried away sometimes."

"She had a hard life," Alvina said, keeping her voice low.

"It made her a bit odd," Jack's mother added.

"I don't mind," said Vivian. "I know I should be seeing a doctor soon."

"She sure puttin' her heart into Emancipation Day," said Dee-Dee. "I like to see a good concert, but Ephie, all she talks about is how from now on Emancipation Day's going to make a new era of pride for coloureds, we going to be accepted into all the white communities, jump right over the colour bar. We'll get jobs that've always been reserved for whites. We'll be able to buy houses in parts of the city we only ever been able to enter as tradesmen or maids before, and sit anywhere we want to in movie theatres and lunch counters. She going to get the mayor to set up something called a task force. *And* she asked Eleanor Roosevelt to speak at the picnic. Imagine that, Eleanor Roosevelt."

"Why Eleanor Roosevelt?" Vivian asked, just as the bird

woman came back from the kitchen carrying a tea tray.

"Because Eleanor Roosevelt," the bird woman said, setting the tray down on the coffee table, "quit the Daughters of the American Revolution in 1939 when the Daughters of the American Revolution wouldn't let Marian Anderson sing in Constitution Hall in Washington because she was coloured."

Vivian was going to ask who Marian Anderson was, but the bird woman's condescending tone made her change her mind. She kept her eyes on the tea tray: on it were a teapot and four cups and saucers, and a white cardboard pastry box. While Jack's mother poured the tea, the bird woman opened the box and took out three squares of vanilla cake and what looked like a hard-boiled egg. When Jack's mother saw the egg she missed Vivian's cup and poured tea into her saucer.

"Ephie, dear," she said, "I don't think—"

But the bird woman set the egg on a plate and handed it to Vivian. Jack's mother looked uncomfortable.

"What's this?" Vivian asked.

"A special Windsor treat," the bird woman said. "We call them Dark Secrets. They don't have them anywhere but here, far as I know. Go ahead, open it up."

Vivian picked up the egg. Alvina and Dee-Dee were quiet. Jack's mother sat down and put her hands in her lap. The bird woman was cackling with anticipation. Vivian touched the egg. It felt solid, like white chocolate. A thin seam ran around it lengthwise, and when Vivian pressed her fingernail into the seam, the egg split in two and lay open in her hand. At the centre of one of the halves was a small curl of brown chocolate in the shape of a fetus. Vivian was so startled she nearly dropped it.

"Ain't it wonderful how they make them so lifelike?" said the bird woman.

Vivian felt the blood draining from her face and was sure she was going to faint. "I . . . I can't eat this," she said. "I'm sorry, I can't." She stood up and placed the confection on the tea tray, where it rattled and lay still.

"Ephie, dear . . ." Jack's mother said, but a roaring sound filled Vivian's ears.

The bird woman's high voice cut through the roar like the cry of a gull through a windstorm. "White people been tellin' us for years that if we got one drop of coloured blood in us, then we coloured. What's wrong with us sayin' the same thing back to them? You and I both know, Josephine, that if that baby got one drop of coloured blood, then it a coloured baby. It belong to us."

"I've got to go," said Vivian, standing. "Jack will be home wanting his . . ."

Jack's mother followed her to the door, wringing her hands. She took Vivian's coat from its hook and helped her on with it. "You'll see a doctor soon, won't you, dear?"

"Yes," Vivian said. "As soon as I can."

Before leaving, she looked back into the room. Alvina and Dee-Dee were studying their tea, and the bird woman's head was pivoting around, she was quite pleased with herself. The feathers in her hat fluttered, as though she were preening, and her horrid chocolate egg lay exposed on the tray.

WILLIAM HENRY

Now William Henry wishes he could see Jackson's wife. She has a nice voice and she sounds smart, but you can't tell much from voices. Radio announcers have nice voices but are probably ordinary people when you meet them face to face. Lying here *is* like listening to a radio program, in a way. *Amos 'n' Andy*, maybe, or *Boston Blackie*. It sure as hell ain't *The Happy Gang*.

How did he get here, anyway? He thinks if he wasn't hit by a bus he might have had a heart attack. He's never had heart trouble before, but when he gets better he'll slow down, stop working so much. He's had enough of slinging plaster. Lifting a hod of wet plaster up a ladder is too damned hard on an old man, and he's old. Time for Benny to take over.

Jackson could make it easier for them if he wanted to. He could put on a good suit, drive out to River Canard and get them a contract in ten seconds flat. But would he do it? Not in this life. Plasterin's coloured work, he'd say. He'd rather sell books to white people too lazy to walk to the store to buy it for themselves. Is that how he thinks he'll earn their respect, by fetching things for them?

He'd like to ask this new wife of his what she sees in him. Is he a good husband to her? This isn't exactly how he pictured their meeting. He thought that maybe once she got used to the idea of Jackson not being who he says he is, the two of them could commiserate about what a blind fool his son turned out to be. They both suffer for it, they have that in common. But neither one of them suffers for it as much as Jackson himself.

"Will," he hears Josie say to him, "you remember Vivian, Jack's wife. She and Jackson are living in their own apartment now. Aren't you, dear?"

"Yes," her sweet voice says, "but only for a short while, until we go back to Newfoundland."

"You hear that, Will? A short while! The faster you get better, the faster these people can get on with life."

Now she comes over to his bedside and says hello in that nice, young voice of hers, not like his, roughened by cigarettes and alcohol and a lifetime of grunt work. Fifty-seven ain't that old, but he needs to slow down. His arm hasn't been the same since the riot, feels like the skin on it shrunk, like it crackles every time he bends it. A lot of things ain't been the same since the riot.

"We got to put all that behind us," he says.

"All what?" Harlan answers, startling him. He thought it was just Josie and Vivian in the room. Harlan doesn't normally come down to the hospital, says he has enough visitors. Besides, he doesn't want his brother coming here, seeing him like this, flat on his back, his hair uncombed and probably needing a shave. He can only imagine what he looks like. He misses his daily shave.

He sees himself in Harlan's barbershop mirror, a bib around his neck and half his face covered with shaving cream. He believes he went home late one night and something happened, he forgets what, maybe his heart, and he didn't get up early the next morning and leave before anyone else was up, and walk down to the British-American for his morning shave, like he usually did, or if he did that was when he was hit by the bus, or whatever it was. He likes that walk, with the sun eating away at the snow and the day still unruined. The lobby always busy with people checking out in time to make the nine o'clock ferry. Harlan leaning against the door of his shop, watching people's hair as they walk past, imagining how he'd cut it, how he'd change the way they look. There's another coloured profession on the way out: barbering. After the riot, whites were wary of coming downtown to get their hair cut, maybe they thought twice about letting a coloured man come at them with a straight razor in his hand. There's white barbers opening shops farther out, up on Wyandotte and Tecumseh, mostly Italians. Harlan was complaining about it just the other day. All them places where they don't have sidewalks and nobody walks anywhere. Won't be long before the coloureds have the whole downtown to themselves; already happening across the river.

"We got to put it behind us," he says again.

"Get on with it," Harlan agrees.

"Slavery ended a hundred and fifteen years ago, at least in this country."

"You goin' to the picnic this year, Will?"

"I ain't missed one yet."

"They say this one's going to be different."

"Who says?"

"Alvina, Josie. They say we're done steppin' aside to let whitey pass."

"We come up here to get away from all that."

"Not an easy thing to get over, though."

"Jackson was never an easy child to get along with."

"Can't say he was."

As soon as he wakes up, William Henry is going to tell Josie that he long forgave her for having a white baby, although he's never really forgiven Jackson for being white. Not that he's a hundred percent white, never mind what he thinks and the way he carries on. If he wants to live white that's his choice, but he can't expect William Henry to turn himself inside out to be white, too. He ain't one of them new electric signs can be one colour one minute and another colour the next. William Henry shakes his head, causing Harlan to step back for a second with the razor so as not to nick him. When Jackson was a baby,

William Henry was ashamed to be seen with him, and now that he's grown up Jackson's ashamed to be seen with William Henry. You reap what you sow.

"She's a bit thick around the waist," Harlan says.

William Henry heard Alvina saying something like that the other day. Thick with child.

"I ain't seen her."

"Me neither."

"About time, though. How long they been married?"

"Three years."

"Be your first grandchild."

"Be another white bugger in the family."

"Maybe, maybe not."

"Yeah, that's right, you never know, do you."

"No, you sure don't. Look at Jackson."

William Henry laughs at Harlan in the mirror. "If that child comes out coloured," he says, "I just might start believin' in God again."

VIVIAN

The trouble was, she didn't know any doctors in Windsor. She supposed she could just look in the telephone directory under Physicians, but that didn't seem a reliable way of choosing a doctor. She wanted someone she knew, or who came recommended by someone she knew. Then she remembered that Peter's father was a doctor. She found the directory in the kitchen and looked up Barnes. Yes, there he was, Howard J. Barnes, MD, residence and office 512 Victoria Avenue. She rang that afternoon, when Jack was out and his mother was at the hospital. She thought of calling Della first, but decided it was best to go through the proper channels. She spoke to a receptionist, explained that she was nearly four months pregnant and needed to see the doctor. She was given an appointment for the next day.

She walked there from Janette. The sky was grey and there was a cold wind, but it was warmer than it would have been in Toronto, she had to admit, there was something spring-like in the air. Gosh, she'd be as big as a house by spring.

At the doctor's office, the receptionist told her to sit in the waiting room. Through the thick windows, their velvet curtains held back by silk ropes, she could see the quiet street lined with leafless trees, the cars parked along the sidewalk, wet but without snow. She remembered the night they had come here before going to Detroit, before she met Jack's father, before she became pregnant. It seemed several lifetimes ago.

Dr. Barnes was tall, with greying hair and smiling eyes behind silver wire-rimmed glasses that glinted in the light from his desk lamp. He looked older than Della, the very portrait of the family physician, a town doctor rather than one from the outports. He wore a three-piece suit, navy-blue pinstripe, with a gold watch chain looped across his vest. He reminded her so much of her father that she felt she knew exactly what he was going to say before he said it. She even knew what he did. At the end of the day, exactly like her father, he would sit stolidly in his chair by the coal fireplace, take a small folding knife from his vest pocket, shave a palmful of tobacco from a plug he kept in a wooden box on the mantelpiece, and light his pipe with a match that he struck on the fireplace fender. Then he would hold a newspaper up to his face and growl at it while Della made supper.

"Well, you're pregnant, all right," he told her. "As if you didn't know that." He had her father's gruff humour, which she understood perfectly. Longed for. "But there's a lot of albumin in your urine. Bet you didn't know *that*, eh? Probably nothing. Been getting much exercise lately?"

"I walked here, does that count? And I do the shopping every day. Is albumin bad?"

"No, it's a protein and the baby needs protein. But a high count could indicate a problem with the kidneys, or a touch of anemia. Probably not in your case, but since you're in the family way we mustn't take chances. We'll do another blood test for iron. You haven't had German measles or chicken pox lately?"

"No."

"No vaccinations?"

"No."

"Do you smoke?"

"No, I quit."

"Good. Do you drink milk?"

"No, I hate milk."

"Too bad. Drink milk. Lots of it. Four glasses a day. Eat calves' liver, too. And green vegetables, spinach. And cod liver oil."

"My father makes cod liver oil in Newfoundland," she said.

"Hmm. Good, you should get some from him. Wouldn't want to have a rickety baby, would we? Come back and see me in a month. Baby's not due until late July or early August, so no reason to panic yet."

But there was every reason to panic. Could a doctor tell her anything about the baby's colour? Could he take X-rays and see from the shape of its head, or the size of its bones? The way it lay in her womb, like a curl of dark chocolate?

"Meanwhile," the doctor said, "do what I've told you and you'll be right as rain. You and the baby." He looked up at her. "Any questions?"

"I want to have the baby in Hôtel-Dieu, if that's all right?"

All the coloured babies were born in Hôtel-Dieu. It was as close as she could come to asking him directly.

"Hôtel-Dieu? I'm afraid I don't have privileges in Hôtel-Dieu," the doctor said, looking at her intently. Or was she imagining that? "I'm with Grace Hospital. If you want to have the baby in Hôtel-Dieu, I could arrange for you to have a—a different doctor. But I think you'd both be much more comfortable in Grace."

She pulled at the buttons on her sweater, remembered the buttons on Jack's Navy tunic that first time on the beach in Ferryland, and stopped.

"I . . . I think you knew my husband during the war," she said. "He was stationed in St. John's."

"Oh?" the doctor said.

"Jack Lewis? He's a friend of your son's."

"Oh, yes, he was here just the other day."

"Jack was here?"

"Yes," Dr. Barnes said, putting away his stethoscope. "He was upstairs, seeing Della. Apparently looking for Peter."

All the objects in the room had been still until that moment, like perching birds, but suddenly they were in violent motion, as though a hawk had flown in through an open window.

"My husband is worried," she said. "About the baby, I mean."

"Well, then," said the doctor, "you've got some good news for him. Everything's fine." But he didn't make it sound like good news.

"Will the baby be . . . normal?" she asked.

"Nothing's normal," the doctor said. "Drink plenty of liquids, preferably milk, and get lots of rest."

The moment passed. The objects around her roosted again.

He took her elbow and led her back to the waiting room, where the receptionist, whose name tag said June, a nice name, gave her a follow-up appointment for early April, a little over a month away. April was a nice name, too.

"Mrs. Barnes saw your name on our appointment book," June said. "She hopes you have time to go upstairs for tea. She's expecting you."

For a second, Vivian thought she had said, "She's expecting, too." She trembled as she left the office.

When she reached the top of the stairs, she saw Della sitting in an old-fashioned wing chair by the fire. The hallways on either side led, Vivian guessed, to bedrooms, and the kitchen and dining areas. There was a bay window fitted with heavy curtains, and a floor-model radio with a framed photograph of Peter on top of it. Soft morning sunlight filtered through the sheers. The layout, the furniture, everything about the place seemed familiar to her. Then she realized this was the house Jack had described to her on the train. He had described Peter's house as though it were his own.

An empty chair faced Della's, and between them a silver tea service had been set on a small table. There were scones and Devonshire cream. It had been a long time since Vivian had had a real English tea. Della was dressed entirely in wool, right down to her stockings; she might have knitted everything herself. There was a knitting basket behind her chair with two long, thin needles sticking out of it, like an insect's antennas.

"Do sit down, Viv," she said. "You look exhausted."

Her worries about the baby and the curious behaviour of the objects in the examining room had left her shaken. "I am a bit flustered," she said, taking the second chair. Sitting, she felt immediately better. Was it the woollen skirt, the English tea, the smell of the fire? How much Dr. Barnes had reminded her of her father? She felt so powerfully at home here that she decided to confide in Della.

"I'm going to have a baby."

A look passed across Della's face that suggested to Vivian that her news either wasn't news or was not entirely welcome. How much did a doctor share with his wife? Or had Della guessed the truth when she saw Vivian's name in the appointment book?

"How wonderful for you," Della said. "How is Jack taking it?"

Della had leaped to the delicate heart of the matter.

"Not well, I'm afraid," Vivian said. "It's a difficult time for him, what with the baby coming and his father's accident."

"How is Jack's father? Any change?"

"No," she said. "No change. He just lies there."

Della poured the tea, a good Earl Grey. She poured expertly, holding the spout above the cup so as not to drip on the white tablecloth.

"Poor man," Della said. "Hôtel-Dieu is a fine hospital, but if he were in Grace I could ask Howie to look in on him."

"Oh," said Vivian.

"And how is the family taking it?"

"They . . . We're all being brave," Vivian said.

"Jack's a brave boy," said Della. "Did he ever tell you about saving me from the riot?"

"What riot?"

"In Detroit, during the war. A mob tipped my car on its side and set fire to it."

"He's never told me anything about it. Were you hurt?"

"No, thank goodness."

"But that must have been dreadful."

There was a lull that Della did not break. Perhaps she found the memory too painful.

"How is Peter?" Vivian asked.

"Oh," said Della, sitting back with her tea. "Peter's Peter. He doesn't seem to be interested in doing much, outside of music." Her gaze went past Vivian. "I tried to talk him into going to college somewhere to study music, and he said that if I could find him a college that taught bebop, he'd go."

"Jack hates bebop."

Vivian saw Della's gaze turn reptilian for a fleeting moment, and she realized she had spoken disparagingly of something that Della's son loved. But it was too late to take it back.

"Many whites say that," Della said. "Bebop is to jazz as Henry Miller is to Proust, they say. Peter disagrees, of course. He says that Miller's is the purer art. Purer than Proust, can you imagine it? Bebop is a refinement of jazz, not a debasement of it, he says, a sort of jazz elevated to the level of mathematics."

"Perhaps that's what Jack meant," Vivian ventured.

"What?"

"Just that it's hard to dance to mathematics." Vivian hoped the subject would change, but Della returned to it with a coldness she no longer pretended to be borrowing from Peter.

"You know, I find it odd," she said. "I was in New York in the twenties, when the first jazz wave hit. I loved it straight off, couldn't get enough of it, but all the whites denounced it as Negro music. Then a few white musicians started playing it and suddenly jazz was this brilliant new art form. Now along comes bebop, and again the whites are calling it jungle music. Well, a few aren't, like my son. But you see what I mean?"

"Maybe Peter will be the next Bix Beiderbecke," Vivian said.

"You mean a kind of white, bebopping Pied Piper? Oh, wouldn't he just love that."

"It won't be Jack, anyway."

"No, it won't be Jackson."

Jackson. She almost missed it. She'd been hearing it from his family so often, but coming from Della it was different. She recalled Dr. Barnes saying that Jack had been in the house recently. Was it the day he'd left after telling her that if the baby was coloured it wasn't his? Had he come here to talk it over with Peter?

"Your husband tells me Jack was here the other day," she said.

Della leaned over the tea service and put her hand on Vivian's arm. "It's all right, dear," she said. "Jackson told me."

"Told you what?"

Della withdrew her hand from Vivian's arm and sat back with her teacup and saucer on her lap. "This is Windsor, darling, we know about Jack's family." The hawk was back in the room. What had Jack told her? What had he told Della that he hadn't told her? "The colour line may be a bit smudged, but it's here all right," Della went on. "We have our little . . . adventures, but we don't usually marry them. Jack understands that."

"But I would have married him," Vivian said, lifting her chin. "I'm not like you."

Della put her cup and saucer on the table. "If Jack had told you about his family before you became pregnant," she said, "would you have wanted to have this child?"

Vivian felt the room burst into movement, as it had in Dr. Barnes's office. She hated Della at that moment, and she hated Della's question. She wanted to say again that she would have married Jack no matter what, that she wouldn't even have asked about the chances, but something wouldn't let her say it.

The truth was, she didn't know what she would have done. She remembered those women in St. John's who had ended their pregnancies, the regret and relief she had seen in their faces. She put her hand on her belly as though to protect the baby from hearing her thoughts.

"You see?" said Della, sensing Vivian's hesitation. "We Windsor women have to ask ourselves that question every day."

Della was telling her she was a fool for believing in Jack. It was what Iris had tried to tell her. Her father, too, in his own way. But what choice did she have? She was in love with him. She is still in love with him. To have said no to him would have been like ending a pregnancy. Before she met Jack she'd lived a life very much like Della's, with everything she knew and valued within reach, prominently on display, no surprises, and certainly no—what had Della called them?—adventures. The word echoed in her ears.

She eyed Della more closely. And then asked, "What did you mean . . . about 'adventures'?"

And from Della's expression as she sat back in her chair, a look at once startled and sad and guilty, Vivian knew. She knew everything. She knew that Della had seduced Jack, because Jack was easily seduced. Vivian knew that because she had seduced him herself. And Vivian knew not just about Della and Jack, but about Jack on his own. He stood stripped before her as in a flash of light. He hadn't come to see Peter that day, he had come to see Della, to find comfort, to renew his faith in himself, to be somewhere where he wasn't a coloured man who had fathered a coloured child, somewhere he'd been accepted into the white world before and assumed he would be again. Della had taken that comfort away from him. And for this, if for no other reason, Vivian hated her.

"What I meant, Viv, darling," said Della, recovering, "is that I know what you're going through."

Oh, do you? Vivian thought. Do you just?

"Jack isn't coloured," she said. "Jack is who he tells me he is."

"But, Vivian, you know he isn't. Everyone knows who he is."

"If Jack says he isn't coloured, then he isn't. I believe him."

"Despite the evidence?"

"Yes, despite the evidence."

WILLIAM HENRY

William Henry doesn't actually feel himself being bathed, but he knows his nurse is touching him because she tells him what she's doing. "Time for your bath, Mr. Lewis," she says, and he hears her swishing the water with the tips of her fingers. Is the water warm? It doesn't matter. The first few times he resisted, as much as he could, tried to think of something else, let his mind drift off, put himself in Harlan's barbershop or at their table in the British-American. Before his heart give out or the bus hit him, he would let himself drift off to them places and before he knew it he would be taking his morning nip from Harlan's bottle, or raising two fingers to Fast Eddy as he walked across the floor of the B-A. But not anymore. Now his mind stays where his body is. It feels better than trying to be two people.

The nurse pulls back the bedsheet and washes him all over with soap and a soft, warm cloth, without, she says, taking out the catheter or the IV drip.

"They're hard to put back in," she tells him. "Now I'm washing your other foot, Mr. Lewis, can you feel that?"

He sees himself shaking his head.

"How about this, Mr. Lewis?"

She washes between his toes, moves the cloth up his legs and around his groin—that's the part he dreaded earlier on, but now he's figured out that that particular part of him's as useless as the rest. Then his stomach and chest. She flips him over, somehow, he doesn't know how she does it, he can't even open his eyes, and she washes his back. "You have a nice back, Mr. Lewis. Strong." She eases his arms away from his sides, she wills them apart and washes under them. Neither of them can coax his hands to open.

"You holdin' on tight to somethin', Mr. Lewis."

Lying here like this, nothing moving, you can't duck away from the thoughts in your head like you can when you're up and about. A thought ain't like an apple you can put down on the table and say, Oh, I'll have that later. A thought is a window you got to look through. If it's dark, it makes everything you look at dark, too, and you might think, Now how'd that yard get so dark, and then you start thinking about that, and pretty soon you're thinking about things you ain't thought about in years, if ever. And if you can't move your entire body, you can't turn away your mind, neither.

And then she shaves him. This here's the best part. She uses a straight razor, near as he can tell. She was a little awkward with it at first, especially around his throat, but she gets the job done. And she combs his hair, at least the front and sides.

"A little white around your temples."

Not white. Grey.

He will make room for this nurse in his dream home. Josie won't mind. It means he won't need Harlan, at least not as a barber, but Harlan will be retired anyway. His father's barber chair, there'll be a place for that, too. Maybe make a special room for it off the tavern, a kind of museum. Let the grandchildren sit in it, pump them up to the top with the foot pedal and then whoosh them back down, like on an elevator. They'll grow up with that sound in their heads, the way he did.

He never thought Jackson would be the first to give him a grandchild. Jackson and his white wife. Ain't all a bed of roses, though, he can hear in her voice that she's worried sick. William Henry would talk to her if he could, tell her what to expect. She won't get a lot of help from Jackson, but Jackson come from a good family.

A lot of things can happen. A lot of things have happened. William Jackson was hard on that boy, and he was hard on Josie, and if there was any way he could make it easier for Jackson's wife, he would do it. Don't turn away from him like I did, he would say. And don't let him turn away from you. He turn away from you, you run around and stand in front of him. He turn away again, you run around again. And you keep doing that until he got nowhere to turn but to you. Easy enough to say, but he never done it.

The truth is he never did right by Jackson. He come at him from the side, like a fox at a thicket, and by the time he decided to raise Jackson as his own, Jackson had his own ideas about who he was. His mother was no help. She never said nothing to him one way or the other. If anything, she encouraged him. He wanted to think of himself as white, fine, let him, maybe there'd be more opportunities for him that way. Maybe she was right, maybe that was how white people got started in the first place, no one told them they weren't.

When Jackson was older, William Henry would take him and Benny to Jackson Park on his days off, to give Josie a break. Sunday at the park was a day off from whites. Coloureds put on their best clothes and went a-walking, arm in arm some of them or in families, and there'd be the smell of chicken from the barbecues, and cases of beer hidden under blankets. That's why they had the Emancipation Day picnics always on the Sunday closest to the first of August. It was like all the normal rules of living were undone and let go of like balloons, and the sheer relief of seeing them lift up into the sky made you feel like it was you floating up there, like your brain was with them but your body was down here on the earth where it belonged. It was the end of slavery, no more whitey, no more waiting in fear for the pounding on the door, or looking over your shoulder to see who else was in the room before speaking, or checking your pocket a hundred times afraid that you forgot your pass. Christ Almighty, it was fine.

Jackson didn't want to go to the picnics after he got to be seven or eight, although they couldn't very well leave him at home. The picnics could get rough at times, lots of drinking, freedom making some people act crazy, but it was safe enough, and anyway it stayed light in August nearly to ten o'clock, the kids could play sneak among the trees and the shrubs, and sometimes they didn't have the fireworks till near midnight. William Henry didn't want Jackson and Benny to miss that. He'd call them, Get over here! when the speeches started about the history of Emancipation Day, and the freeing of the slaves, and the Underground Railroad, and how the park was named after Cecil E. Jackson, the former mayor of Windsor. They needed to hear all that, especially Jackson. "Hear that, boy? This here park named after a white man. That's how far we come." But you couldn't teach that boy nothing.

William Henry'd be drinking pretty steady from lunchtime, but just beer, mostly, and he'd eat a lot of roast pork and bread and baked beans. His good shirt might have a few stains on it and maybe not be tucked into his pants all the way. Just meant he was having a good time. The sky was purple and green, the way a bruise gets just before it goes black. William Henry and Josie would make the children sit and look up at it, gauging its suitability for fireworks. Still not dark enough, but what was wrong with sitting on a bench in a park with your mother and father and brother for a few minutes? William Henry could always tell when there was something eating Jackson. After the speeches were over, the boy just sat on the bench with his hands under his knees, head down, not even swinging his feet, and said he wanted to go home. Jackson was the only one ever give him any backtalk.

"Don't you want to see the fireworks, Jackson?" Josie said.

"I want to go home."

"Don't you want to go up on the stage with Alvina and hear her sing?"

"I want to go home."

"Well you can't," William Henry cut in.

"Why not?"

"Because I say so. We take you home now, we miss the fireworks too."

"I don't want to see the fireworks."

"What do you mean, you don't want to see the fireworks?"

"Are you tired, Jackson honey? Do you want to sit on Mommy's lap and go to sleep?"

"I want to go *home*!"

"Jesus Christ!"

"Never mind, Will, he's just tired. I'll take him home."

"No, you won't. Didn't you just hear me say he can't go home?"

Benny said, "Maybe he's scared of the fireworks."

"Then he got to learn not to be. There's plenty things in life scarier than fireworks."

Then it got dark, finally, and lots of people were standing around looking up and they were lucky to have a bench, except that some of them put their trash in the trashcan right beside it. They didn't put the street lamps on because of the fireworks, but there were little fires here and there in the barbecues, and some of the cars had their lights on. Still, it was dark enough and there was smoke in the air. Some people were shouting. The sky got pitch black, not even a moon, and when the fireworks started they were nothing much, a few sizzlers and whirligigs, and Josie said, "See, Jackson, they ain't so bad, are they?" And William Henry was thinking they ain't so good, neither. But when Jackson didn't answer and they looked around for him, he wasn't there.

"Where's Jackson?" Josie said, and he could already hear the worry in her voice even though the boy probably just went off to the bushes to pee.

When he didn't come back, they looked for him, calmly at first, but there was a lot of people in the park, and they all had kids, and there was a lot of places he could have gone. Josie called him again and again, her voice getting more and more anxious. William Henry called, too. He went to the bandstand to get Alvina to help them look, and Josie took Benny and went through the bushes, but none of them found him. He was gone. They must have come back to that bench fifty times, thinking if he got lost he would go back to it, and every time they got there and no Jackson, Josie would get worse.

"He been taken," she wailed at him, grabbing his arm and shaking it. "Somebody took my boy."

You hear about it happening but you don't give it much thought. A little girl down the street from them went missing one day and they all went out to help search for her, turned the whole Settlement upside down and never found nothing but her coat, which her mother went around clutching to her for the next four days until the police found the body. And now you remember the papers saying maybe one person in ten thousand was a child snatcher, and you think there's a couple thousand people in this park, and you start to look at each one of them different. But these are your people. Which ones do you ask for help? William Henry remembers saying to himself, there ain't no one here going to hurt a child.

Pretty soon they had fifty people looking for him, everybody beating at the bushes and calling, "Jackson!" They spread outside the park, up and down the nearby streets, knocking on doors, looking in people's garages and sheds and parked cars. Josie and William Henry went around with them at first, but after a time she just sat on the bench and looked like she never going to leave it. That bench was her coat. People brought all kinds of boys up to her, but they was all coloured. None of them was Jackson. She said to William Henry, all quiet like, did he think they ought to tell them they were looking for a white boy? And William Henry thought about it, about telling that crowd of his people that they lost a white boy, and he said no, let them keep bringing up any stray kid they find.

When an hour went by like that, they called the police.

After a long time the police came and told them to go home.

Josie said, Uh-uh, she wasn't going to leave that bench. Jackson might come back to that bench, he might be out there looking for that bench right now, so they asked how were the police going to contact them if they find him, and Josie said to William Henry he could take Benny and Alvina home, but she would sit on that bench till kingdom come if she had to. So that's what William Henry did. He was pretty sober by then and he put Benny and Alvina in the back seat and on the way home they drove up and down the streets looking on porches and in between houses. He was sorry for the way he spoke to Jackson, and if Jackson had appeared at that moment he would've picked him up and told him so. But they never found him that night. The boy didn't appear.

The next morning he brought Josie some breakfast at the park, but it turned out he didn't need to because there was still people from the picnic there and some of them was sitting with her and feeding her. She was still on the bench, a shawl wrapped around her and her eyes sunk so deep he was afraid to look into them. She was like a holy woman. He always thought holy women got that way because they had something extra that nobody else had, but looking at Josie he realized they got holy by losing something, something so precious that when it was gone, all that was left of them was the part nothing could touch.

The police didn't call that day. There was nothing about a missing child in the papers. One or two neighbours who been at the picnic dropped by, and when they learned there was no news they shook their heads. Police ain't even looking, they said. At the park, they must have said the same thing to Josie,

he had a scar on his left cheek just below the eye where a dog bit him when he was a baby.

"What about his skin?" the detective sergeant asked him.

"Light," said William Henry. Then, when the detective sergeant didn't say nothing, he said, "Real light."

"What do you mean?" the detective sergeant asked shortly.

"Jackson's a coloured boy," William Henry said, "but he looks white. To some. Probably to you."

The detective sergeant looked at William Henry for a long time. William Henry thought he should say something else, then decided he'd said enough.

"We got to be real sure about this."

"Real sure about what?"

"We got a kid here. Fits the description, I guess."

"You got Jackson?"

"We got a kid that fits the description. Says his name is Jack."

"Yeah, that's what he calls himself when he's talkin' to whites."

"He also says his parents are dead. He says he's an orphan."

"We ain't dead."

"He wants us to put him in a new home."

"He already got a home."

"Boy says a *white* home."

That stopped him like a pole between the eyes. This wasn't a conversation, it was an investigation. Word of a white kid against his. The police weren't going to give Jackson up.

"Let me see him," William Henry said.

"All right, but you can't say nothing to him."

The detective sergeant took him into a back room, and there was Jackson sitting on a chair talking to another police officer. The cop was Ted Lepage, William Henry used to play poker with him before the Fox Theatre job. William Henry relaxed a bit. Ted would know about Jackson.

When Jackson saw William Henry come in, he went still and the detective sergeant and Ted Lepage looked at each other.

"Hey, Jackson," William Henry said, then remembered he wasn't supposed to say anything.

"This ain't my father," Jackson said.

"Who said it was?" said the detective sergeant, but Jackson didn't realize he give himself away.

"My father works in one of them big buildings downtown," Jackson said. "He goes up in an elevator and he has a secretary. We live in a big house, it's wide like this and it's got conker trees in front of it, and we have a maid, a coloured woman named Rosie, and my mother takes me to school every day in a car."

William Henry sat down on an empty chair in front of his son.

The detective sergeant cleared his throat. "I thought you said you was an orphan."

"I *am!*" Jackson screamed up at the ceiling, his little fingers clawing at the front of his shirt like he was trying to rip it off.

"Don't you tear that shirt, boy," William Henry said.

"My mother and father were both killed," Jackson said, looking over at William Henry, his face twisted into an expression William Henry never seen on him before. At first he thought it was just hatred, then he saw other things in it—fear, and anger, and something else, like you see in a caged animal. Helplessness.

Jackson raised his finger and pointed at William Henry. "He killed them. Him and another man, they jump out from behind some bushes and killed my parents, and they tried to kill me, too, but I ran away."

"Don't leave town," the detective sergeant joked when the two cops escorted William Henry and Jackson to the front door of the station. "We get a report of a missing white boy or a couple of dead white parents, we know where to find you." Detective Constable Ted Lepage didn't say anything to William Henry but put a friendly hand on his shoulder when he opened the door for him and Jackson to leave.

William Henry was so mad he could barely see to drive. Only thing kept him going was thinking about all the stripes he was going to put on Jackson when he got him home. He was going to give him something make his backside start hurting the minute he even thought about doing this again. The boy sat beside him in the front seat, hands under his knees, staring straight ahead out the window, not saying a word, like he was riding in a hearse, like he was being driven to auction, and it wasn't so long ago he might have been, running away like that.

When Josie saw Jackson she whooped and run down the hall from the kitchen and threw her arms around him like he the prodigal son come back from the dead. William Henry was still mad but he didn't have the heart to take the boy away from her again and whip the living daylights out of him like he wanted to. So he went down to the basement where he kept his spare liquor and sat on a coal sack and thought about what he was going to do about that child once all the merrymaking was done. He had a glass down there because he didn't like to drink straight from the bottle in the mornings. He could hear Josie upstairs in the kitchen, slaughtering the fatted calf, and he just sitting there getting madder and madder, until finally he went back upstairs and hit Jackson such a smack on the head it made his teeth rattle. No, he didn't, but that's what he was seething to do, and he thinks now that since that day he never stopped seething to do it. The look Jackson give him in the police station, that twist of hatred, never left William Henry, stayed burned into his eyes like when you look into a lamp and then turn it off before going to sleep. From that day on William Henry treated him like he was someone else's child. He saw that look again every time Josie pleaded with him to pick the boy up, take him to a ball game, show him how to hammer a nail into a piece of wood, saw it for the next ten years until Jackson was eighteen and went off to join the Navy, saw it every time he looked at his own self in Harlan's goddamn mirror. For what was joining the Navy but his own son finishing what he started all them years ago at the Emancipation Day picnic?

When William Henry woke up from this, he would do what he should have done then. He would hit his son. And then he would hug the boy to him and he would say what he should have told him long ago, he would tell Jackson, You are my son.

The nurse rolled him over on his back. "Help me now, Mr. Lewis, you too big for me to move all by myself." She changed his catheter bag and put fresh saline solution in his IV.

"All this salt water in your veins," she said, "we're going to turn you into a sailor, just like your boy Jackson."

VIVIAN

During her May appointment, Dr. Barnes came into the examining room drying his hands. He told her to lie back on the table and to unbutton her maternity blouse up to her bra, and to loosen the hook and zipper on her skirt and to slip it down to expose her lower abdomen. She had had to come back to him because she didn't know any other doctors and because, yes, she trusted him despite what she knew about Della and Jack. Perhaps she even felt a kind of sympathy, almost a kinship, with him, both of them victims of the same deceit. He palpated the lump in her belly like a child trying to guess what gift was inside the pretty pink wrapping paper.

"How big is it?" she asked.

"About a pound and a half," he said, applying his stethoscope to the mound. "The size of a muskmelon."

Muskmelons were brown and felt like they had a baby's caul stretched over them. She shuddered. "Can you hear anything?"

He took the rubber earpieces from his ears and put them in hers. At first there was a lot of rumbling and gurgling, then he moved the disk to a spot on her right side, just under the rib cage, and it was as though he had turned the dial on a marconi set. VONF, Newfoundland's newest singing sensation. She could clearly make out two distinct sets of drumbeats, one muted but insistent, ponderous, that was her heart, a bass drum heard from a block away. The other was closer, small and quick and tentative as a tom. The two drums were playing off each other, question and answer, call and response, Is everything all right? Boom! Is everything all right? Boom! and the tom sending back, Yes-yes, yes-yes.

"How's the milk coming?" Dr. Barnes asked her.

She took the earpieces from her ears. "Isn't it a bit early for that?"

"I mean your drinking milk. Four glasses a day." He pulled down her lower eyelid and peered in. "Your iron seems fine," he said. "Having headaches?"

"No."

She wanted to tell him that he had been right not to come to their wedding, to begin missing her before she was even gone. Her empty room in the house in Ferryland, her empty place at the dinner table. She had filled both for so long, and then Jack had come and almost overnight had taken her away. She'd left her father without saying a proper goodbye, and now it looked as though she might never return. She hadn't sent the stamps, she must do that tomorrow, but what would she say in the letter? And what if she went home now with a coloured baby? Wouldn't he think she had been with a sailor from the Islands, some night when Jack was out playing at a dance? Wouldn't he take Jack's side? Wouldn't it be the same nightmare?

So she had lost her father, and Iris would just say she'd tried to warn her, and Freddie would back Iris up, and her mother would throw up her hands and go to bed for a week. She'd lost touch with Frank and Jeannie. And Della, she never wanted to lay eyes on that woman again. Even Alvina and Jack's mother had become distant, preoccupied with the approaching Emancipation Day picnic. Who else but Jack was left?

She gave the earpieces to the doctor. "Are you sure everything's . . . okay?" she asked, as though he, too, had heard the drums. "Is there something you're not telling me?"

"Everything's fine," said the doctor. "Is there something you're not telling me?"

"No," she said. "Nothing."

salesman. He told them he'd been a salesman in Toronto, but they said they were full up. He was hired to patch up a house on Factoria Road, near the Chrysler plant, for a quick sale, which meant he could do a better job on it and get the jump on other house buyers and buy it himself. He'd be paid to fix up his own house. That was what he'd had in mind when he ordered the furniture, a surprise for Vivian when she came home from the hospital with the baby. A new house, new furniture, everything brand spanking new right down to the dishcloths. They'd start fresh, never look back, just the three of them. Him and Lily White, and little Baby White.

They wanted too much for the house, fifteen hundred dollars, but he thought he could swing it if he landed a job at Chrysler's. With the union threatening to come in, they were always looking for someone willing to work for what they were offering.

He was too wide awake to go home. He needed time to think and maybe sober up before facing Vivian. She'd be asleep by now anyway, she always was, even though the light bulb in her bedside lamp was usually still warm whenever he got home. She was as big as the *Enola Gay* and the baby was ready to drop any minute, although she still looked good to him. He'd tried to tell her that a few times, but she just looked at him like he was lying. The few times he'd tried to put his hand on her stomach, to feel the life that they'd made together, she'd gone all tense, like he was hurting her, or trying to hurt the baby. Jesus, what did she think he was?

He drove down Ouellette with the window open, taking in the sweet, vegetal smell of the elms that lined Jackson Park.

Lights were still on in the bandstand even though it was after one o'clock in the morning: coloureds setting up for Emancipation Day, he supposed. His mother and Alvina were probably there. As he approached Sandwich East, he saw the Merc parked by the ferry dock. What was Benny doing down here? He was probably in the British-American, drinking with Uncle Harley in the barbershop with the blinds drawn. Benny often slept there these days, slumped in the barber chair like their grandfather used to do. The light in the old, fly-specked barber's pole in the lobby would be turned off until morning, when Jack imagined Uncle Harley gave Benny his morning shave.

Jack parked behind the Merc, in front of a low, wooden building, a former warehouse that had seen better days. It had a crooked porch and the windows were boarded up, but a sign above the door said "The Flatted Fifth." It looked dark from a distance, but this close he could see light between the slats and when he turned the Hup's engine off he could hear music and voices pouring out onto the street. A speakeasy! Whoever owned the place was paying a fortune to someone, the cops, the mob, bootleggers. They were probably smuggling their booze across from Detroit by boat. He got out of the car and pissed against a bollard, which reminded him of his days in St. John's, the number of times he'd pissed against trees and buildings as he made his way up from Water Street to the barracks, rolling home dead drunk.

As he was getting back into the car, the door of the speakeasy opened and a woman came out and stood on the top step. The band must have been taking a break, because it was quiet except for the sound of crickets and water gently lapping against the ferry dock. He looked up at her.

"Hello, Della," he said.

"Jack?" It was like she was having trouble recalling his name.

The thought angered him. It angered him even more that he still needed something from her.

"What are you doing here?" he asked.

"I own the place."

"The hell you do."

"The hell I do."

He climbed the steps and stood beside her.

"Someone's going to kill themselves on these steps," he said.

"Nowhere's safe these days," she replied.

They stood watching the Detroit skyline, the dull yellow arc of the Ambassador Bridge, the flashing red light on top of the Penobscot Building, the softer lights of Belle Isle and the Ford plant, steady above their flickering reflections in the silently flowing river. There was something about looking out over water at night, he remembered it from the Navy. The Black Bottom looked dark and deserted, as it had the night of the riot.

Della asked him how Vivian was.

"She's fine. The baby's late, but your husband says that's normal for a first child."

"My husband says nothing's normal," she said.

Inside, the band started up again. Jack recognized the tune. "Autumn Leaves."

"This joint a black-and-tan?" he asked. He tried to keep the sneer out of his voice, but wasn't sure he'd succeeded.

"Yes. You'll fit right in." She turned to go back.

He caught a hint of her scent as she passed and followed it.

The only other whites he saw besides her were his brother, Benny, who was standing at the bar, and Peter, who was on the stage at the far end, holding his trumpet in front of his stomach and looking down into it as though he expected flowers to sprout from the mouthpiece. Peter looked older. He'd let his hair grow long, his face was even thinner than usual, and his eyes, when he looked up, seemed to glaze off through his horn-rims as though he were studying some enormous painting no one could see but him. Dee-Dee, in a long, sequined dress with a feather boa around her neck and a fascinator in her hair, was standing at a mike beside him. Behind them were a piano, drums and a tenor sax. They'd left "Autumn Leaves" behind and were off somewhere on their own. Jack looked around the room. The lights were low and there was a pall of cigarette smoke in the air. People sat with their chairs turned towards the stage, nodding their heads. Benny waved from the bar and he went over.

"No change," Benny said. He'd been drinking twenty-cent shots.

"What?"

"In the old man. I was there this afternoon. No change."

He looked at his brother and saw that he'd teared up, as though his body was filling with liquid and it had just reached his eyes. In the red light from above the bar the tears looked like blood, and for a split second Jack was back in the riot, watching Benny's pulped face go down. The barman gave him a drink and he knocked it back, and when he looked again at Benny he was staring sadly into his glass.

"Come on, Benny, nobody blames you for what happened."

"Nobody has to," Benny said. "I know my own self what I done."

Jack held out his glass for a refill and the barman obliged. He swallowed that down, too. Benny's words burned into his chest.

The barman put a third shot in front of Jack, but he left it there and turned to face the stage when the band started a new song. Della had gone to sit with a tall, light-skinned man Jack recognized as the trumpet player from the Horse Shoe. Jonesie. Well well. And a few tables over he saw Alvina. Christ, the whole family. Where was his mother, and Alvina's alcoholic husband? Peter's trumpet picked up an F-sharp from the tenor sax and held it for a while, waving it like a flag, a key with only two naturals in it. Peter rang a few changes up and down the scale and then somehow slipped into C, which should have been a jolt but he made it sound right. Jack found himself listening hard. Then Peter was back in F-sharp again, then back in C, it was like he was playing a scale with fifteen notes in it. And then he got it: C was the flatted fifth for the key of F-sharp. Very clever. Every time Peter slipped from F-sharp to C, Jack swung his eyes over to Della, and when Peter returned to the home key Jack looked back at the stage. How the hell did he make that work? It was like he was combining music with something that was so far outside music it wasn't even sound anymore. It went through the skin and straight into the heart. Then Dee-Dee started singing and Benny faced the stage, too, and there they were, two brothers, standing elbow to elbow like the first humans responding to a sound never heard before, both of them listening to the same thing but hearing something different.

Whatever it was, it wasn't music, and Jack hated it.

There was applause when it ended. Benny sighed and went back to his drink. "She's good, huh," he said.

Jack saw that his own glass was in Benny's hand, empty.

The set was over, and Peter and Dee-Dee came to the bar. Dee-Dee stood up on her tiptoes and kissed Benny's ear, and Benny lost some of his glumness.

"What was that last song?" Jack asked. "I didn't recognize it."

"Peter wrote it," Dee-Dee said.

"You *wrote* it?"

"I got it written down somewhere," Peter said. "Some of it."

"What's it called?"

"'Blues Meridian,'" said Peter. "Go get your horn, you can join us for the next set." Jack thought about his trombone in the trunk of the Hup.

"How much do you pay?" This was met with silence, and that vague, faraway look returned to Peter's eyes. "Thanks anyway," Jack said, "but I gotta get home. Viv'll be waiting up."

He drove back to Janette Avenue and parked in the alley behind the apartment. Boxcars were being shunted on the tracks, but they weren't making much noise. Vivian had asked him once about hobos coming to the door and he had told her not to be such a worrywart, but he had taken to locking the car at night and listening for soft voices in the shadows. He climbed the back stairs to their apartment and let himself in through the screened-in balcony. The apartment was dark, and he closed the bathroom door before switching on the single bulb above the sink. In the bedroom he undressed and was almost in bed before he realized Vivian wasn't there. When he turned on the bedside lamp, he saw the note and almost fainted, it sounded so much like something on a gravestone:

"Gone to Grace."

VIVIAN

It was the first day of August. Her contractions were coming at regular intervals, like ripples from the passing of a distant ship. Alvina was probably up already, making last-minute preparations for the Emancipation Day parade. If Vivian were in Hôtel-Dieu instead of Grace Hospital, she could watch the parade from Jack's father's room as the high-school marching bands boogied their way up Ouellette to Jackson Park. She could wave to Alvina, who would be in the Cadillac convertible, sitting up on the back of the seat with Mayor Reaume and Eleanor Roosevelt. Another surge came in, bigger this time, and she straightened her back to meet it. There. Alvina would look up as they passed and wave back.

Vivian had decided that if the baby came out dark, she would stay in Windsor and raise it in the Settlement, with Alvina and Jack's mother and Benny and Dee-Dee. She would get a job, typing or filing. She would get a lift to work every morning with Benny. Dee-Dee would sing to the baby all day. She wouldn't even mind if Ephie the bird woman came around; Jack's mother said she had once been a midwife. Vivian lay back in the bed. Another wave, but this time she was ready.

Her nurse was from the Annapolis Valley in Nova Scotia and said she believed in the Bible because it put apples in Paradise. When she checked Vivian for dilation, she said, "Crikey, the little bugger's head's sticking half out. Where's the bloody doctor at?" And hurried out. Vivian tried to look down to see it, but her stomach was in the way. A full minute went by and she began to worry. Then she heard Dr. Barnes's name on the loudspeaker and the nurse returned.

"You can't have the baby until the doctor's here," she said. "Keep your ankles crossed, my dear. Think of the ocean, the gentle sea, not all of it crashing in."

The nurse must have been thinking of the Bay of Fundy.

A second nurse arrived, and the first nurse said, "Cover her up, we'll wheel her in to Delivery."

In the hallway she was racked by a pain so sharp she thought it would rend her. She was breaking up on the rocks. "I can't," she said, trying to will herself back out to sea.

"Don't push, Mrs. Lewis."

She wasn't pushing. She wasn't doing anything. She was

floating, rising and falling with the pain.

The delivery room was large and cold. She wanted the red cashmere scarf that Iris had sent her. The nurses hoisted her onto a bed and lifted her legs into the stirrups.

"Give her the scopolamine now," the first nurse said.

"This'll just put you to sleep, Mrs. Lewis," said the new nurse, and Vivian looked away, up into the light on the ceiling. "When you wake up you'll have a beautiful baby to hold. There, now, tell me the names of your family."

The names of her family? Well, there was Daddy and Mother and Wat and Iris and Freddie and . . . and the twins . . . and there she was standing on top of the cliff above Ferryland, looking down at the ocean. There were whitecaps on the waves, rows and rows of them, moving steadily towards her without coming any closer, and the wind that made them was whipping her hair, filling her nostrils with a salt-laden tang. A gull hovered at eye level, its unblinking eye fixed on her. The sea was the earth's life-blood, her father always said, the land was its flesh, the sky its full lungs heaved with air. Heave, heaved, heaven. Newfoundland. God's country. Fairy Land. There were fairy caps in the fields and fairy pipes in the bog, and many times she'd been fairy-led in places she knew like the palm of her hand. If she threw her head back now and looked up at the clouds she would become dizzy, and the gull's cry would make a fairy tune, and she'd step forward, she wouldn't be able to stop herself, she would step off the cliff and float up into the clouds. A schooner appeared at the mouth of the harbour, its pure white topsails straining against the wind. She could make out her father's red pennant on the mainmast. Was he back from England so soon, with a white porcelain doll for her? Or back from Barbados with a tar-baby? Which would it be? Without turning her head she could see the wharf with the longliners tied up to it, all named after counties across the sea, the *Wicklow*, the *Shrop*, the *Ayre*. If she were on the wharf now she would hear their rigging snapping against the masts, and the bowlines creaking on the stays. She wished them tight lines and bloody decks. She wished them no hungry waves.

When she opened her eyes Dr. Barnes was there and the nurse was holding her wrist.

"Your husband's in the viewing room," the nurse said. "I'll go fetch him for you."

"Wait!" But the pressure on her wrist eased and was gone.

Dr. Barnes was at the foot of her bed, looking at her chart.

"Doctor," she said.

"Yes, Vivian?"

She looked at the door behind him. She could still hear the roar of the waves, so close they must be just outside the room. She brought her voice down to a plea. "What colour is it?"

PART VI

ME

I live at 1856 Factoria Road in Windsor, and my telephone number is Whitehall 4-9528. My father works at Chrysler's, on the assembly line. I have to remember that in case I get lost. Today is Sunday, August 1, 1956, and it's my birthday. My friends are playing at my house. Uve Petruniak, Helmut Rheinhart and Marcel Smolinski. My father calls their parents DPs, but he's friendly with them, cuts their lawns, helps them fix their cars. The church we go to is Christ Anglican, on the other side of Ouellette. My father wears a black cassock and a white surplice because he sings in the choir, and he says when I'm older I can sing in it, too. Except when there's a funeral. My grandfather died when I was born, so I never went to the funeral.

For my last birthday my uncle Benny gave me a rifle that he made out of a piece of wood and it looked like a real one. It was painted brown and had a trigger and a rubber band that could shoot stones and marbles, but my father took the rubber band off because he said I could put someone's eye out and we couldn't afford that. But in the winter Uncle Benny was killed in a car accident on River Canard Road, and I was not allowed to go to his funeral because my father said his head had been chopped off and seeing it would give me nightmares.

My grandmother says that August first is called Emancipation Day. "You should be proud to be born on this day," she says. "It's a sign." She says my aunt Alvina is in charge of Emancipation Day, but I've never met her. My father says I shouldn't believe everything my grandmother says, because she's old.

For my birthday lunch today we had tomato soup from a can. My father says that canned vegetables are better than vegetables from a store because they're fresher. We also had bread and butter and, because it is my birthday, a can of fruit cocktail for dessert. After lunch we went to Riverside Park, beside the Detroit River, where there are pony rides and a Ferris wheel and a small bandstand where my father played in a band. When he sang "Has Anybody Seen My Gal?" I ran to get my mother. She laughed when I told her that Dad wanted her, and said, "Oh, that's just a song." My mother has brown eyes, like me, and comes from a place called Fairy Land. My father sometimes calls her Lily White.

When my father comes home from work he empties his

Thermos bottle in the kitchen sink and rinses it out and puts it upside down on the drainboard. Then he stretches out on the chesterfield and rests his eyes until supper is ready. But because today is Sunday and my birthday, he set up the drum set he got me as a present. It has a big bass drum, a snare drum, a tom and a brass cymbal, and he taught me to hold the sticks a certain way, sort of like pencils. He set the drums up on the front porch because my mother said they'd give her a headache. Then we had lunch and then we went to the park.

After that, Uve, Helmut, Marcel and I caught six garter snakes in the field across from our house, in the ditch that runs between Factoria Road and the railroad tracks, and we were throwing them high into the air to see if we could wrap them around the telephone wires. We had three snakes hanging in front of our house when a kid we didn't know rode his bike down the street. Factoria Road is a dead end, but most people who don't live here don't know that. And yet here was this kid, who is not from around here, riding full speed like he knew where he was going. But no one on our street knew any black kids.

"Hey!" I shouted, but the kid didn't stop, so I yelled again. "Hey, nigger!"

The kid seemed to slow down without changing his pedalling, like he was going by in slow motion, or his wheels were half sunk in soft tar. He turned his face towards me, his eyes looking at the four of us on the sidewalk but focusing on me. He wasn't mad or anything, his face was kind of blank. I think he was just wondering how I'd made his pedalling harder, or if I had some kind of power over him, like in a comic book.

But then I heard the screen door on our house open behind me, and my father coming out onto the porch.

"Wayne!" he yelled. "You get over here!"

I didn't go in right away because I was still watching the black kid. He was halfway down the block. My father came down off the porch and I could hear my cymbal rattle, and he hurried to where we all were on the sidewalk beside our bucket of snakes. He grabbed my arm and almost lifted me off my feet. He looked frightened, and that made me frightened, too.

"Don't you ever, *ever* call anyone by that word!" he yelled. I was staring up at him, and then he turned to look down the street to where the black kid was riding away.

"Do you *hear* me?" He shook me a little until I nodded.

"Do you *hear* me?" he yelled again, louder. I nodded again. "That is a very bad word! You *know* that. You know better than to call a person by that word!"

But I didn't. No one had ever told me not to use that word.

My father looked up again and saw that the kid on the bike was at the end of the street, that he hadn't stopped and was no longer looking back. Then my father took my face in his hands and lowered his voice, so only I could hear.

"Son," he said, "don't you know those people carry knives?"

ACKNOWLEDGEMENTS

This novel has gone through many changes in the twenty years it has taken me to write it. Early versions were impossibly long and unwieldy, and it was Patsy Aldana who persuaded me that a family saga covering nearly two hundred years and five generations might be too much for a first novelist. My agent at the time, Bella Pomer, was a model of patience while I reassembled, rejected, reimagined and rewrote the book into something she could go back to potential publishers with.

I was still at sea when Nita Pronovost, senior editor at Doubleday Canada, took me aside at a party and in five minutes told me exactly what I should do with it. By then I was smart enough, or desperate enough, to do it. Several bouts of reassembling, rejecting, reimagining and rewriting later, I held the book in my hands that had been living in my head and heart for two decades. If anyone tries to tell you that writing a novel is easy, send them to Queen's University Archives and let them read the twenty-two drafts that trace *Emancipation Day*'s metamorphoses.

Many people have lent a sympathetic and restorative ear to my lamentations. Among them I would like to thank Matt Cohen, Andrea Levy, Virginia Lavin-Moss, Lawrence Hill, and Jamie Swift. Jane Warren gave me some very practical advice, and Zoë Maslow provided much appreciated encouragement on a number of important levels.

I also thank my new agent, Anne McDermid, who has been very helpful with suggestions and tactical support; the Canada Council for the Arts and the Ontario Arts Council for their invaluable financial contributions; and, of course, my wife, Merilyn Simonds, for her seemingly boundless patience and inspiration.

DISCUSSION QUESTIONS

1. Why do you think Wayne Grady chose William Henry, Jack and Vivian as the narrators? Would you have chosen someone else?

2. What are your thoughts on Jack's character? Did you sympathize with his plight, with his cool nature, or were you repelled by it?

3. Throughout their courtship and marriage in St. John's, Jack never reveals to Vivian his African-American heritage. Why do you think this is? Does Jack consider himself to be "passing" as a white person, or does he honestly believe he is white?

4. The novel is predicated on racism, denial, and willful misunderstandings. Jack never admits to being black, not even to himself. William Henry is as ashamed of his fair-skinned son as Jack is of his true racial background. The exploration of what race is and the influence of family is thought provoking. Discuss.

5. Have you ever denied or lied about anything to do with your heritage to get ahead? Have you ever reinvented yourself?

6. What were the advantages that came to Jack as a result of taking on a white identity?

7. Why do you suppose Vivian doesn't pointedly question the increasingly elaborate excuses Jack offers for why she still hasn't met William Henry? Why does she want to love a man who she suspects is a liar?

8. Do you find it believable that Vivian would fall in love with Jack? Do you believe that she would stay with him when she begins to suspect his treachery?

9. How much did you know about the history of World War II in Canada and the Battle of the Atlantic before you read this book? Are you compelled to read more about the era?

10. The tone, the timbre and the pacing of the novel are steeped in music. What kind of a role did jazz and big band play in the lives of the characters and their identities (Jack and Peter, in particular)?

11. Vivian and Della are strikingly different women but are both archetypes of their era. On page 54 Vivian says that, "You can't belong to a thing you belong to a place." How do you think the places they "belong" to shaped them as individuals?

12. Two events precipitate Jack's joining the Navy—the Detroit Riot and his brief affair and subsequent rejection by Della Barnes. Which of the two events was the more significant, from Jack's point of view? How are they related?

13. How did the issue of race play out differently in Windsor during this era than it may have in other parts of Canada?

14. Discuss the gravity of the first sentence, the importance of name, and the implications of the last sentence.

15. The novel takes place more than a century after the Slavery Abolition Act of 1833 ended slavery in the British Empire. Discuss the blatant and subtle ways Grady shows that racism and racial tensions still existed in Canada.

16. Have you read any of Wayne Grady's non-fiction works? Can you see a similarity in writing styles, especially considering this novel is loosely based on his family history?

17. What is the significance of the title, *Emancipation Day*? Who, by the end the novel, is emancipated?

18. What did you take away from this novel?